Murder
Over Easy

**Center Point
Large Print**

**This Large Print Book carries the
Seal of Approval of N.A.V.H.**

Murder Over Easy

Jimmie Ruth Evans

CENTER POINT PUBLISHING
THORNDIKE, MAINE

This Center Point Large Print edition
is published in the year 2007 by arrangement with
The Berkley Publishing Group, a division of
Penguin Group (USA) Inc.

The text of this Large Print edition is unabridged. In other
aspects, this book may vary from the original edition. Printed in
Thailand. Set in 16-point Times New Roman type.

ISBN-10: 1-58547-929-2
ISBN-13: 978-1-58547-929-0

Library of Congress Cataloging-in-Publication Data

Evans, Jimmie Ruth.
   Murder over easy / Jimmie Ruth Evans.--Center Point large print ed.
     p. cm.
   ISBN-13: 978-1-58547-929-0 (lib. bdg. : alk. paper)
     1. Waitresses--Fiction. 2. Restaurateurs--Fiction. 3. Murder--Investigation--Fiction.
   4. Sex-oriented businesses--Fiction. 5. Extortion--Fiction. 6. Mississippi--Fiction.
   7. Large type books. I. Title.

PS3610.A43M87 2007
813'.6--dc22

2006031066

For Charlaine Harris

Her books have never failed to enthrall me,
and her friendship has never failed to sustain me.

Acknowledgments

As always, thanks to my agent, Nancy Yost, who asked the question that inspired this series. I can never thank her enough for that!

My editor, Natalee Rosenstein, with whom I've now worked for more than a decade, continues to be the kind of editor every writer dreams about having. I can never thank her enough for the opportunities she has given me.

Margaret Nimri provided assistance with certain culinary matters by sharing her family recipe for fruit cobbler, for which I offer grateful thanks.

My friends never fail to give me support and encouragement. Tejas Englesmith is always there, spurring me on and not grumbling when I have to spend time with the computer instead. Julie Wray Herman and Patricia Orr deserve medals for continuing dutifully to read everything I bombard them with and offer constructive criticism. I couldn't do it without them!

One

Wanda Nell Culpepper smiled sleepily into the early morning sunshine as she pulled out of the parking lot of Budget Mart and onto the highway toward home. She had her window down, enjoying the cool, fragrant air of this second week of June. It wouldn't be much longer before the mornings would be hot and sticky, and she'd have to drive with the windows up and the air conditioner blasting, even at seven o'clock in the morning.

She was looking forward to a rare Sunday off. After working an evening shift at the Kountry Kitchen, and then all night at Budget Mart restocking the shelves, she was glad the restaurant was closed today. She could sleep for a while, then get up and spend the day relaxing. Heck, maybe she could even finish that new Caroline Burnes book she had sitting on her nightstand. Miranda would be out of the house, working her own shift at Budget Mart, and Juliet would be taking care of Lavon, Miranda's little boy. Wanda Nell could actually have a little time to herself.

The streets of Tullahoma, Mississippi, were almost deserted. Wanda Nell made it out to the turnoff to the lake in record time, and she passed only one truck once she turned off the highway. A few minutes later, she came to the driveway leading to the Kozy Kove Trailer Park and turned.

Pulling her red Cavalier into its parking place beside her double-wide trailer, Wanda Nell glanced over at her neighbor's place. A light shone in the kitchen. She wondered how long Mayrene had been up and how her date last night had gone. Smothering a yawn, she decided she'd wait until later to get all the details from her best friend.

Inside the trailer, everything was quiet. Wanda Nell frowned as she dropped her purse on the counter in the kitchen. Miranda should be up by now, getting ready for work. Her shift started at nine, and it took the girl a long time to get up and get going in the morning. Shaking her head, Wanda Nell headed down the hall to the back of the trailer to wake up her older daughter.

The door was partly open. Wanda Nell knocked, then called, "Miranda. You awake yet?"

Mumbled words greeted her as she pushed the door further open. Lying in a tangle of sheets, Miranda peered balefully at her mother. "I ain't going to work today, Mama. I don't feel good."

Wanda Nell eyed her daughter doubtfully. Miranda was always claiming she was sick, trying to get out of going to work. She was the laziest seventeen-year-old on the face of the earth, as Wanda Nell had complained many a time. She stepped forward, leaned over, and placed a hand on Miranda's forehead.

"You're not running a fever," Wanda Nell announced. "And you don't look sick to me."

Miranda pulled a pillow over her head and said·

10

something. Wanda Nell pulled the pillow off, and Miranda scowled up at her.

"What did you say, Miranda?" Wanda Nell asked tartly.

Miranda knew that tone. "Nothing, Mama," she mumbled.

"I expect you better be getting up from there and start getting ready for work." Wanda Nell dropped the pillow back on the bed.

Excited chatter from the nearby crib claimed her attention. Miranda's sixteen-month-old son Lavon was awake and wanting his grandmother to pick him up. Wanda Nell stepped over to the crib and scooped the baby up in her arms, kissing him several times.

"Miranda," she said after a moment, "this baby's sopping wet. I hope you haven't let him lie here all night without changing his diaper."

Wanda Nell didn't wait for Miranda to answer. She took Lavon into the bathroom and patiently stripped off his soggy diaper and dropped it into the diaper pail. She refused to have disposable diapers in the house, even though it meant she often had to wash the baby's diapers herself when Miranda neglected to do so.

Lavon stood on the toilet seat and talked to her while she got a washcloth and soaked it in warm water. As she bathed her grandson, Wanda Nell noted that more of what Lavon had to say actually sounded like real words. Right now he seemed to be telling her some story about his stuffed bunny. He giggled as she

11

rubbed him dry with a towel.

Carrying the baby back into the bedroom, Wanda Nell noted with disgust that Miranda was still lying there. She set Lavon down on the changing table and, without turning to look at her daughter, began to put a fresh diaper and a clean shirt on the baby. She spoke as she worked, trying hard not to let her irritation with Miranda color her voice.

"Miranda, you'd best get on up out of that bed and start getting ready for work. You're not too big for me to take a belt to, but I'm sure you don't want me to embarrass you like that, do you?"

"No, Mama," Miranda said, her voice sullen.

"Besides," Wanda Nell went on, still not looking at her daughter, "remember what you promised your brother. T.J.'s gonna be mighty disappointed in you if he finds out you're already slacking off before you've even worked a whole month at Budget Mart."

"All right, Mama," Miranda snapped. "I get the message. I'll get up and get ready for work. I already worked three days this week; seems like I oughta be able to have a little time off."

With Lavon cleanly dressed and riding comfortably on her left hip, Wanda Nell came over to Miranda. She had to keep a firm hand on her temper, or she and Miranda would get into a fight. She didn't want that. She was trying hard to be more patient with the girl.

With her right hand, Wanda Nell reached out and stroked her daughter's head. "I really do appreciate you helping out, Miranda. It means a lot to me, you holding down this job. And Dixie McBride tells me you're doing good."

Miranda glowed under her mother's rare praise. "Thanks, Mama. I guess I don't mind working that much, but I sure do hate getting up early."

"I know, honey, I hate it too," Wanda Nell said, turning and heading for the door. She paused a moment and looked back at Miranda. "But if you're gonna be an adult and be treated like one, you've gotta behave like one."

Not waiting for Miranda's response, she took Lavon into the kitchen for his breakfast. She got him settled in his high chair and brought his favorite spoon and a jar of baby food. She had just sat down in a chair to feed Lavon when her younger daughter, Juliet, appeared.

"Morning, Mama," Juliet said, coming forward to give her mother a kiss on the cheek. "I'll take over, and you can go on and get to bed if you want. I know you're plumb worn out by now."

"I'm okay, sweetie," Wanda Nell said. "Open up, little bird," she told her grandson, and his mouth obligingly popped open.

"You hungry, Mama?" Juliet asked. "I'll scramble you some eggs if you want."

Wanda Nell shook her head. "No thanks. After I finish feeding Lavon, I'm going to bed for a while."

"Okay," Juliet said. She went to the cabinet and pulled out a box of cereal, setting it on the table. She found a clean bowl and spoon in the dishwasher and retrieved the milk from the refrigerator. She sat down at the table across from her mother and poured cereal and milk into the bowl.

Wanda Nell watched her daughter for a moment as she munched on her Cheerios. Juliet was everything her older sister was not: smart, mature, responsible, obedient. Wanda Nell had to give Miranda some credit, though. She was making an effort to get her act together. Wanda Nell was just thankful that Juliet, nearly three years younger than her sister, didn't need the same kind of constant pushing.

"What're you and Lavon gonna do today?" Wanda Nell asked, offering the baby another spoonful of his food. While Miranda was working at Budget Mart this summer, Juliet was earning some money taking care of Lavon.

"T.J.'s gonna come by and get us after he and Grandmother Culpepper leave church, and we're going to Grandmother's for lunch and spend part of the afternoon. Is that okay with you?" Juliet regarded her mother anxiously. Wanda Nell and her ex-mother-in-law didn't get along very well, but Wanda Nell didn't begrudge the old woman time spent with her granddaughter and her great-grandson, now that she had finally admitted they existed.

"No, honey, that's fine," Wanda Nell said. "I'm sure your brother will enjoy having you over there." She shook her head. "I don't know how he stands being cooped up with that old battle-ax all the time in that big old house."

14

Juliet laughed. "T.J.'s got her eating out of the palm of his hand, Mama. You know that. She'd just about stand on her head and sing if he asked her to do it."

"And that's the truth," Wanda Nell said, smiling. T.J., her eldest, was the spitting image of his late father, Bobby Ray Culpepper, old Mrs. Culpepper's only child. Half the time, Wanda Nell figured, old Mrs. Culpepper couldn't remember whether he was T.J. or his daddy.

"It sure is good to have T.J. back, isn't it, Mama?" Juliet said. "Even if he's living with Grandmother and not with us."

"That it is," Wanda Nell replied, wiping some stray baby food from Lavon's face. She still couldn't quite get over the change in her son. At twenty-two, he seemed like he'd finally grown up. No more bar brawls, no more brushes with the law, no more running around town raising hell with his buddies. He was like a different boy entirely.

Maybe his father's murder had something to do with that, Wanda Nell reflected. They'd all been affected by Bobby Ray's death and the investigation into it. By dying, Bobby Ray had made them a family again, something he'd never quite managed to do while he was alive.

Shaking off her morbid thoughts, Wanda Nell got up and poured some milk into a sippy cup for Lavon. She handed him the cup, then ruffled his curly black hair. With his pale chocolate skin, he was a little brown angel. He looked up at her and giggled.

"Mama," Juliet said. "Did you hear me?"

"What?" Wanda Nell turned to face her daughter. "No, sweetie, I'm sorry. I guess I was off on another planet somewhere. What'd you say?"

Juliet laughed. "I didn't think you were listening to me, but that's okay. I know you're tired." She pushed away from the table and took her bowl and spoon to the sink. Facing her mother, she said, "I was telling you about the computer T.J.'s gonna give me."

"Computer? What computer?" Wanda Nell asked, bewildered. "How on earth is T.J. gonna afford a computer?" Her eyes narrowed. "Unless his grandmother bought it for him." The old woman had showered numerous gifts on her grandson, but she remained stingy when it came to her two granddaughters and her great-grandson.

Juliet shook her head. "No, Mama, it's nothing to do with Grandmother. Mr. Tucker is replacing the computers in his office, and he told T.J. he could take a couple of the old ones."

"Oh," Wanda Nell said, thinking it over. Hamilton Tucker, who insisted on being called Tuck, was a lawyer they had met during the investigation into Bobby Ray's murder. Since then, he'd been very helpful to T.J., offering him a part-time job so T.J. wouldn't be totally dependent on his grandmother for money.

"T.J.'s been learning all about computers," Juliet said, "and this afternoon he's going to show me how mine works. I'll be able to do a lot of my work for

16

school on the computer, Mama, and there's even a printer to go with it." She eyed her mother anxiously. "Are you sure it's okay?"

Wanda Nell wasn't real fond of accepting something that seemed like charity, but she couldn't think of a way to turn down the offer without offending Tuck Tucker. She owed him a lot already for what he'd done for her and her family, and she didn't like feeling beholden to anyone.

"I guess so," Wanda Nell said. She decided she'd talk to T.J. and see if there wasn't some way she could pay Tuck for the computers, or at least for the one Juliet would be bringing home with her.

All of a sudden, she yawned. Waves of tiredness washed over her, and she yawned again.

"You go on to bed," Juliet said. "I'll take care of Lavon, and I'll make sure Miranda gets off to work okay."

"Thank you, baby," Wanda Nell said. She kissed both Juliet and Lavon, then almost stumbled on her way to her bedroom. All those hours on her feet had worn her out.

Stripping off her clothes and slipping into a nightgown, Wanda Nell was in bed less than three minutes after she left her daughter and grandson in the kitchen. She was vaguely aware of sounds coming from the other end of the trailer as she drifted off.

An insistent ringing pulled Wanda Nell from a deep sleep. Bleary-eyed, she stared at the digital clock on her bedside table. The ringing continued as she tried to focus on the time. Finally, she registered that it was 12:03 P.M. and that the ringing was from the phone beside the clock.

Grumbling, Wanda Nell reached for the phone. "Hello," she said.

"Wanda Nell, you gotta help me," a man's voice said. "They said I killed her, but I didn't, I swear. You gotta help me!"

Two

"Melvin," Wanda Nell said, "are you drunk? What are you talking about?" As she spoke, she sat up in bed, awake now. She pushed several strands of long blonde hair out of her eyes.

"No, Wanda Nell, I ain't drunk," Melvin Arbuckle snapped back at her, "though I wish to hell I was right now. I can't believe this is happening."

"Where are you, and what the hell happened?"

"I'm at the county jail, and this is my one phone call," Melvin said, making an obvious effort to speak in a calmer tone. "Fayetta's dead, Wanda Nell, and they think I killed her."

Wanda Nell sat, shocked into silence, the phone still stuck to her ear.

"Wanda Nell? You there?" Melvin asked, his voice strained.

"Good lord, Melvin! Fayetta?" Wanda Nell couldn't

believe it. Fayetta Sutton was one of the waitresses at the Kountry Kitchen, Melvin's restaurant. She and Fayetta had worked together there for several years, and they had despised each other the whole time. "Did y'all have a fight? Is that what happened?"

"We had a fight last night," Melvin said, his voice low, like he was trying to keep someone else from hearing him. "But when I left her place she was still alive." He paused for a deep breath. "I went back over there this morning, and I found her." His voice broke on a sob.

Wanda Nell got a hollow feeling in the pit of her stomach. What he found had to have been pretty bad.

"It was awful, Wanda Nell," Melvin went on, his voice jerky as he tried to hold back the sobs. "Like somebody was slaughtering a pig. There was blood all over the place . . ." His voice trailed off.

Wanda Nell shuddered and almost dropped the phone. Her imagination let her picture the scene all too clearly. "Good lord, Melvin," she finally managed to say.

"Look, Wanda Nell, they ain't gonna let me talk any longer, so you gotta do something for me."

"What?"

"You know that lawyer that helped you when Bobby Ray was killed?" Melvin didn't wait for an answer. He rushed on. "You gotta call him for me, Wanda Nell. See if he'll take my case. Tell him I got money. I can afford to pay him."

Wanda Nell took a deep breath to steady herself.

"Okay, Melvin, just hang on. I'll talk to him."

"Thanks," Melvin said, and then the phone clicked in her ear.

Wanda Nell dropped the receiver in the cradle and sat for a moment, staring into space. She had to get her mind around this. Fayetta brutally murdered, Melvin arrested for it. She'd known them both for years, and she just couldn't see Melvin killing anybody. Fayetta was enough to drive some men crazy, but Melvin seemed to have had her number.

But could something have caused him to snap? Fayetta wasn't content to have just one man on a string, and Melvin didn't seem to like being two-timed. *Or three-timed or four-timed,* Wanda Nell thought sourly. Fayetta was a real piece of work.

She didn't deserve to be slaughtered like a pig, though, and Wanda Nell briefly felt ashamed of herself.

Getting out of bed, she padded barefoot down the hall and into the kitchen. She kept her list of phone numbers in a drawer near the phone there, and she pulled the list out and scanned it for Tuck Tucker's number.

Around her, the house was silent. Miranda was presumably at work, and Juliet and Lavon should be at Mrs. Culpepper's by now. Wanda Nell punched in the numbers and waited. After four rings, an answering machine came on to advise her that the law offices of Hamilton Tucker were closed today, but if this was an emergency, she could reach him on his cell phone. She scrambled for a pencil and managed to jot the number down in time.

Wanda Nell broke the connection, waited for a dial tone, then put in the new number. After a couple of rings, Tuck answered.

"Hey, Tuck, this is Wanda Nell Culpepper," she said. She still felt awkward talking to him. He was so polished and smart, and so *lawyery,* she always felt like a hick around him, even though he went out of his way to put her at ease.

"Wanda Nell," Tuck said, "we were just talking about you. How are you?"

Momentarily diverted by this unexpected statement, Wanda Nell forgot about the reason for her call. "Who's 'we'?"

"Oh, T.J., Juliet, and I," Tuck said. "I'm having lunch with them at Mrs. Culpepper's. Can't you join us?"

"Uh, no," Wanda Nell said, taken aback. He and T.J. sure had been getting pretty chummy lately, but he was a good influence, that much Wanda Nell had decided. Better than T.J.'s old buddies in Tullahoma, the good Lord knew.

Wanda Nell remembered the reason for her call. "Tuck, my boss at the Kountry Kitchen, Melvin Arbuckle. You know him?"

"No," Tuck said after a brief pause, "can't say as I do. He need a lawyer?"

"Yeah," Wanda Nell said, sighing heavily. "They've got him down at the county jail. He called me and asked me to call you for him."

"What's the charge?" Tuck asked when Wanda Nell hesitated.

"Murder," she said. "He says they arrested him for killing one of the waitresses at the restaurant. Fayetta Sutton."

"I see," Tuck said. "Well, I guess I'd better get on over to the jail and try to talk to him. Lunch will have to wait."

"I'm sorry," Wanda Nell said, but Tuck just laughed.

"That's all right, Wanda Nell," he said. "After all, it's my job."

"Tuck," Wanda Nell said quickly, before he ended the conversation. "Um . . . can you let me know how it goes?"

"He a friend, in addition to being your boss?"

"Yes," Wanda Nell said without hesitation. Melvin had been a good friend to her. He'd made it plain more than once over the years that he'd like to be more than that to her, but she had shied away from that kind of relationship with him. As a result, he'd turned to Fayetta.

"Okay, I'll see what I can do," Tuck said. "I'll speak to you later."

"Thanks," Wanda Nell said, and then the connection was broken. She hung up the phone and stared at the wall.

She was still staring at it in some kind of trance when it rang a couple of minutes later. Shaking herself back to reality, Wanda Nell answered the phone.

"Hello."

"Mama, you okay?"

She appreciated T.J.'s obvious concern. He was much more thoughtful these days. "Yeah, honey, I'm okay. A little shocked, I guess."

"Anything you want me to do? Why don't you let me come get you, and you come on and have lunch with us?"

Wanda Nell laughed. "Now, honey, I wouldn't wanna watch your grandmother choking down her food with me sitting at her table."

Over T.J.'s protests that it wouldn't be like that, Wanda Nell remained firm. Despite what T.J. said, the old woman disliked her, and it was mutual. They got along slightly better now, in the aftermath of Bobby Ray's murder, but they still didn't care to spend any time with each other.

"Okay," T.J. sighed. "Then I guess I'll bring Juliet and Lavon home later on, like we planned. She tell you about the computer?"

"Yes, she did," Wanda Nell said, "and I want to talk to you about that."

"It's okay, Mama," T.J. said, a bit defensively. "Tuck is doing a nice thing, and you don't have to think of it like it's a handout."

"Whatever," Wanda Nell said, not totally convinced. "But we'll see. In the meantime, y'all enjoy your lunch and try not to think about any of this."

She hung up the phone and wandered over to the refrigerator. Completely awake now, she was aware of how hungry she was. First she poured herself a glass of cold Coke, then she examined the fridge to see what there was to eat. All the while her mind was fretting over Melvin's situation and the awful news of Fayetta's death.

As she munched on some cold fried chicken, she thought about what she could do. She had to believe Melvin was innocent. Surely someone else had done this. Fayetta didn't exactly have a spotless reputation in Tullahoma, and there was probably some married man in town who'd finally had it with her and chosen a drastic way out.

Or maybe it was somebody's wife. The good Lord knew there were more than a few of them around who had reason to despise Fayetta.

But to hate her enough to kill her like that? Wanda Nell's imagination was a little too vivid for her sometimes. She pushed away the rest of the fried chicken. She'd lost her appetite.

What could she do? A couple of ideas had occurred to her. She might get into trouble, she reckoned, but she hadn't let that stop her before.

Wanda Nell got up from the table and went back to the phone. She knew the number by heart. A couple of months ago, she had used it often.

The dispatcher at the sheriff's department answered.

"I'd like to speak to Deputy Johnson," Wanda Nell said. "Elmer Lee Johnson."

"I'll see if he's available, ma'am," the dispatcher said.

24

"Tell him it's urgent," Wanda Nell added quickly.

Elmer Lee wasn't going to be too happy with her sticking her nose in like this. Wanda Nell figured he was probably the one who'd be investigating, and she might as well try talking to him. He'd given her a real hard time during the investigation into Bobby Ray's murder, but eventually they had come to some kind of understanding. She hadn't seen Elmer Lee since Bobby Ray's funeral, and the memory of that last conversation was on her mind as she waited to speak to him.

Another couple of minutes passed, and Wanda Nell was about to hang up.

"Deputy Johnson," Elmer Lee barked into the phone. "How can I help you?"

"Elmer Lee, it's me, Wanda Nell," she said, and waited for the explosion.

At the other end of the line, she heard a deep breath being taken. "And what, pray tell, do *you* want? I'm kinda busy right now, Wanda Nell."

"I know, Elmer Lee," Wanda Nell said. She hated feeling defensive with him. "But Melvin called me, and I'm concerned. Did you really arrest him for killing Fayetta?"

"Yes, we did arrest him," Elmer Lee said with exaggerated patience. "We caught him red-handed, so to speak, and there don't seem to be much reason to look any further. That okay with you?"

He sure knew how to push her buttons, Wanda Nell reflected. But she wasn't going to let him make her lose her temper. "I'm not trying to do your job for you, Elmer Lee," she said, and the unspoken words *at least this time* hung between them. "I just find it hard to believe that Melvin could, well, butcher somebody."

"And how do you know she was butchered?"

"Cut the crap, Elmer Lee," Wanda Nell said sharply. "You don't need to play some stupid game with me. You know Melvin, too. Do you really think he could do something like this?"

"You're pushing your nose into something you better stay out of," Elmer Lee said. "I've seen some bad stuff in the twenty-two years I've been in the sheriff's department, but this was about the worst. You don't want to have anything to do with this."

Chilled by the bleakness of Elmer Lee's tone, Wanda Nell couldn't speak for a moment. Then she rallied. "It just don't sound like Melvin."

"I know that," Elmer Lee replied. "But you're just gonna have to butt out and let us do our jobs. Good-bye, Wanda Nell."

The phone clicked in her ear. Wanda Nell put the receiver back on the cradle.

She rubbed her arms up and down. Talking to Elmer Lee had shaken her resolve, but then she thought of the desperation and fear in Melvin's voice. She couldn't just abandon him. He had stood by her when she was accused of murdering Bobby Ray. She owed him some loyalty.

Her mind made up, she peered out the window of her kitchen. It faced her friend Mayrene Lancaster's trailer. Lights shone in the living room, so Mayrene must be home. Wanda Nell picked up the phone and dialed.

"Hey, Mayrene," Wanda Nell said when her friend answered.

"Hey yourself, girl. How're you doing?" Without waiting for an answer, Mayrene plunged ahead. "Honey, I have just *got* to tell you about my date last night. You won't believe this guy."

"I want to hear all about it, I promise," Wanda Nell said, interrupting before Mayrene could really get going, "but something's come up, and I need your help."

"Uh, sure," Mayrene said. "Is something wrong with the baby? Or one of the girls?"

"No, nothing like that," Wanda Nell assured her. "Listen, if you ain't got anything to do for the next hour or so, I need you to go with me somewhere."

"Well sure, honey," Mayrene said, obviously puzzled. "But what the heck is this all about?"

"I'd rather tell you on the way. I can be ready in about five minutes."

Mayrene laughed. "Then I guess I'll meet you outside at my car in five minutes."

Wanda Nell hung up the phone, smiling. Mayrene was one in a million. When you needed her, she didn't ask questions. She hurried back to her bedroom to brush her hair and get dressed.

Five minutes later, as promised, she met Mayrene at her car. Mayrene, as usual, looked like she'd just

27

stepped out of a bandbox. Wanda Nell marveled at her friend's ability to appear without a hair out of place and her makeup perfect, even on such short notice.

But then Mayrene didn't have any kids to worry about, only herself. About a dozen years older than Wanda Nell, Mayrene had been single as long as Wanda Nell had known her, though there were at least two ex-husbands in her past.

"Okay, now what's going on?" Mayrene asked as they got into the car. She commenced backing out of her parking space.

Quickly, Wanda Nell began to explain. Mayrene's eyes widened in horror and sympathy, but she didn't interrupt. They had turned onto the highway before Wanda Nell finished.

"Awful," Mayrene commented. "She was a real piece of work, but she sure didn't deserve nothing like that."

"No," Wanda Nell said, "and I just can't believe Melvin did it."

"Sure don't sound like him," Mayrene agreed. "Now, where're we going? To the jail, to try to see Melvin?" She turned her big Buick onto the highway into town.

"No," Wanda Nell said. "I doubt they'd let me see him right now, anyway. Elmer Lee is pissed at me."

"You called him?"

"Yeah," Wanda Nell said. Mayrene just rolled her eyes at her. "I wanna go by Fayetta's house."

"What?" Mayrene's hands jerked on the steering

28

wheel. Muttering, she righted the car on the highway. "Are you nuts, honey? They ain't gonna let you in her house. What do you expect to see, anyway?"

"I've got a plan," Wanda Nell said. "I know I won't be able to get inside, but I might be able to see something." She threw her hands up in the air. "I just gotta do something."

"Okay, honey, I'm with you," Mayrene said. "It can't be any worse than what happened in Greenville." She looked at Wanda Nell and grinned. They both laughed, remembering.

"I don't think you'll need your shotgun today," Wanda Nell said, sobering. "At least, I sure hope not."

She directed Mayrene to Fayetta's house in a section of town not far from the Kountry Kitchen, where the houses were old, small, and on the shabby side. Not the best neighborhood in Tullahoma, but at least Fayetta could afford a place for her and her kids.

Her kids! It finally hit Wanda Nell. Where were Fayetta's children when all this was going on? Then she relaxed against the seat. *Probably with Fayetta's mother.* Wanda Nell had met her once, a prim, sour-looking older woman who'd made it clear she didn't think much of her daughter.

"And your plan?" Mayrene prompted Wanda Nell when they were close to the house.

"Fayetta's house is on the corner," Wanda Nell explained, "and I figure if the sheriff's department has somebody on watch there, he's probably at the front of the house. You can stop and let me out around the corner, and I can come through the backyard and sneak a peek inside. In the meantime, you go to the front and park and go up to the house like you're coming to visit Fayetta."

"I get you," Mayrene said. She shook her head. "You may be heading for a whole mess of trouble if they catch you snooping, girl."

Wanda Nell shrugged. *So be it.* She looked ahead. "Okay, stop here," she said. She pointed before she got out of the car. "That's the house, there on the corner. Just go on around and see if there's anybody there."

Wanda Nell shut the door, and Mayrene drove off. Wanda Nell moved to the edge of the street and walked slowly toward Fayetta's house. As she approached the backyard, she scanned for any signs of activity.

The closer she came, the more she could see. Fayetta had few curtains up, so most of the windows were bare. Wanda Nell's breath quickened as she drew closer to the house.

She was in the backyard now, and she couldn't see any sign of anyone in the house. She could hear Mayrene, however, hailing someone as she came up the walk to the front door. A deputy on duty, she reckoned, and maybe the only one at the moment.

Wanda Nell edged closer to the house, into the shade of a couple of old oak trees just a few feet from the house. She pushed her way cautiously into the overgrown hydrangeas in the flowerbeds at the back

30

of the house and peered into the first window she came to.

It was the kitchen. Nothing looked out of place there.

She moved down to the next window. Fayetta's bedroom, if she remembered correctly. She hesitated, steeling herself.

Wanda Nell gasped as she gazed inside. Bile rose in her throat and she turned away, trying not to vomit.

Three

Wanda Nell forced herself to breathe deeply. She focused on the shade beneath a tree in the backyard and worked on controlling the urge to throw up. When she thought she could handle it, she turned her head and looked into Fayetta's bedroom again.

The mattress sat slightly askew on the box spring, and the sheets, rumpled and bunched up here and there, had deep crimson splashes across them. Wanda Nell's eyes followed the trail of blood. Fayetta must have crawled out of the bed and across the room toward the door. A pool of blood had collected on the bare linoleum by the door, and a dark blob marred the paint near the knob.

Convinced she had seen enough, Wanda Nell turned away, only to find a large, scowling sheriff's deputy standing right behind her.

"Would you like to explain what you're doing here,

ma'am?" He stood with arms crossed over a broad, powerful chest.

Wanda Nell stared up into implacable, unfriendly eyes. She drew a shaky breath. "Sorry, Deputy Stover," she said, reading the name off his nameplate. "I came over to check on my co-worker. Fayetta and I work together at the Kountry Kitchen. And I just came over to check on her . . ." Her voice trailed off. She could see Stover wasn't buying any of this.

"What's your name, ma'am?"

Wanda Nell swallowed hard. "Wanda Nell Culpepper."

The deputy's face relaxed for a moment. "Yes, ma'am, I reckon I heard tell of you," he said. "Well, Miz Culpepper, I think you'd better get on home. Ain't nothing you can do around here. Your friend is waiting around front for you."

"Thank you, Deputy, I will," Wanda Nell said. She risked one last glance at his face, but the stern mask was back. As she scooted around the house, she wondered what kind of tales Elmer Lee Johnson had been telling about her around the sheriff's department.

Mayrene was sitting in the car, the engine running and the air conditioning blasting. Wanda Nell was grateful for the cool air, because she discovered she was sweating profusely when she dropped into the passenger seat.

"Did he yell at you?" Mayrene asked as she put the car into gear and drove off.

Wanda Nell mopped at her face with some Kleenex

32

from her purse. "No, thank the Lord," she said. "He was actually nicer about it than I guess I should've expected. When I told him my name, he seemed to know who I was."

"Elmer Lee's been doing some talking," Mayrene said, grinning.

"Must've been," Wanda Nell agreed. "Because I don't remember seeing this Deputy Stover around before. He must be new."

"He sure is cute," Mayrene said.

Wanda Nell laughed. "And about twenty years younger'n you, too."

"And your point would be?" Mayrene said airily.

"Never mind that," Wanda Nell said. "I need to tell you what I saw. There ain't no way Melvin killed Fayetta."

Quickly she described the horror of what she had seen. Even now, the violence of it made her stomach knot up.

"Pretty damn vicious," Mayrene said, her face paling as her hands tightly gripped the steering wheel. "And you don't think Melvin could've done it?"

"No, I don't," Wanda Nell said firmly. "For her to bleed that much, whoever done it must've stabbed her a bunch of times. Like in some kind of frenzy, I guess." She shook her head. "I don't think Melvin'd do something like that."

"You know him a lot better than I do," Mayrene said, her tone dubious. "But sometimes a person snaps, and they do things you don't think they would."

33

"I know that," Wanda Nell acknowledged. "But I just don't think Melvin cared that much about Fayetta to do something that deranged to her."

All of a sudden, tears started streaming down her face. She had been thinking of everything but Fayetta herself, and now it hit her. "Lord knows I hated that girl something awful," Wanda Nell said shakily. "But to die like that. She was meaner'n any snake you ever wanted to see, but even she didn't deserve this." She clutched more Kleenex in her hand and dried her eyes.

Mayrene reached over and patted her arm. "I know, honey," she said. "And I wish now I hadn't brought you here to see that. After what happened with Bobby Ray, you didn't need to see something like that."

"No, I'll be okay," Wanda Nell insisted. "I had to know. Melvin told me a little about it, but I had to see it for myself. And now I've seen it, I'm going to have to do what I can to help Melvin. I don't believe he did this, and he's going to need help if Elmer Lee's convinced he's guilty."

"That's for dang sure. He's worse than an old bulldog when he gets ahold of something," Mayrene agreed. She turned off the highway onto the lake road. They'd be back home in another two minutes.

"Now, tell me about your date last night," Wanda Nell said.

Mayrene grinned at her. "Ain't much to tell, except I will say that I think I got me a live one this time. He may seem real quiet, but you know what they say about them still waters. I think they may be running pretty deep."

That's all she would say, and Wanda Nell didn't press her further. Mayrene would divulge the details when she was ready.

When they turned into the drive at the Kozy Kove Trailer Park, Wanda Nell could see T.J.'s brand new pickup parked in her parking space. She frowned. That pickup gave her a slight headache every time she saw it. Old Mrs. Culpepper had bought it for T.J., and Wanda Nell hadn't wanted her to do it.

Mrs. Culpepper had argued that T.J. needed to be able to get around town on his own and not to have to be dependent on anyone. She still insisted on driving herself around in her old Cadillac, scaring the life out of anyone foolish enough to get in her way. She also didn't want to have to interrupt her schedule of bridge parties, gossip sessions, and church committee work to ferry her grandson back and forth to his part-time job and to visit his mother and sisters.

Wanda Nell had given in. She'd worn herself to a frazzle, trying to argue with the old battle-ax, and she had to admit T.J. having a way to get around sure made things easier for her. But she still wished she could've bought that truck for him.

"You wanna come over for a while, have some coffee, and visit with T.J.?" Wanda Nell asked before she opened the car door to get out.

"Thanks, honey," Mayrene said, "but I got some things I need to tend to." She grinned as her car door clanged shut. "I reckon I've had about enough excitement for one day."

Wanda Nell felt guilty. "I'm sorry, Mayrene," she said. "I know I shouldn't get you into things like this."

"Now, you just stop right there, Wanda Nell," Mayrene said, acting real stern. "I'm a big girl, and I know how to say *no* when I want to." She grinned. "If I didn't have me another hot date later this afternoon, I'd come on over and visit. But Mr. Padget is taking me over to Greenwood for a movie and dinner afterwards, and I got to get ready."

Wanda Nell grinned back at her. Then her eyes widened in surprise. "Mr. Padget? You mean the guy that works at the funeral home? That Mr. Padget?"

"Yeah," Mayrene said, her face taking on a slightly mulish look. "And what's wrong with that?"

"Uh, nothing," Wanda Nell said, "nothing at all. I was just a bit surprised. He don't seem like the kinda man you usually go for."

"Which would be?" Mayrene asked, one eyebrow arched.

Wanda Nell almost blurted out what she was thinking, and that would rile Mayrene for sure. "Well, you usually like a man who's got a bit of fire to him, and this Padget guy seems awfully cool and quiet the times I've seen him."

"Some fires are way down deep," Mayrene drawled. "But they're there, honey. They're there." Then she winked at Wanda Nell. "Just like those still waters."

Wanda Nell just shook her head. Mayrene talked

awful big sometimes, and Wanda Nell didn't know whether to believe her half the time. "Y'all have fun in Greenwood," she said, giving a little wave as she headed for her trailer.

"Oh, we will. I can guarantee that." Mayrene's teasing laughter rang in the hot afternoon air.

Wanda Nell opened the door of her trailer to the happy squeals of her grandson. Lavon was bouncing up and down on T.J.'s leg as they played horsey on the couch. Wanda Nell watched for a moment, leaning back against the door. She had a lump in her throat all of a sudden.

"Hey, Mama," T.J. said. "Look at this big ol' cowboy I got on my leg. Can't he ride real good?"

"Gamma," Lavon said between giggles.

"Yeah, he rides real good," Wanda Nell said as she sat beside T.J. on the sofa. "But I expect it's about time for cowboys to be heading to the bunkhouse for a little nap. What do you think, Lavon?"

T.J. stopped bouncing his leg and, still holding his hands, let Lavon slide down to the floor. Still giggling, Lavon got up and climbed into his grandmother's lap. "Gamma nap," he said.

Wanda Nell smiled down at him. He was such a good child, nothing like his mother had been at this age. "Yes, baby, it's nap time." She stood up, Lavon in her arms. "T.J., you're not going anywhere, are you? I hope you can stay awhile and visit." She waited for T.J.'s nod, then headed off to the bedroom Lavon shared with his mother. "Just let me get this here cowboy settled, and I'll be back."

Wanda Nell checked to make sure Lavon was dry, then put him in his crib. She crooned to him for a few minutes and, worn out by playing with his uncle, Lavon was soon sound asleep.

T.J. was sitting in the kitchen, drinking a Coke out of the can. "Where's Juliet?" Wanda Nell asked, retrieving a can for herself from the fridge.

"She's in her room, playing around with her computer," T.J. said as his mother sat down at the table across from him. He held up a hand to forestall what he thought his mother was going to say. "I know you're not real thrilled with the idea of Tuck giving Juliet and me computers, Mama, but please don't make a big deal out of it."

"I wasn't planning on making a big deal out of it," Wanda Nell said mildly. "I appreciate what Tuck's done for you, and for all of us. But I just don't want anybody getting in the habit of thinking somebody's gonna come along with handouts every time we need something."

T.J. grinned. "I know that. Otherwise I wouldn't be working. I'd just let Grandma Culpepper foot the bill for everything."

Wanda Nell grimaced. The old witch had done far too much as it was.

"Come on now, Mama," T.J. said in a wheedling tone. "Just think of it like this. Think of all those years Grandma and Grandpa Culpepper didn't give any of us Christmas presents or birthday presents. Think

38

what all that would add up to."

Wanda Nell rolled her eyes at her son. There was some truth in what he said, since the elder Culpeppers had managed to ignore the existence of their grandchildren for many years, just because they despised *her*. Mrs. Culpepper was trying to make up for some of that, though she was going overboard where T.J. was concerned. He got far more from her than either of his sisters or his nephew did.

"So what's going on with Melvin?" T.J. asked. "You think he really killed Miz Sutton?"

Wanda Nell shut her eyes for a moment, hoping to block out the vision of Fayetta's bedroom. It didn't work. "I don't think he could do something that vicious," she said. "Whoever killed her hated her something awful, and I just don't think Melvin cared that much about her."

"And how do *you* know how vicious it was?" T.J. asked suspiciously. "What were you and Mayrene up to, Mama?"

"I got Mayrene to go with me to Fayetta's house." Wanda Nell squirmed a bit in her seat. The tables were definitely turned, with her on the defensive for once. "And I had a look into Fayetta's bedroom where it happened."

"Mama!" T.J.'s face darkened. "What do you mean, messing around in something like that? You're lucky they didn't haul you off to the sheriff's department for poking around like that. Unless they didn't catch you."

Wanda Nell squirmed some more.

"They did catch you," T.J. said flatly.

"Yeah, there was a deputy on guard," Wanda Nell said. "But he let us go. I told him I was coming by to check on Fayetta, pretending like I didn't know what had happened. I don't think he much believed me, but Mayrene had been flirting with him, so he didn't fuss too much." She blushed at the memory of what the deputy had actually said to her.

"You were lucky," T.J. said. "What do you think Mr. Johnson's gonna say if he catches you nosing around another murder?"

"I don't give a flying flip what Elmer Lee Johnson thinks," Wanda Nell said, annoyed. "That man's not the boss of me, and if I want to help out a friend, he's not going to stop me."

"Whoa, Mama," T.J. said, holding up a hand. "I know you want to help Melvin, but you still got to be careful. You don't know what you could be getting into. I mean, you said whoever killed Miz Sutton must've hated her. Do you think that person's gonna like you poking your nose in?" He leaned forward. "Think about it, Mama. If Melvin didn't do it, whoever did it'll be pretty happy to have Melvin in jail for it. And if you go around messing things up, then the killer might come after you."

Wanda Nell sighed. "I know that, T.J. I'm not a dimwit, despite what Elmer Lee thinks. But I can't just sit by and watch Melvin get railroaded for something I don't think he did. I didn't sit still and let you

40

go to prison for killing your daddy, did I?"

"No, Mama, you didn't," T.J. said, sighing heavily. "But that was a little bit different. I'm your son. I'd do the same thing for you. We're family. But Melvin's not. He's just some guy you work for."

"Yeah, I work for him," Wanda Nell said, trying—and failing—to keep her temper under control. "He's been a damn good friend to me many a time. And if it wasn't for him, a certain Mr. Thaddeus James Culpepper the second wouldn't've got his sorry ass bailed out of jail a couple of times." She paused for a deep breath. "Your daddy and your sainted grandma sure as hell weren't gonna come up with the money, and I had no one else to turn to. Melvin helped me out when nobody else would—or could."

T.J. flushed a deep red. "Lord, Mama, I'm sorry. I had no idea. I never even thought about the money. One of these days maybe I'll be able to pay you back."

Her anger spent, Wanda Nell reached across the table to pat her son's hand. "I don't want the money back, T.J. I did what I did because you're my son and I love you. I'd do it again if I had to, but I don't expect I'll have to. But at least you ought to understand why I feel like I should help Melvin when he needs me."

"I do," T.J. said, but he didn't sound any too sure. "But you've got to be careful, Mama."

"Careful about what?" Juliet padded into the kitchen in her bare feet, so quietly that neither T.J. nor Wanda Nell had heard her.

41

"Oh, about working so much," Wanda Nell said, hating to lie to her daughter, but not wanting her to be burdened any more than she had to be.

Juliet eyed her mother suspiciously. "Uh-huh, and I'm gonna be homecoming queen this year, too."

"Never you mind your smart mouth, missy," Wanda Nell said, attempting to make light of it. "Besides, you're pretty enough to be homecoming queen, and don't you think any different."

"Mama's right about that, Bug," T.J. said, using the nickname guaranteed to annoy his baby sister.

"Honestly," Juliet said. She went to the fridge and extracted a can of Diet Coke. "You people need to go to the eye doctor and get some glasses." Tossing her shoulder-length blonde hair, she stalked out of the kitchen and back to her bedroom.

"You're not gonna be able to keep Juliet from knowing about this, Mama," T.J. said. "Especially if you get yourself mixed up in it."

"Then I'll deal with that when I have to," Wanda Nell snapped. She got up to throw her empty can into the garbage bin under the sink.

Glancing out the window, she saw a car pulling into the parking space behind T.J.'s truck. As she watched, Tuck Tucker climbed out of his late-model Mercedes and walked up to the door.

"Go let Tuck in," Wanda Nell instructed her son. T.J. got to his feet and hurried through the living room to the door. Wanda Nell followed slowly.

Catching sight of Wanda Nell, Hamilton "Tuck"

Tucker took his hand off T.J.'s shoulder, where it had been resting lightly. "Afternoon, Wanda Nell," he said, coming forward to offer his hand. "I hope you don't mind me dropping by like this, but I thought I ought to let you know what's going on."

A year or two over thirty, Tuck was as tall and dark as T.J. but even more handsome, Wanda Nell thought, and her son was no slouch. Like T.J., Tuck wore jeans and black cowboy boots that emphasized his lean, muscular frame, but Tuck's shirt and sport coat were made of silk. T.J.'s shirt was simple cotton.

"Thanks, Tuck," Wanda Nell said, releasing his hand. "I appreciate that. Let's sit down." She motioned toward the couch and two chairs. "Can I get you something to drink?"

"No, I'm fine," Tuck said, waiting until Wanda Nell was seated in one of the chairs before sitting down on the couch next to T.J. "Now, ordinarily I wouldn't be talking to anyone about some of this, because of attorney-client privilege. But Melvin particularly wanted me to talk to you, Wanda Nell, and let you know what's going on." He smiled briefly. "He has more faith in you, I think, than he does in me."

Wanda Nell didn't quite know what to make of that. Was Tuck teasing her? He didn't sound mad, at least.

She cleared her throat. "I guess he figures I'm going to meddle anyway, and I can maybe get away with things you can't, Tuck."

Tuck laughed. "I expect so. Frankly, I'll take all the help I can get on this one." His tone had darkened.

43

"Is it that bad?" Wanda Nell asked, her heart sinking.

Nodding, Tuck said, "Yes. It's pretty bad."

Before he could continue, T.J. spoke. "Mama's already been to Miz Sutton's house to have a look-see." He frowned at Wanda Nell.

Wanda Nell shot him a look. "Yeah, I did. I had to see for myself."

Tuck didn't comment, other than to say, "Then you know how bad it was." He leaned back on the couch, his knee brushing against T.J.'s. "But the worst thing is the murder weapon."

"What was it?" Wanda Nell asked, suddenly afraid to hear the answer.

"A knife that came from the Kountry Kitchen," Tuck said. "Melvin identified it himself."

Four

Wanda Nell blanched. She bet she knew which knife it was, and she felt like throwing up.

"Mama, you okay? You want something to drink? Some water?"

Glancing up, Wanda Nell saw T.J. bent over her, concern in his face. Slowly, she shook her head. "No, I'm okay. Just give me a minute."

"Sorry, Wanda Nell," Tuck said as T.J. sat down beside him again.

"Not your fault," she said. "I'm okay." *As long as I*

44

can keep that awful picture out of my head, she thought.

The two men eyed her doubtfully, but neither one said anything more until she had regained her composure.

"That makes it look pretty bad for Melvin," Wanda Nell stated.

"It does," Tuck agreed. "But until they get a report back from the state crime lab on the knife, we won't know if there's any other link to Melvin. I can think of several reasons why the knife could've been in the victim's house without Melvin bringing it there himself."

"One of them being," Wanda Nell spoke bitterly, "that Fayetta Sutton was liable to help herself to whatever she wanted, even if it belonged to someone else."

"You didn't like her." Tuck made it a statement rather than a question.

"No, I didn't," Wanda Nell said, "and I had plenty reasons not to. She was conniving and two-faced, and those were her good points." Then she felt ashamed of herself, talking about the woman this way after she'd been brutally killed.

"De mortuis nil nisi bonum," Tuck said, then grinned wryly when Wanda Nell and T.J. stared blankly at him. "Sorry, just a quotation. You can blame all the Latin I studied in high school. Basically, it means, 'Don't say anything but good about the dead.'"

"Then I doubt anybody'd have much to say about

Miz Sutton," T.J. said smartly. "From what I've heard," he added hastily after getting a sharp look from his mother.

"No point in fiddle-farting around," Wanda Nell said, ignoring the two grinning men. "You know what I mean. I'm sorry it happened to her. As much as I despised her, I wouldn't've wished that on her. But trying to whitewash her now won't help Melvin none."

"No," Tuck said. "It sure won't. And in order to help him, Wanda Nell, I'm going to need to know everything I can about the victim. If Mrs. Sutton had the kind of character I'm being told she had, then I'm going to have to know about it."

"I'll tell you what I know, things she did to me or that I saw her do at the Kountry Kitchen," Wanda Nell said slowly, "and then I'll tell you what I heard." Her mouth twisted in a bitter grin. "The men at the Kountry Kitchen are bigger gossips than any woman ever dared to be."

"Let's just start with things you know," Tuck said. He pulled a small notebook and a pen from his inside jacket pocket. Poised to take notes, he watched Wanda Nell.

Turning her eyes away from that notebook, Wanda Nell thought about Fayetta. "It was about four years ago, around the time Fayetta started working at the Kountry Kitchen. I started missing money from my purse. It was never very much, two or three dollars now and then, sometimes five. And at first it was real occasional, but then it started happening more regularly." Wanda Nell shrugged. "At first I didn't think much about it. It's easy to lose track of a few dollars here and there. But when it started happening more and more, I knew it wasn't me spending it and forgetting about it.

"I thought maybe Miranda was taking it. It would've been like her to help herself without asking me first." Wanda Nell grimaced. "I almost called her on it, but I realized something else was going on at the same time. I realized my tips at the Kountry Kitchen had gone down. I couldn't understand it. I've always gotten real good tips, and all my regulars were still wanting me to wait on 'em."

"So Miz Sutton was stealing your tips and money out of your purse?" T.J. asked.

Wanda Nell nodded. "Didn't take me long to catch her lifting some of my tips off my tables. But I had to set a trap for her with my purse. I marked some dollar bills and a coupla fives and left them in my purse. Didn't take her a day or two to get into my purse and take three dollars out of it. Now, she'd always take the ones she got for tips and exchange them in the cash register. Melvin didn't mind, and we all do it. So I waited that day till I saw her doing that, and then I got Melvin and asked him to look in the register."

"What happened?" Tuck prompted when she fell silent.

"It was real unpleasant," Wanda Nell continued after a sigh. "He found the marked ones, just like I told him he would, but Fayetta swore up and down she hadn't put them in there. I could see Melvin wanted to believe me, but I couldn't really prove I hadn't put them in there myself."

"Melvin oughta known you don't lie or cheat, Mama," T.J. said hotly.

"He knew," Wanda Nell said. "But without better proof he couldn't do much. He did tell Fayetta he'd known me a long time and I'd never lied to him before. He was going to give her the benefit of the doubt this time, but if anything like this happened again, he'd have to reconsider." She paused. "That was before he started sleeping with her."

"Did she stop stealing from you?" Tuck asked.

"Yeah, she sure did," Wanda Nell answered. "Soon as Melvin walked off, I got up in her face and told her that if I found any more money missing from my purse or from one of my tables, I was calling in the sheriff. And since he and my daddy had been real good friends, I'd see him haul her sorry rear end off to jail where it belonged."

T.J. snorted, then tried to turn it into a cough.

"From that point on, Fayetta tried to do me dirty any way she could," Wanda Nell said. "She didn't steal from me any more, but she talked about me behind my back like you wouldn't believe. And the next time Bobby Ray showed up in town, she made sure she got him into bed, and then told me all about it."

"That was pretty foul," Tuck commented. "Even if he was your ex-husband."

"That was the way she was," Wanda Nell said. "She hated it because Melvin and the customers respected me, and nobody in her whole life ever respected her. She never did nothing to earn it, and it galled her that men in the restaurant treated me different." She shook her head. "Pretty pitiful, when you get right down to it."

"What else can you tell me about her?" Tuck asked.

"Well, she had four kids," Wanda Nell said, after thinking a moment. "Each one of them had a different daddy, from what I heard. The oldest one's about ten, and the youngest one's about four. She had it right before she started working at the Kountry Kitchen."

"Is there someone to look after them? Their fathers?"

"Fayetta's mama probably has them," Wanda Nell said. "None of their daddies ever paid much attention to them. Far as I know, they're probably all married men, because that's mostly what Fayetta went after."

"Sounds like a soap opera," T.J. commented. "Those poor kids."

"*Those poor kids* is right," Wanda Nell said, heat coloring her voice. "Fayetta for a mama was bad enough and then not having no daddy around, but Fayetta's mama is . . ." Words failed her.

"What?" Tuck asked.

Wanda Nell shrugged. "Her name is Agnes Vance, and she belongs to one of them real strict churches. No dancing, no playing cards, no drinking, all that kind of thing. And her and Fayetta didn't get along, not by a

49

long shot. She'll be the one to look after Fayetta's kids, and if they don't turn out like their mama, I'll be surprised." She sighed. "You can't raise kids like that, never letting them have any fun, and expect them not to run wild when they get old enough."

"And sometimes they run wild even if you do let 'em have fun growing up," T.J. said wryly.

Wanda Nell nodded. "Yeah, ain't that the truth! But at least you saw the error of your ways, honey. And look at you now."

T.J. smiled, blushing a little. "Thank you, Mama."

Tuck patted him on the knee. "He's turned himself around, no doubt about that." He and T.J. exchanged grins. Then Tuck turned back to Wanda Nell.

"What about Mrs. Sutton and Melvin Arbuckle?" He regarded Wanda Nell intently.

Wanda Nell took her time before answering. "I've known Melvin a long time," she finally said. "He was three years ahead of me in school, and he asked me out once when he was a senior and I was a freshman. I wanted to go, because a lot of the girls would've given anything to be asked out by him. But my mama and daddy said I was too young to be going out with a senior." She broke off for a moment, lost in the memories of twenty-six years earlier.

"Anyway," she went on, "I've known Melvin a long time. He's always had women after him, but he never got married. Don't know why. Maybe he liked playing around too much." She shrugged. "Fayetta made it clear from the get-go that she was available. She was always brushing up against him, that kind of thing. Melvin ignored her for a long time, but about a year ago, I could tell they were, well, involved, I guess."

"Was it a serious relationship?" Tuck asked.

Again Wanda Nell shrugged. "I think maybe Fayetta might've wanted it to be, but Melvin didn't act like he wanted anything permanent. I think he had enough sense not to marry her, and her with those kids. So one week they'd be going hot and heavy, and the next week Fayetta would hardly talk to him."

"That might not look good for Melvin," T.J. said.

"Maybe not," Wanda Nell said, "if he was the only man Fayetta'd been involved with the last coupla years."

"Do you know for a fact that she was seeing another man, or other men?" Tuck had his pen ready to write down names.

Wanda Nell hesitated. She wanted to help Melvin, but she didn't want to drag someone else into the mess, someone who might be innocent, too.

"If it can help Melvin, Wanda Nell, I need to know," Tuck prodded, his voice gentle. "I know it's distasteful to talk about these things, but in a situation like this, it's unavoidable."

"You're right, I know," Wanda Nell said, sighing and leaning back in her chair. T.J. watched her, his face expressing his sympathy.

"Tuck's got to be able to come up with reasonable doubt, Mama," T.J. said when his mother failed to continue. "If he can show that someone else had a

51

motive, then it'll help Melvin."

"Yeah," Wanda Nell said, rubbing a hand tiredly across her face. "Well, here goes. A coupla times I overheard Melvin and Fayetta arguing about her seeing other men. Fayetta wasn't real shy about naming names, and I couldn't help but hear a couple of them."

"Who were they?" Tuck asked.

"Deke Campbell was one of them," Wanda Nell said. "And the other was Billy Joe Eccles."

Both Tuck and T.J. whistled at the same time. Deke Campbell was president of the bank in Tullahoma, married with several grown children, while Billy Joe Eccles was one of the leading businessmen. He owned the biggest grocery store in town, along with several gas stations and a clothing store on the town square. He had a finger in a lot of pies, as did Deke Campbell.

"Two prominent and powerful men in Tullahoma," Tuck said, his voice slightly strained. "Both married and rich."

"Uh-huh," Wanda Nell said, "and ain't neither of them gonna take kindly to someone poking into their private business."

"You could say that again," Tuck said, his voice stronger. "And that means this case is going to take some delicate handling." He slapped his notebook against his knee. "Mind you, I'm not afraid of rattling a few cages if I have to. But I don't want to if I don't have to."

52

"I think that would be pretty smart," Wanda Nell said. "I don't know that much about Deke Campbell, but I heard that Billy Joe Eccles is pretty mean if you get crossways of him."

"Then we just won't get crossways of him," T.J. said firmly. He turned to look at Tuck. "Will we?"

Tuck grinned. "Maybe not. But I can be pretty tough if someone gets crossways of me. You just remember that."

T.J. stared at him. Wanda Nell watched them both, aware of some odd tension between them.

"I'm not aiming to get crossways of anybody," she said firmly, ending the moment of uncomfortable silence. "But I'm going to do what I can to help Melvin."

Tuck and T.J. focused their attention on her. "I won't be able to do much until Melvin goes before the magistrate," Tuck said, "when we hear the charges and the evidence against him. But I'm going to do some digging, and if you find out anything helpful, Wanda Nell, I'd appreciate knowing it. I don't want you to put yourself in danger, though."

"I won't," Wanda Nell said. "And if I do, I'll have backup." She thought with a smile of Mayrene and her shotgun. Mayrene would face down anybody with that shotgun.

"There's one other thing," T.J. said. "What about the Kountry Kitchen?"

Wanda Nell stared at him, dismayed. She hadn't thought about the restaurant even once. She'd been

53

too focused on the murder itself and proving Melvin's innocence.

"Well, shoot," she said. "You're right, T.J. Somebody's got to keep the restaurant open. We can't just close it down while Melvin's in jail."

"Can you run it, Wanda Nell?" Tuck asked.

"Yeah, I guess so," Wanda Nell said slowly. She'd certainly worked there long enough to know all she needed to keep it running the way Melvin would. "But that's not my only job. I can't afford to miss my shift at Budget Mart, and I can't be at the restaurant all day and then work at Budget Mart, too."

"Could you take any time off from Budget Mart?" Tuck asked. "Say a couple of weeks? Do they give you any vacation time?"

"I got some hours built up," Wanda Nell said. "I'll talk to my supervisor and see if I can work something out." She had been hoping to take a couple weeks off later in the summer, before Juliet had to go back to school, so they could go visit her cousin in Jackson for a few days. But this was more important.

"Would you have to be at the Kountry Kitchen all day long, Mama?" T.J. asked. "Couldn't someone else open up, maybe, and you close up? Or vice versa?"

Wanda Nell thought for a moment. "We're gonna be short-handed without Melvin and Fayetta both." She shook her head. "You know, I can't believe this is all happening. It's just too weird. But I guess it is happening, and that means we have to deal with it. I know somebody I can call who'll probably be willing

54

to work. I can trust her to open up in the morning and work through lunch. Then I can come in at lunch and work through closing at night. But we're still gonna need at least one more waitress."

"What about me, Mama?" T.J. asked. "Can I help somehow? I've got a little experience. I worked in a restaurant in Houston for a few months."

"You hadn't told me that," Wanda Nell said, surprised. T.J. had yet to tell her much about the time he had spent in Houston, just prior to returning to Tullahoma a few months ago. He hadn't seemed to want to talk about it, and she hadn't pushed him.

T.J. shrugged. "Yeah, well, it wasn't that exciting, but I can bus tables and do things like that, if you need me. I can probably even wait on tables, too."

"Don't forget I'm going to need you helping *me* on this case, and the other ones I'm working on right now."

T.J. flushed slightly at Tuck's words, which Wanda Nell thought were a mite sharp. "I reckon I can get by," Wanda Nell said mildly into the awkward pause. "I don't want to waste T.J.'s valuable time busing tables if he's got something more important to do."

Now it was Tuck's turn to flush slightly. "I'm sorry, Wanda Nell," he said. "I didn't mean it that way." He smiled, fully aware of the effect of his charm when he did so. "It's just that I've gotten to where I really count on T.J.'s help in the office. He's the best assistant I ever had."

"Then he's better off working with you," Wanda

55

Nell said, accepting the apology with a smile of her own. "I doubt it'll take me long to turn up some help. There's always somebody wanting a job, and with the kids out of school for the summer, I can probably find one real quick."

"Good. That's settled," Tuck said, getting up from the couch. "I'm heading back to the office. You coming, T.J.?"

"Yeah," T.J. said. "I'll be along in a few minutes."

Tuck nodded, said good-bye to Wanda Nell, then disappeared out the door. Moments later they heard his car pulling out of the driveway.

T.J. sat on the couch, an odd look on his face.

Wanda Nell watched him for a moment, waiting for him to speak. When he didn't, she said, "I'm not mad, honey. I'm really proud of you for working so hard at such a good job. The kind of training you're getting, maybe you'll want to go to college and law school yourself."

T.J. drew a deep breath. "Actually, Mama, Tuck and I've been talking about that. Maybe one of these days, but not right now. But there's something I need to talk to you about." He stopped abruptly and looked away from his mother.

Wanda Nell had a strange feeling in the pit of her stomach. She almost jumped out of her chair when she heard the phone ring.

"Hang on a minute," she said, gratefully heading into the kitchen to answer the phone.

Before she even had time to say hello, a voice

barked in her ear. "Wanda Nell, is that you?"

Without waiting for a response, Lucretia Culpepper, Wanda Nell's former mother-in-law, kept talking. "You tell T.J. I need him at home right this minute. I fell, and I need help."

"It's for you," Wanda Nell said to T.J., who had followed her into the kitchen.

"Grandma?" T.J. asked.

Wanda Nell nodded.

"Yes, ma'am," T.J. said into the phone. "Do you need something?" He listened for a moment. "I'll be right home, Grandma. Don't move." He hung up the phone.

"You think she really fell?" Wanda Nell asked.

T.J. shrugged. "Probably not. She knew I was here, and I guess she thought I'd stayed long enough. So now I got to go back there."

"Sorry, honey," Wanda Nell said.

"I won't have to stay long," T.J. said with a slight grin. "Soon as I tell her I'm needed at work, she won't mind. Tuck's got her eating out of his hand like you wouldn't believe."

"I'll just bet he does," Wanda Nell muttered. *And the old witch ain't the only one,* she added silently.

"We'll talk later, Mama," T.J. said, giving her a quick peck on the cheek. "Give Bug and Lavon a hug for me." Then he was gone.

Wanda Nell stood staring at the closed door, deep in thought, until she could hear Lavon yelling "Gamma" from his and Miranda's room.

She was real curious to know what T.J. wanted to talk to her about, and half afraid she wouldn't want to hear it when she did. Shrugging, she walked down the hall to take care of her grandson.

Five

Wanda Nell got Lavon changed into a fresh diaper and brought him into the kitchen for an afternoon snack. While her grandson happily ate animal crackers and sipped his milk, she got on the phone and did some calling around, trying to arrange for help at the Kountry Kitchen.

Her first call was to Ovie Ashmore, a semi-retired waitress she knew would probably be willing to help out for a while.

"Why, sure, Wanda Nell," Ovie said, her voice roughed by nearly fifty years of heavy smoking. "My daughter and her kids are down in Florida right now, visiting their other grandma and grandpa. So I'm getting a break from babysitting." She chuckled. "And bored out of my skull just watching TV all day long. I sure wouldn't mind earning a little extra money neither."

Or keeping up with what's going on, Wanda Nell thought, grinning. Ovie loved to talk and to know everybody's business, but she was a darn good waitress, and reliable to boot. Wanda Nell would need someone like Ovie until this whole mess was straightened out.

"You don't mind opening up in the morning?" Wanda Nell asked.

"Naw," Ovie said. "I wake up early anyway. Might as well be working."

"Thanks. I appreciate it," Wanda Nell said. After a slight pause, she continued. "People are gonna be talking about Melvin. You know how that goes. But I have to tell you, I don't think he did it."

"Damn straight," Ovie said firmly. She'd known Melvin since he was a boy and had worked for him before. "He's a good man, and I don't think he could do something like that." Wanda Nell had filled her in on the situation, as much as she could, before she had asked Ovie to help out at the Kountry Kitchen.

"Good, then I can count on you," Wanda Nell said, relieved. "I'll come over in a little while and drop off the key I've got." Melvin had insisted she keep one, in case of emergency. Neither one of them had ever expected something like this. "And if you got any questions, we can talk about it then."

"I'll be watching for you," Ovie said.

Wanda Nell hung up the phone, her mind busy gathering the details of everything that needed doing. She ticked them off in her head: Tell Ovie where to find the spare cash Melvin kept on hand for the cash register. Explain what shifts everybody was supposed to work. Call the cook and the dishwasher and make sure they'd show up like they were supposed to. Just for a start.

Half an hour later, she had covered the basics. She

was satisfied the Kountry Kitchen could open as usual on Monday morning. They should have enough food to get them through the day, but she'd need to talk to Melvin's various suppliers to make sure deliveries would continue as scheduled.

Juliet came into the kitchen at some point and took over looking after the baby. Wanda Nell waved a hand at her gratefully, and Juliet smiled back.

Her last call was to her supervisor at Budget Mart. She explained the situation to Mr. Tompkins, and he agreed she could use some of her vacation hours on such short notice. "Ordinarily I couldn't okay a last-minute request like this, Wanda Nell," he said, "but seeing as it's you asking, and you having such a good record here, well, I guess we can be lenient this one time."

"Thanks, Mr. Tompkins. I sure appreciate it, and I'm sorry I had to bother you at home," Wanda Nell said. "I'm hoping that it'll only be for this week."

"That would be good," Tompkins replied. "We'll look forward to having you back. Things get done like they should when you're here."

Wanda Nell breathed a sigh of relief as she hung up the phone. That had been easier than she expected.

"What all's going on, Mama?" Juliet asked as she came back into the kitchen. "I put Lavon in his playpen in the living room and put on one of his Barney videos."

That purple dinosaur gave Wanda Nell a headache, but Lavon loved him. "Sit down, honey," she told

60

Juliet and waited until the girl was sitting at the table with her before continuing. "I guess you heard what happened. I mean, about Fayetta Sutton getting murdered, and Melvin being in jail."

Juliet nodded. "T.J. told me, but that's about all he told me." Her eyes grew round as she stared at her mother. "Mama, did Mr. Arbuckle do it?"

"No, honey, I don't think he did," Wanda Nell said. "Mr. Tucker's taking the case, and I'm going to help out. I'm going to be looking after the Kountry Kitchen as long as Melvin's in jail."

"You think they'll let him out on bail?"

"I don't see why not, but you never know. I'm just hoping it's soon, because I can't take too long off from Budget Mart."

"Can I do anything to help, Mama?"

Wanda Nell patted Juliet's hand. "You just keep on doing what you're doing now, sweetie. Look after Lavon, and try to keep your sister going to work like she should."

"I'll do my best," Juliet promised.

Wanda Nell checked the clock on the stove. It was nearly four. Miranda should be home soon, and Wanda Nell needed her car. If Mayrene hadn't gone off to meet her new boyfriend, she could've borrowed Mayrene's car.

A couple minutes past four, the phone rang. Wanda Nell answered.

"Mama, is it alright if I keep the car awhile?" Miranda's voice had that whiny, wheedling tone that

61

drove Wanda Nell crazy. "Me'n Chanelle're maybe gonna go get a bite to eat. It won't be more'n hour or so. And since you don't have to go to work tonight, I thought it'd be okay . . ." Her voice trailed off.

Wanda Nell took a couple of deep breaths before answering. At least Miranda had called to ask permission, instead of just not showing up at home until the good Lord knew when, like she used to. "If it was any other time, honey," she finally said, "I wouldn't mind. Truly, I wouldn't. You've been working hard, and you deserve a little fun."

"But not tonight."

Regretting the hurt in Miranda's voice, Wanda Nell spoke even more gently. "I'm sorry, Miranda. But something's happened, and I'm gonna need the car for a little while. Mayrene's gone, or I'd borrow her car. Right now, though, I need the car."

A long sigh came down the line. "Okay, Mama, I'm on my way." Then Miranda gave a squeak of alarm as the full import of her mother's words finally sank in. "Whatta you mean, something's happened? Is it Lavon? Is my baby okay?"

"Lavon is fine," Wanda Nell said firmly. "It's nothing to do with him. Something to do with work, and I'll tell you about it when you get here. So just come on home."

Miranda promised she would, and Wanda Nell hung up the phone, feeling pleased. Miranda was changing a bit, too. She wasn't as responsible or mature as her older brother, or even her younger sister half the time, but she was learning. Wanda Nell took heart at that.

True to her word, Miranda pulled into the driveway about ten minutes later. Wanda Nell quickly explained what was going on, leaving out a lot of the details, while Miranda stared at her, bewilderment on her face. "Good Lord, Mama," she finally said. "That's awful. That poor woman."

Wanda Nell nodded. She didn't want to think any more about what she had seen at Fayetta's house. She squeezed Miranda's arm. "Thanks for coming right home, honey. I'll make it up to you later, I promise."

"That's okay, Mama. I understand." Miranda shivered. "I just can't get over that poor woman."

"I know," Wanda Nell said. "Now you go on and help Juliet with Lavon, and I'll be back as soon as I can, okay?"

"Yes, Mama," Miranda said dutifully.

Wanda Nell grabbed her purse and picked up the chicken casserole she'd found in the freezer. After she had stopped by Ovie's to drop off the key, she thought she'd make another stop, and the chicken casserole would give her a good excuse.

The drive to Ovie's house, in a neighborhood near the high school, took only a few minutes. Wanda Nell handed over the key, gave Ovie a rundown on the things she needed to know, then politely refused a cup of coffee.

"I'm sorry," she said. "Any other time I'd love to,

63

Ovie. It's been a while since we've had a good visit. But right now I've got so much to do. You don't mind?"

"Sure, honey," Ovie said, "I know. We'll catch up tomorrow at the restaurant."

"Great," Wanda Nell said, relieved. She dearly loved Ovie, but the woman could talk the horns off a billy goat. "I'll see you then."

Back in her car, she pulled a scrap of paper from her purse. Before she'd left home, she'd looked up Agnes Vance in the phone book and scribbled down the address. If she was remembering rightly, the street wasn't far off the town square, in an old and slightly run-down, but still respectable, section of town.

She headed for Main Street and followed it all the way up to the square, casting a glance at old Mrs. Culpepper's house as she passed it. She turned off the square onto a street leading east, and a couple blocks later she found Parker Street. Stopping at the corner, she squinted in the mid-afternoon sun at the numbers on the street sign, then turned left.

Agnes Vance's house, a modest one-story red-brick dwelling with a front porch and detached garage, was the next-to-last house on the right. Wanda Nell pulled her car to a stop in front of it and examined the house for signs that someone was home. She noted absently that the paint on the porch was peeling and the steps leading up to the porch sagged a bit, but she could see no sign of anyone at home. The garage door was shut as well.

Taking a deep breath, Wanda Nell grabbed her purse, picked up the casserole, and headed up the walk to the porch. Gingerly climbing the steps, she saw that everything was neat and tidy, despite the need for a good paint job. Holding the still-cold casserole dish in her left hand, she rang the doorbell with her right and waited.

She was about to turn and walk back to her car when she heard footsteps inside the house. The door opened slightly, and a face appeared in the opening, shaded by the screen door.

"Miz Vance?" Wanda Nell said. "I'm Wanda Nell Culpepper. I work at the Kountry Kitchen. I'm real sorry about what happened, and I thought maybe this would come in handy." She held up the chicken casserole for Mrs. Vance to see.

Wanda Nell peered at the older woman through the mesh of the screen. At first she thought Mrs. Vance was just going to shut the door in her face without even saying a word, but just as the silence began to get awkward, Mrs. Vance pulled the door further open and pushed at the screen door.

"Come on in, Miz Culpepper," she said, standing aside and motioning Wanda Nell in with a hand.

Wanda Nell stepped inside, smiling uncertainly. Mrs. Vance's voice was cold and distant, but her actions were welcoming.

"I worked for several years with your daughter, Miz Vance," she said as the older woman accepted the casserole dish. "I can't tell you how shocked I was

65

when I heard what happened. It's a terrible, terrible thing."

Agnes Vance stood staring at her, the dish in her hands, saying nothing. Wanda Nell looked back at her, trying not to appear nervous, but the woman's unblinking stare was beginning to unnerve her. Tall and gaunt, she must have been about sixty, Wanda Nell reckoned. She wore a neat but faded house dress, and her dark hair, streaked liberally with gray, was caught up in a large bun at the back of her neck.

"The Lord's judgment is a terrible thing," Mrs. Vance said, her voice taking on some color, "but now she rests in the arms of Jesus. I've been praying for her, Miz Culpepper, and I hope you will too. Pray for the Lord to forgive her for the sinfulness of her ways and the wickedness in her heart."

Without waiting for a response, Mrs. Vance turned and walked down the hall. Not knowing what else to do, Wanda Nell followed her. The house was dark and chilly, and Wanda Nell shivered slightly as she walked into the kitchen behind Mrs. Vance.

Here at least was some light, the paint on the walls a bright yellow to contrast sharply with the darker colors of the hall. Afternoon sun streamed in through the windows, hitting the chrome legs of the kitchen table and chairs. Wanda Nell remembered her parents having a set like them when she was growing up. She stood there uncertainly, waiting for Mrs. Vance to say something.

The older woman set the casserole dish on a counter

where several other, similar dishes resided, then turned back to Wanda Nell. She gestured for Wanda Nell to take a seat at the table, and she did, setting her purse on the floor beside her.

"You will pray for her, won't you, Miz Culpepper?" Mrs. Vance regarded her intently.

"Oh, yes, ma'am," Wanda Nell said.

"You look like a good Christian woman," Mrs. Vance said. "Would you like some coffee or some lemonade?"

"Lemonade would be nice," Wanda Nell said.

Mrs. Vance turned away to get a pitcher of lemonade from the fridge and a couple of glasses from a cabinet near the sink. She poured two glasses, then returned the pitcher to the fridge. Handing Wanda Nell one of the glasses, she sat down at the table across from her guest.

Casting about for something to say, Wanda Nell took a sip of the lemonade to give herself a little more time to think. The lemonade was cold and tart, but delicious. She set the glass down on the table.

"How are the children doing, Miz Vance?" she asked. "I just can't imagine what a shock this is for them."

"The children were with me last night," Mrs. Vance said. "Thank the Lord they were spared the sight of His judgment upon their mother." She shook her head. "They've suffered enough from their mother's wickedness, but now I can be sure they will be raised without the taint of evil in their lives."

Wanda Nell wasn't sure how to respond to this. "I'm glad they were with you," she said. "They shouldn't have to see, well, you know . . ." Her voice trailed off.

Mrs. Vance nodded. "They've seen enough already, Miz Culpepper. The things those children were exposed to, you just wouldn't believe. I did my best raising that girl, I want you to know, and I never have understood how she came to be so wicked. Her father died when she was only twelve, and I reckon if she'd had her daddy to make her toe the line, she might've been a good girl. But I had to raise her by myself, and she was wild." She sighed. "She was just plain wild, and nothing I could do or say made a bit of difference to her. I prayed on my knees every night for the Lord to show her the way to righteousness, but it never happened."

Wanda Nell had some sympathy for Mrs. Vance, thinking about her own struggles with T.J. and Miranda. She had said more than a few prayers over them both, and she understood Mrs. Vance's anguish.

"I'm sorry she was such a trial to you," Wanda Nell said, trying to choose her words carefully. "I know what it's like to have a wayward child. No matter what you tell them, they just have to learn things for themselves."

Mrs. Vance nodded and sipped at her lemonade.

"Where are the children now?" Wanda Nell asked.

"They're all in their room," Mrs. Vance replied. "The older ones are doing their Bible study, and the youngest is taking her nap. With the Lord's help I aim to see they're not tainted with their mother's wickedness."

Wanda Nell didn't say anything for a moment. She had no quarrel with the woman's devotion to her faith, but she felt sorry for the children having to live under the care of someone who seemed not to have the slightest joy or humor in her. But there was nothing she could do about that. It wasn't her place, and it was Mrs. Vance's right to raise her grandchildren how she saw fit.

She remembered how Fayetta used to gripe about her mother. A time or two Fayetta had repeated the words Mrs. Vance had said to her, and the memory of the names Fayetta had called her mother almost made Wanda Nell blush now. She was thankful she and her own mother had had a very close relationship, nothing like the one between Fayetta and Mrs. Vance.

"If there's anything I can do to help," Wanda Nell said finally, "please let me know."

"Thank you kindly," Mrs. Vance replied. "As a matter of fact, there is something you can do, if you can. I heard they arrested Mr. Arbuckle. Is that true?"

"Yes, ma'am," Wanda Nell said. "But I have to tell you, Miz Vance, I don't think he did it. It must've been somebody else, and if you have any idea who else it could've been, please tell me."

Mrs. Vance's eyes narrowed. "She was fornicating with that man, and the Lord only knows how many other men. As far as I'm concerned, they all ought to be in jail."

Wanda Nell clutched her lemonade. Obviously she wasn't going to get any help for Melvin out of Mrs. Vance.

"She had some money coming to her from work," Mrs. Vance continued, "and I sure would appreciate it if I could get it. The children are going to need it, and I barely have enough for myself as it is."

"I'll take care of it," Wanda Nell said. She would talk to Tuck about it, and between them they could figure out the money situation. There might be enough in the petty cash to pay Mrs. Vance whatever Melvin owed Fayetta. She also decided, right then, that she'd start taking up money at the Kountry Kitchen for Fayetta's kids. All of Fayetta's regulars, and hers too, would probably chip in.

"I don't even know how I'm going to afford to bury her," Mrs. Vance said.

"Maybe we can get you some help for that," Wanda Nell said gently.

"I have to trust the Lord will provide," Mrs. Vance said, sighing tiredly.

"Is there anything else I can do?" Wanda Nell asked. Now was not the time to try to question Mrs. Vance about what she might know about her daughter's life. Wanda Nell genuinely did want to help, despite the way she had felt about Fayetta. Her heart went out to Fayetta's children, and she was determined to help them somehow.

Mrs. Vance just sat there, so quiet that Wanda Nell thought she hadn't heard the question.

70

"I don't want to go back to that house alone," Mrs. Vance said, her eyes cast down. "But the children are going to need their things, and somebody's going to have to clean up the house. Would you go with me? I don't know who else to ask."

"Yes, ma'am," Wanda Nell said. "I'll go with you." She felt a little guilty, because this was what she had been hoping for. "I'll find out from the sheriff's department when they'll let us do that, and I'll let you know."

"Thank you," Mrs. Vance said. "I appreciate that."

"I'd better be going," Wanda Nell said, standing up. "Thank you for the lemonade. It was delicious."

Mrs. Vance stood up and accompanied Wanda Nell to the door. The house was quiet except for the noise they made walking. If Mrs. Vance hadn't told her the children were there, she never would have known it.

"If you think of anything else I can help with," Wanda Nell said after she had stepped onto the porch, "you just give me a call. My number's in the book, or you can call me at the Kountry Kitchen."

Mrs. Vance nodded and thanked her again, then closed the door.

Wanda Nell made her way carefully down the porch steps and back to her car. She sat there a moment, feeling depressed by how horrible the whole mess was, then started up the car and headed for home. She didn't look back. That house, so cold and quiet, had unnerved her, and she couldn't wait to get back to her own, warm and full of life as it was.

Six

Wanda Nell barely got inside her door before Miranda was on the way out.

"I'll see you later, Mama," she said, hopping down the steps.

"Now, hold on a minute, Miranda," Wanda Nell said, standing in the doorway. Miranda turned to stare up at her, the sulky look already forming on her face.

"For one thing," Wanda Nell said mildly, "I've got the car keys, and you're not gonna get very far without them." For all she knew, Miranda'd had a set made for herself, though if she had, she'd been smart enough to hide that fact from her mother.

"Oh, yeah," Miranda said, her face clearing. She walked back a few steps to accept the keys from her mother's hand. "Thank you, Mama."

"And another thing," Wanda Nell said as her daughter was turning away.

The sulky look came back. Miranda stood, hands on hips, waiting. Wanda Nell breathed deeply before she spoke. "I just wanna remind you not to be out too late, honey. You've gotta get up and go to work in the morning, remember? I think it'd be a good idea if you were home by ten, then you can get plenty sleep."

"Yes, Mama," Miranda said in a bored tone. Wanda Nell was surprised the girl hadn't started arguing with her, the way she used to. *Thank heaven for small miracles,* Wanda Nell thought.

"We're gonna have to work out something about the car for the next few days," Wanda Nell said. "I'm gonna be working at the restaurant in the afternoon and closing out in the evening, and with you on the morning shift, it's gonna be hard for both of us to get to work and back."

"I could take a week off," Miranda said eagerly, "if that'd be a help to you, Mama. And then we wouldn't have to worry about the car."

Suppressing a sigh, Wanda Nell said, "No, honey, I can't ask you to do that. I'm gonna talk to your brother and see if he can't help us out somehow. We'll manage one way or another. You can't afford to be missing any work, and neither can I."

Miranda frowned, but she didn't say anything for a moment. Then she mumbled something under her breath. Wanda Nell decided to let it pass. "Now go on and enjoy yourself, honey," she said. "Just try to be back by ten."

Without waiting for a response, she stepped inside and closed the door. Shaking her head, she thought about what Mrs. Vance had said about Fayetta. At least Miranda was making an effort, however grudging, to straighten herself up a bit. Fayetta apparently never had, to hear Mrs. Vance tell it.

Before calling T.J., Wanda Nell checked on Juliet and Lavon. Moving quietly down the hall toward Juliet's room, she paused at the threshold and peeked

73

inside. Juliet was busy doing something on the computer and Lavon crouched on the floor near her, playing with some of his toys. Deciding they'd be fine by themselves for a while longer, Wanda Nell stole away to the kitchen.

Hoping that her son would answer and not his grandmother, Wanda Nell punched in the number.

"Hello," said an old, thin voice.

Wanda Nell grimaced. "Hello, Miz Culpepper, this is Wanda Nell. How are you?" She was going to be polite to the old biddy if it killed her.

"I was resting until the phone disturbed me," Mrs. Culpepper replied, her voice stronger. "What do you want, Wanda Nell? I hope you're not calling to bother T.J. He can't be running over there every other minute when I need him here."

Before Wanda Nell could get a word in edgewise, Mrs. Culpepper continued her litany of grievances.

"Since Charlesetta had the nerve to up and quit on me, I need T.J. here to help me. I keep thinking I'll try to find me another woman to help out here, but you know the blacks these days have some uppity ideas. None of the young ones want to work like they ought to, and the older ones say they're too old to work in a house like this with all the stairs. You think they'd be honored to work here, but that doesn't mean a thing to them."

With that kind of attitude toward black people, Wanda Nell reflected, it was no wonder nobody wanted to work for the old woman. She was a

74

dinosaur, but there were still a lot of people around who thought just the way she did. "Well, Miz Culpepper, Charlesetta *is* in her seventies," she pointed out mildly, "and after she had that heart attack, the doctor told her she couldn't work no more for you. Going up and down those steps like to've killed her as it was."

"I'm just as old as Charlesetta, or near about," Mrs. Culpepper snapped. "And I still make it up and down those steps several times a day."

Wanda Nell decided there was no point in answering that. Instead she said, "If you can't find some black lady to come in and work for you, maybe you could find some nice white woman or a girl who'd do it. There's bound to be people out there looking for jobs."

"I don't know," Mrs. Culpepper said. "I'm getting to where I don't want strangers in my house. I don't like the idea of some white trash coming in here and looking at my things and then stealing me blind behind my back."

Gripping the phone tightly in her hand, Wanda Nell did her best to hold her temper. "At some point you're gonna have to have some help, Miz Culpepper. You can't expect T.J. to be there all the time, doing the housework and everything, not when he's got a job. I mean, it's only part-time right now, but he could maybe start taking classes at the junior college this fall and still work, too. Don't you want him to improve himself?"

That was the old woman's weak spot. She doted on her grandson, and even though she did her best to control him, she did sincerely want the best for him. Or so Wanda Nell believed and hoped.

"I guess maybe you're right," Mrs. Culpepper said, her tone grudging. "Maybe I'll start asking around and find out if there's a good Christian white woman who'll come in and work for me a few days a week."

"That's a good idea," Wanda Nell said. "And if I hear of anybody suitable, I'll let you know." Before Mrs. Culpepper could comment on that, she hurried on. "Is T.J. there? I need to talk to him for a minute."

"No, he's not here," Mrs. Culpepper said, sounding aggrieved. "He's with Mr. Tucker down at his office. They're working on something down there, something to do with that boss of yours who hacked up that slutty waitress you work with. What's her name?"

Though Wanda Nell couldn't argue with Mrs. Culpepper's description of Fayetta, she despised the tone of malicious glee in the old woman's voice. "Her name was Fayetta Sutton," Wanda Nell said, trying not to snap back at her. "And no matter how she lived her life, she didn't deserve to die that way." She probably sounded self-righteous, but she didn't care. Mrs. Culpepper had no call to talk like that about someone she probably had never even met. Then a thought struck her.

"How do *you* know how she died?"

There was silence on the other end. Then Mrs.

Culpepper hesitantly said, "I heard it."

"Where did you hear it?" Wanda Nell demanded. Surely T.J. hadn't told his grandmother anything. Was the story of Fayetta's death already racing through the Tullahoma grapevine?

"If you must know," Mrs. Culpepper said, her voice suddenly prim, "I just happened to overhear T.J. and Mr. Tucker talking about it right after T.J. came back from your place this afternoon."

Rightly figuring that meant Mrs. Culpepper had been listening in on a phone conversation, Wanda Nell decided she'd better warn her son the old woman was probably listening to every phone call he made. He didn't have a cell phone, but maybe he ought to get one if he wanted any privacy.

"You need to be real careful about talking to anyone about it," Wanda Nell said, knowing that trying to tell the old witch what to do was a lost cause.

"For your information, Wanda Nell, I do not gossip." The chill in her voice amused Wanda Nell, because she knew Mrs. Culpepper liked nothing better than to spread any kind of tale she heard, even about people she'd never met.

"I guess I'll try calling T.J. at the office, then," Wanda Nell said. She started to say good-bye, but Mrs. Culpepper interrupted her.

"Now, don't be in such a rush, Wanda Nell," the old woman said in a friendlier tone. "Since you've already disturbed me, there's something I reckon you and I ought to talk about."

"What's that?" Wanda Nell asked warily, ignoring the jibe.

"It's T.J.," Mrs. Culpepper said. "I've been introducing him to some real nice girls at church. They're pretty too, so it's not that. They're all from good families, the kind of girls he ought to be associating with. I can see they're interested in him. After all, why shouldn't they be? He's a very handsome boy, just like his daddy was, and he's a Culpepper, too, despite the way he was raised. I've been teaching him proper manners, and he knows how to behave with a young lady. But he won't call any of them or go out with them."

Wanda Nell ignored the thinly veiled insult, though she dearly wanted to slam the phone down. Instead, she waited a moment, then calmly said, "T.J.'s already got a lot on his plate, Miz Culpepper. He's working, *and* he's looking after you. That don't leave him a whole lot of time to socialize." She didn't mention the fact that T.J. also didn't have the money to be taking these girls out to the kinds of places they'd expect to be taken, although she didn't doubt Mrs. Culpepper would come up with the money if T.J. would only cooperate. "Besides, he's barely twenty-two. He doesn't need to be rushing into anything. He's got to figure out what he's going to be doing with himself, and he doesn't need some little ol' girl hanging on his arm, wanting attention all the time."

"I'm only thinking of his best interests," Mrs. Culpepper said, her tone huffy. "After all, if he's going

78

to succeed in this town, he's going to need to marry the right kind of girl. Surely *you* of all people know that. If he marries the wrong girl, it could ruin his life."

Wanda Nell thought the top of her head was going to come off, her temper flared so quickly. She wanted to say something, but she was so angry she couldn't think clearly enough to respond.

"I guess I won't try to force him," Mrs. Culpepper continued, "because he's as stubborn as his daddy ever was, the Lord rest his dear soul. But you try talking to him, Wanda Nell; tell him how important it is to marry the right girl."

Wanda Nell hung up the phone before she started screaming into it. No one else had the power to make her this angry. She fussed at herself for letting Mrs. Culpepper get to her. She started taking deep breaths to calm herself. After a minute or so, she felt better, more in control.

She sat down at the kitchen table and stared into space. She sure would be talking to T.J., she decided, but she for damn sure wasn't going to do what Mrs. Culpepper wanted her to. Instead she was going to let him know he wouldn't be hearing any of that non-sense from her, and not to let his grandmother push him into something he didn't want to do or wasn't ready for.

She got up and poured herself some Coke. She drank half the glass before she went back to the phone. She consulted her list of numbers for Tuck Tucker's office number and punched it in.

"Law offices of Hamilton Tucker," T.J. said after the phone had rung three times. "How can I help you?"

"T.J., it's me," Wanda Nell said.

"Hang on a minute, Mama," T.J. said before she could continue.

He must have put his hand over the mouthpiece, Wanda Nell decided. She could hear the sound of talking, but everything was muffled. She thought she heard somebody laugh, but she wasn't sure. She was getting pretty annoyed with T.J. and was about to hang up when he came back on the line.

"Sorry, Mama," he said, his voice a little breathless. "I, uh, I knocked something over, and we had to clean it up before it ruined some papers."

"That's okay," Wanda Nell said. "Did you need something?"

"Well, I need to talk to you about your grandmother," Wanda Nell said, "but that can wait. Right now I need to talk to Tuck about a few things."

"Hang on," T.J. said.

The line went quiet, then Wanda Nell heard music. She couldn't believe it, but he'd put her on hold. Surely Tuck couldn't be that busy on a Sunday afternoon, even if he did have a brand-new murder case to work on.

After nearly a minute, the music cut off and Tuck came on the line. "Sorry for making you wait, Wanda Nell. I was on another line. What can I do for you?"

Slightly soothed by the apology, Wanda Nell told

80

him about her visit to Agnes Vance. She concluded by saying, "I need to be able to give her whatever Melvin owed Fayetta in wages. Is that okay? She sure sounded like she needed the money. I don't know if she has a job or anything, but with them three kids to look after now, I'm sure she's going to need anything she can get."

"I'll talk to him about it," Tuck said. "I'll be going by the jail in the morning anyway, and if there's anything else you want me to discuss with him, let me know."

"Do you think I might be able to go see him?" Wanda Nell asked.

"I'll see," Tuck said. "It depends on the sheriff, but since he knows you, I'm guessing he'll probably okay it."

"Thanks," Wanda Nell said. She needed to see Melvin for herself, talk to him face to face. If she did, she could put to rest any doubts she might have.

"Is there anything else?"

"Yes," Wanda Nell said. "You might want to write some of this down."

"Shoot," Tuck said. "I'm ready."

She told him of the various arrangements she had made to keep the Kountry Kitchen running while Melvin was in jail. "I can probably get the suppliers to let us have what we need for a week, but after that they're gonna wanna be paid, so we need to arrange for that somehow."

"We will," Tuck assured her. "I'm sure Melvin will

81

be very glad to know that you're handling everything for him, Wanda Nell. Just from the conversation I had with him earlier today, I know he has a lot of respect for you."

"I'm just doing what anybody would do to help out a friend," she said. Compliments made her uneasy.

Tuck didn't embarrass her any further. Instead he said, "Just let me know if there's anything else you'll need at the restaurant. You have my cell phone number, don't you?"

Wanda Nell assured him she did, then before he rang off, she asked if she could speak to T.J. for a minute.

"What is it, Mama?" T.J. sounded slightly impatient.

Ignoring that, Wanda Nell explained the dilemma of having only the one car.

"What time do you wanna be at the Kountry Kitchen?" T.J. asked.

"By two, I guess," Wanda Nell said.

"Then I'll come pick you up and take you there," T.J. said. "I'll get me some lunch, and by then Miranda'll be getting off work. She can come there, too, and leave the car for you, and I'll take her home. Let me just check with Tuck."

Wanda Nell waited while her son held another muffled conversation with his boss. "Tuck said that's fine with him. He'll only need me part of the day this week."

"Good," Wanda Nell said. "But what about your grandmother?"

"Don't worry about Granny," T.J. said. "I'll work it out with her."

"Thank you, son, I appreciate it," Wanda Nell said, "and lunch will be on me, how's that?"

"It's a date," T.J. said. "See you tomorrow, Mama."

"Bye," Wanda Nell said and hung up the phone. She decided she'd wait till the next day to talk to T.J. about his grandmother and her plans for his social life. She glanced at the clock. It was about time for somebody to start thinking about dinner for her and Juliet and Lavon. She got up from the table and set to work.

After dinner, and after getting Lavon settled for the night, Wanda Nell wearily sat down on the sofa in the living room, planning to read for a while. Juliet was back in her room, playing with the computer again. Wanda Nell hoped she wasn't going to put her eyes out with the darn thing, but she supposed it was good for Juliet to be learning about it. She picked up her book, a new one by Caroline Burnes, one of her favorite writers, and tried to concentrate.

The closer the time edged toward ten o'clock, the less she could focus on the book. Ten o'clock came and went, and no sign of Miranda. No phone call either. Wanda Nell put her book aside, trying not to feel either anxious or angry.

Ten-thirty. She was pacing around the living room and kitchen, unable to settle down. She should have given Miranda her cell phone to take with her. Maybe she was having car trouble and couldn't get to a phone. Next time she'd insist on Miranda taking the cell phone with her. Or maybe she'd suggest that Miranda start saving some money to get one of her own.

Ten-forty-five. Should she go out looking for her? Wanda Nell checked, but Mayrene still wasn't home. She might be able to borrow a car from one of her other neighbors, but at this late hour, she hated taking a chance on waking them up.

She picked up the phone in the kitchen and punched in Mrs. Culpepper's number instead. Her former mother-in-law usually turned the ringer on her bedside phone off during the night so no one would disturb her. It should be safe to call T.J., though she hated to wake him up.

The phone rang and rang. Wanda Nell let it ring fifteen times. Mrs. Culpepper didn't have an answering machine, considering them vulgar devices. Frustrated, Wanda Nell put the phone back on its cradle. Why hadn't T.J. answered the phone? Surely he ought to be home and in bed by now.

Maybe he and Tuck were still working at the office. Wanda Nell knew that Tuck sometimes worked long hours, and on occasion T.J. had stayed on to help him, long after Tuck's secretary had gone home. She picked up the phone and called Tuck's office.

The answering machine came on, advising her to call Tuck's cell phone if this was an emergency. Wanda Nell found the piece of paper where she'd written down the number earlier in the day. Should she call it? Maybe Tuck knew where T.J. was, but she

84

hated to disturb him if he was at home and asleep. But, she reasoned, if he didn't want to talk to anybody, he would turn the phone off.

Frustrated and not sure what else to do, she decided to call. The phone rang three times, and Wanda Nell thought she was about to get Tuck's voice mail, when Tuck answered.

"Tuck Tucker," he said.

"Tuck, this is Wanda Nell," she said, rushing her words. "I'm sorry to bother you so late at night, but I need to talk to T.J., and I don't know where he is. I tried calling him at his grandmother's, but nobody answered the phone, and I'm a little worried." She came to a halt, almost out of breath.

"It's okay," Tuck said after a brief pause. "Actually, T.J.'s here with me, at my house. We worked right through dinner, and I figured the least I owed him was something decent to eat. Hold on a second, and I'll hand him the phone."

"Thanks," Wanda Nell said.

T.J. spoke after a moment, sounding both irritated and frightened. "What's wrong, Mama? Why are you calling Tuck so late at night?"

"It's Miranda, honey. She was supposed to be home by ten o'clock, and here it is, nearly eleven, and I'm getting a little worried."

"Now, Mama," T.J. said, soothingly, "you know Miranda. She's just out having a good time and forgot to pay attention to the clock. I bet she'll be home any minute now, and you can fuss at her then."

"Maybe," Wanda Nell said, "but it just makes me nervous. I don't like the idea of her being out so late when she's got to go to work in the morning."

"I know," T.J. said, "but give her another half hour or so, Mama, and I bet she'll be home. If you don't hear from her by midnight, call me back and I'll go out and look for her."

"Where will you be?" Wanda Nell asked. "Surely you're not going to stay that late at Tuck's house and leave your grandmother all by herself."

T.J. didn't say anything for a minute. "Actually, Mama," he said hesitantly, "I was gonna spend the night here. I'm really tired, and we had a little wine with dinner, and I don't feel like driving back to Granny's. She'll be okay one night on her own."

"Well, I guess so," Wanda Nell said slowly. There was something odd about T.J.'s voice, and she couldn't quite put her finger on it. Maybe he was just slightly drunk from the wine. She was about to say something to him when she realized a car had pulled into her driveway.

"Listen, honey, there's Miranda now. I'll talk to you later," she said. She hung up the phone, forgetting all about T.J. Instead, she started telling herself to keep calm and not yell at Miranda and went to open the door.

Seven

The next morning, Wanda Nell woke up with a headache. After she shut off the alarm clock, she lay there for a couple of minutes with her eyes shut, massaging her temples and forehead, hoping the pain would ease. That didn't help much, so she went into the bathroom she shared with Juliet and found some aspirin.

Staring at herself in the bathroom mirror, she decided she looked hungover. Since she rarely ever drank these days and sure hadn't last night, that hardly seemed fair. She splashed her face with cold water, then brushed her hair. Feeling a little more human, and sensing the pain begin to recede, she went back to her bedroom and pulled her robe on over her nightgown.

In the kitchen, Juliet was spooning cereal into Lavon's mouth. As soon as he spotted his grandmother, he started banging his hands on the tray of his high chair and crooning "Gamma." Wanda Nell kissed his sticky face and ruffled his hair. They talked nonsense to each other for a moment while Juliet waited patiently with the spoon. She eyed her mother critically as Wanda Nell wiped some cereal from her cheek.

"You look terrible, Mama. Didn't you sleep well?"

Wanda Nell poured herself some coffee and brought

it to the table before answering. "Not too well, honey. Took me forever to get off to sleep last night." She yawned.

"I guess so," Juliet said. "The way you and Miranda were arguing last night, it's a wonder the neighbors didn't call the sheriff's department."

Wanda Nell grimaced. "Were we really that loud?"

Juliet laughed. "Maybe not *that* loud. But loud enough. I'm just glad Lavon didn't wake up and start crying. You know he hates it when y'all argue."

"I know, honey, I know." Wanda Nell sipped at her coffee. "I told myself I wasn't going to lose my temper with her, even though she was way over an hour late last night and didn't have the decency to call and tell me she was okay."

" 'And not lying dead on the side of the road somewhere,' " Juliet quoted, grinning at her mother.

"Very funny, missy," Wanda Nell said sourly. "You just wait till you have kids, you'll see."

"My children will be perfect and never cause me a bit of trouble," Juliet said loftily, then laughed.

"Uh-huh," Wanda Nell said. "I hate to even ask this, but did Miranda get up and go to work?"

"She sure did," Juliet said. She had such an innocent look on her face that Wanda Nell was immediately suspicious.

"How'd you get her up and out the door, or shouldn't I ask?"

"I have my ways," Juliet said, gazing blandly at her mother.

88

Wanda Nell regarded her for a moment, then shrugged. "As long as she got up and went to work, it don't matter, I guess."

"Can I fix you some breakfast, Mama?"

"I'm not real hungry just yet," Wanda Nell said. "I'll fix me some toast or something in a while." She drained the last of the coffee from her cup and got up for a refill. "What are you and Lavon going to do today?"

"Oh, we're gonna play outside and build us a sand castle or two, and maybe we'll watch a little Barney and have a bath and a nap at some point." Juliet rubbed her nephew affectionately on the head. "Doesn't that sound like fun, Lavon?"

Lavon agreed so enthusiastically that a few blobs of cereal that had been stuck on his hands went flying through the air. Laughing, Wanda Nell snatched up a paper towel and cleaned up the small mess he'd made.

"Sounds like a good plan to me," Wanda Nell said, dropping the paper towel into the trash bin under the sink. "Y'all just be careful while you're outside. Be on the lookout for snakes. T.J. did a good job with that little sandbox he made for Lavon, but you can never be too careful with snakes." She shuddered.

"I know, Mama," Juliet said. "Don't worry." She pulled Lavon from his high chair. "I'll clean that up later, Mama, so don't you bother with it. I'm going to get Lavon dressed, and we're going outside to play for a while."

Lavon held out his arms for another hug from his grandmother before he'd let Juliet take him out of the kitchen. After a couple of hugs, Wanda Nell waved bye at him as Juliet carried him off.

She glanced at the clock. It was nearly nine. She resisted the impulse to call the Kountry Kitchen and check on how things were going. If there were any problems, Ovie would've called her before now.

She did need to call Tuck Tucker though. Lying awake last night, she'd thought back over the day and realized she'd forgotten to ask Tuck about something. She needed him to find out from the sheriff's department when she and Agnes Vance would be able get into Fayetta's house to retrieve the things Mrs. Vance needed for Fayetta's kids. There had been so many distractions, it was a wonder she hadn't forgotten more than that.

Thinking about Tuck also reminded her that she was real peeved with T.J. She didn't like the idea of him leaving his grandmother alone at night like he'd done. She could understand him wanting a break from playing nursemaid and housekeeper, but as long as he'd agreed to live with his grandmother, he should stick to his part of the deal. They were going to have a little talk about that when he came to take her to the Kountry Kitchen.

Wanda Nell picked up the phone and called Tuck's office. After one ring a cheerful voice answered, "Hamilton Tucker's office. How may I help you?"

"Hey, Blanche, this is Wanda Nell."

"Hey, girl, how're you doing? You and that cousin of mine getting up to anything lately?" Blanche Tillman, Tuck's secretary, was Mayrene Lancaster's cousin. Mayrene had suggested Wanda Nell call Tuck's office a couple of months ago when T.J. had needed a lawyer. Since then, with T.J. working there, Wanda Nell had gotten to know Blanche quite a bit better.

"Mayrene's busy with a new boyfriend," Wanda Nell said. "She tell you about him?"

"No, she sure as heck didn't," Blanche said. "Come on now, tell me what you know."

They gossiped amiably for a couple of minutes about Mayrene, with Blanche making a few jokes about Mayrene dating an undertaker. All of a sudden Blanche interrupted the flow of confidences. "I believe Mr. Tucker can speak with you now, Miz Culpepper."

"He just walked in there, didn't he?" Wanda Nell almost laughed.

"Yes, that's correct," Blanche said primly. "I'll transfer you to his private line."

Wanda Nell heard a couple of rings on the line, then Tuck picked up.

"Morning, Wanda Nell," he said. "What can I do for you this fine day?"

"You sure sound happy today," she said, slightly disgruntled by the cheery tone of his voice.

"That's because I am, I guess," Tuck said, laughing. "Now, what can I do for you?"

Wanda Nell tried not to sound peevish when she responded. "I forgot to ask you about something last night. When I talked to Agnes Vance yesterday, she asked me if I'd go with her to her daughter's house. She needs to get the children's things and some other stuff. Can you find out from the sheriff's department when we might do that?"

"Sure thing," Tuck said. "I'm heading over to the jail in a few minutes and I'll talk to Deputy Johnson. I'll see if y'all can't go over there sometime tomorrow, but of course there'll have to be someone from the department there with you."

"Thanks, Tuck," Wanda Nell said. "Tomorrow morning would be fine. Just let me know, and I'll talk to Miz Vance."

Tuck told her to have a good day, and Wanda Nell wished him the same, then hung up the phone. "I guess if I was a rich lawyer, I'd wake up all chirpy like a bird every day, too." She addressed her remark to the kitchen table, stared at it blankly for a moment, then got up to make herself some breakfast.

After finishing her toast and coffee, Wanda Nell started in on some of the household chores she hadn't had time for the day before. She did several loads of laundry, mopped the kitchen floor, and was about to start in on the bathrooms when the phone rang. She picked up the receiver after removing her rubber gloves and dropping them in the sink.

"Wanda Nell, it's Tuck."

"What's up?"

"Are you where you can come on down to the jail right now? Sorry for the short notice, but Melvin insists on talking to you, and I've got the okay from the sheriff's department."

Wanda Nell sighed into the phone. "Well, considering I look like I've been rode hard and put away wet after doing housework all morning, I need a little time to take a shower and get dressed."

"That's fine," Tuck said hastily. "We're not in that much of a hurry."

"Good. One more thing, though," Wanda Nell said.

"What's that?"

"I don't have a way to get there." She explained the car situation.

"Don't worry," Tuck said. "T.J. can come get you. I know he was planning to come get you later anyway to take you to work. He can just come early."

"That's fine," Wanda Nell replied. "Tell him to give me thirty minutes and I'll be ready."

"He'll be there," Tuck said, then rang off.

Wanda Nell put her cleaning supplies away. The bathrooms would just have to wait awhile longer. Miranda was supposed to have cleaned them a couple days ago, but Miranda and housework weren't on real familiar terms most of the time.

A quick shower made her feel better. Wanda Nell washed her hair, wondering if it was time to get it cut. She combed it out and let it dry as she dressed, then pinned it back out of her face. By the time T.J. knocked on the door, she was ready to go. She'd even had time to tell Juliet where she was going and to reassure herself that her daughter and grandson hadn't found any snakes in the sandbox.

"You look nice, Mama," T.J. said as he held open the passenger door of his truck for her.

"Thank you, honey," she said. "You look real nice, too." Since he'd come back to Tullahoma a couple months ago, T.J. had stopped dressing like a derelict cowboy. He still wore jeans and boots most of the time, but the jeans were clean and pressed and the boots highly polished. He'd had his long, unkempt black hair cut short, and though he still sported a small gold ring in his left ear, he now looked like a nice, clean young man. Wanda Nell was thrilled with the transformation, but T.J. had never really confided in her about what had caused it all.

"Thanks," T.J. said, smiling at her. He backed the truck out of the driveway and headed for town. His eyes on the road ahead, T.J. spoke again. "I'm sorry about last night, Mama. I know I shouldn't have left Grandma alone all night. I promise it won't happen again."

"I know how wearing it can be," Wanda Nell said, "having to look after someone like that. Especially when you been used to doing what you want, when you want, and not having to think about somebody else."

T.J. started to say something, but she put her hand on his arm. "I'm not fussing at you, T.J. I'm just saying what's what. I understand how you feel. But

94

sometimes you gotta do what you don't want to because it's the right thing to do. You and your grandma made a deal, and she expects you to stick to it. So do I."

"I know that, Mama," T.J. said. "I said I won't let it happen again."

"I'm proud of you," Wanda Nell said. "But I also want you to know, if it gets to be too much for you—trying to look after your grandma and work and everything—you'll tell me. Ain't no sense in you running yourself into the ground trying to please your grandma all the time."

T.J. grinned at her. "I'd like to see the person alive who could please her all the time. I'm doing pretty good, but there's some things she just won't let alone." His face darkened. "I sure wish she'd stop trying to fix me up with these girls she knows."

"What's wrong with these girls she keeps shoving at you?" Wanda Nell asked curiously. "Are they all ugly or stupid or something?"

"No, it's not that," T.J. said, his voice suddenly strained. "I'll tell you about it later, Mama." He pulled the truck into a parking space at the jail. "Besides, we're here."

Wanda Nell sat and looked at him a moment, not answering. She patted his arm. "Okay, honey. You wanna wait out here for me?"

"Yeah," T.J. said. "I don't really wanna go back in there if I don't have to." He'd been arrested and had spent a few days here when his daddy had been murdered. Wanda Nell couldn't blame him for wanting to wait in the truck.

"I won't be too long," Wanda Nell said.

She was a bit nervous as she walked slowly to the door and on into the jail. She paused for a moment just inside the door, adjusting to the light, taking a couple of deep breaths to steady herself. She was glad to see Tuck there waiting for her.

The lawyer took care of the particulars, and soon a deputy was escorting Wanda Nell down the hall to the interview room. She'd been here before, and she liked it less each time.

She sat down at the desk the deputy indicated and stared through the glass dividing her part of the room from the inmates' side. Moments later a door opened, and Melvin Arbuckle entered, escorted by a deputy.

Wanda Nell kept her head down for a moment, waiting until Melvin was seated opposite her. She was afraid to look into his eyes. What if she'd been wrong? What if he really was guilty? She'd know it as soon as she looked into his face. He wouldn't be able to hide it from her.

"Wanda Nell. Look at me." Melvin's voice was quiet, raspy from too many cigarettes.

Slowly Wanda Nell raised her head until her gaze was level with his.

Eight

Wanda Nell stared right into Melvin's eyes. He met her gaze without flinching.

Wanda Nell read several things in his eyes: sadness, anxiety, maybe even despair, but not guilt. She relaxed. Not guilt. Melvin hadn't killed Fayetta.

"How're you doing, Melvin?" Wanda Nell said softly.

"Okay, I guess, considering." He shrugged.

His face was pale, the skin under his eyes dark. Otherwise he was neat as a pin, as always, which made his jail attire look almost natural.

"They treating you okay?"

"Not too bad."

"You didn't do it." Wanda Nell made it a statement, not a question.

"No, I didn't." Melvin's face brightened for a moment, and his eyes shone with gratitude. "You know I couldn't do something like that."

Wanda Nell shuddered involuntarily as a mental picture of Fayetta's bedroom flashed through her mind. "I know," she said, her voice low. "I went there to see it for myself."

"You shouldn't have done that," Melvin said. "You don't need to be seeing things like that."

"I had to know," Wanda Nell said. "And when I saw that, I knew you hadn't done it."

Now Melvin shuddered, his eyes closed. "God, Wanda Nell, it was horrible. I ain't never seen anything like it. Like somebody was butcherin' a hog." A few tears trickled down his cheeks. He wiped them away with a shaking hand.

"She didn't deserve that," Wanda Nell said gently.

Melvin shook his head. "God knows she could be a bitch when she wanted to be, but ain't no way she should've died like that."

Wanda Nell waited a moment while he regained his composure. "You got any idea who could've hated her that much?"

"That's all I been thinking about," Melvin said. He cast a glance over his shoulder at the deputy standing in the corner of the room. He leaned forward. "I know she was fooling around with a couple of married men, or had been. Might've been one of them. Or their wives."

"Deke Campbell? Billy Joe Eccles?" Wanda Nell kept her voice low.

Startled, Melvin just stared at her. Finally he nodded.

"You think it could be one of them?"

"Maybe," Melvin said. He frowned. "Lately Fayetta was being real pushy about money. She was always trying to get some outta me, I know that much. And I heard her on the phone a coupla times, talking to somebody. It sounded to me like maybe she was trying to blackmail whoever it was."

"Any idea who she was talking to?"

98

"Naw. I asked her about it, and she like to've bit my head off," Melvin said ruefully. "Told me since I didn't have the decency to marry her, it wasn't none of my business."

"Why'd you go over there yesterday morning?"

"I was gonna try to make up with her after that fight we had," Melvin said. "And I was gonna finish putting the computer together. I bought one for her and the kids, and I was putting it all together in her bedroom when the argument started." He paused, taking a deep breath. "When she didn't come to the door, I let myself in, and that's when I found her." He looked away for a moment.

"How about the knife?" Wanda Nell asked, hating to have to mention it. "They say it's one from the Kountry Kitchen."

"Yeah," Melvin said, "it was. I told 'em that myself." He shrugged. "All I can figure is Fayetta took it home with her. Wouldn't've been the first time she took stuff from the restaurant. She just took whatever she wanted. Didn't matter what it cost anybody else."

Wanda Nell grimaced in sympathy at the bitter note in his voice. She knew exactly what he meant. But she had to ask Melvin something.

"Why'd you want to see me so urgently today?"

Melvin's face tightened. When he spoke, his voice was so low Wanda Nell had to strain to hear him. "I had to know you believed me. I couldn't face all this if you didn't."

99

Behind her the deputy cleared his throat. "Time's up, ma'am."

Wanda Nell nodded at him. "Just one more minute, deputy." She turned back to Melvin. "Don't you be worrying now. I believe you, and we're gonna get this thing figured out and get you outta here."

"Thanks, Wanda Nell," Melvin said, almost smiling. "You're a good friend, and I appreciate that. And I appreciate you running the Kountry Kitchen while I'm stuck in here."

"Glad to do it," she said. "And if I have any questions, I'll get Tuck to get in touch with you. I don't reckon they'll let me call you." She grinned briefly.

"But you be careful," Melvin said. "I don't want anything to happen to you."

"It won't," Wanda Nell assured him.

"Fayetta was bad news," Melvin said, "and she was mixed up in something. I don't know what, but whatever it was, it wasn't any good. You be real careful if you start poking your nose in. I know you."

"I'll be careful," Wanda Nell said.

The deputy on Melvin's side had come to lead him away. Wanda Nell stood and watched him until he had disappeared through the door. Then she turned and followed her deputy back down the hall to where Tuck was waiting for her. Tuck thanked the deputy on duty and was leading Wanda Nell toward the door when a voice hailed them.

"Yo! Wanda Nell! Hang on a minute."

Recognizing the voice, Wanda Nell wanted to keep

100

on walking toward the door. Instead, she stopped and turned around.

"Howdy, Elmer Lee," she said. "How are you?"

Elmer Lee Johnson, chief deputy of the Tullahoma County Sheriff's Department, stood a couple feet away from her and Tuck. His dark hair was slicked back with some kind of gel, and his mouth was twisted into a scowl.

"I'd be doing just fine if I knew you wasn't gonna be sticking your nose into this," Elmer Lee said, his right hand resting on the butt of his gun. "Morning, Tucker." He nodded at Tuck.

"Morning, Deputy," Tuck said equably.

"You got the wrong man, Elmer Lee," Wanda Nell said. "Melvin didn't do this, and the sooner you realize that and start looking for the real killer, the better off we'll all be."

Elmer Lee shook his head. "We're just gonna have to recruit you for the sheriff's department, Wanda Nell. We need somebody like you to come in here and tell us what we been doing wrong all these years. It's a wonder we ever get anything done without you."

Don't let him get to you, Wanda Nell kept telling herself. She waited a moment before she spoke. Smiling sweetly, she said, "Why, thank you, Elmer Lee. I sure would love to take you up on your kind invitation, but I guess I'll just have to decline this time. Sooner or later you're gonna have to admit you're wrong, but I'm not the kind of person who's gonna rub it in."

101

"Well, thank *you*," Elmer Lee said, his voice dripping with sarcasm. "It's nice to know you're still every bit as pigheaded as you always was. But I'm warning you, Wanda Nell, and you, too, Tucker: you better not stick your nose in. You're liable to get it cut off." He stomped off.

Wanda Nell didn't say anything until she and Tuck were outside. "That went well," she said.

"What is it with you and him?" Tuck asked. "I know you can't stand each other, but why?"

Wanda Nell shrugged. "We've known each other since high school. He and Bobby Ray was like brothers, and he's hated me ever since I came between them. He's always blamed me for everything that went wrong in Bobby Ray's life." She paused for a moment, thinking back to that strange scene between her and Elmer Lee after Bobby Ray's funeral, when Elmer Lee had come close to admitting he'd once had feelings for Wanda Nell. "I guess you could say he's jealous."

"Well, whatever it is," Tuck said, "we've got to be careful about antagonizing him. Even if he is wrong about my client." He examined Wanda Nell's face.

"He is wrong," she said firmly. "After seeing Melvin, I'm more convinced than ever he didn't do it."

Tuck escorted Wanda Nell to the truck. He and T.J. exchanged greetings. "Now, look, Tuck," Wanda Nell said. "Melvin pretty much confirmed what I told you about Fayetta and those married men."

102

"You mean Campbell and Eccles?" Tuck asked.

"Yeah," Wanda Nell said. "And it's gonna mean stirring up a real hornet's nest, but we gotta find out what was going on with Fayetta and them two. The answer's gotta be there somewhere."

Tuck sighed deeply. "Maybe so. But the you-know-what's gonna hit the fan when we start digging."

"Then you better put some overalls on over them nice clothes of yours," Wanda Nell advised him half-jokingly.

"Now, Mama," T.J. said, trying to sound stern.

"Seriously," Wanda Nell said. "I'm not gonna sit around and let Melvin take the blame for this, not just because some rich guy in town doesn't want his precious behind in jail."

"No, of course not," Tuck said firmly. "I'm going to start looking into this as discreetly as possible. Let me handle this."

Wanda Nell nodded, but she wasn't going to make any promises. She figured she had a better chance of rooting up the dirt than Tuck did. People were a lot more cautious talking to a lawyer than they would be to a waitress.

"I guess you'd better take me on to work," Wanda Nell told T.J.

"Yes'm," he said, starting the truck. "Hey, Tuck, I'm gonna have some lunch there, and then I can come back to the office if you need me."

"Sure," Tuck said. "I can always find something for you to do." He grinned, and Wanda Nell thought once again how attractive he was. Too bad he was too young for her.

The truck idling, T.J. sat watching Tuck walk to his car. Wanda Nell poked him in the side. "Let's get going, T.J. Stop woolgathering. I need to get to work."

"Yes'm," T.J. said, putting the truck into reverse and backing out of the parking space.

"Do you still have time to run Miranda home after she drops off my car at the restaurant?"

"Yes'm," T.J. said. He glanced at his watch. "By the time I finish eating lunch she oughta be getting off work."

"She better not be late," Wanda Nell muttered.

They finished the short drive to the Kountry Kitchen in silence. T.J. parked and followed his mother inside. He took a seat at the counter and picked up one of the menus stuck in a holder in front of him. Wanda Nell waved at a few of her regulars and indicated to Ovie and Ruby Garner, the other waitress on the morning shift, that she'd be back in a minute.

She went through the kitchen, pausing briefly to greet the cook, Lurene, and Elray, the dishwasher and cook's assistant. Wanda Nell assured them everything was okay with Melvin and that everything would get sorted out soon. In the meantime, she'd be in charge, and if they had any questions or concerns, they should come to her.

"That Fayetta was a bad woman," Lurene said suddenly. "She wasn't nothing but trash, and it ain't right, they be thinking Mistuh Melvin do something like that. He a good man, and they oughta be knowing that. Some other man done that to her."

"That's what we're gonna find out," Wanda Nell assured her. "And if you should happen to hear anything, you let me know, you hear?"

Both Lurene and Elray promised they would. Wanda Nell figured if there were any news making its way through the black folks' grapevine, Lurene would hear it.

She stowed her purse in the small storeroom that served as a locker room for the waitresses. She pulled an apron on over her clothes. Since Fayetta had talked Melvin into letting them wear regular clothes instead of uniforms a month ago, she'd been very pleased with the change. One good thing Fayetta had done, she acknowledged.

Back out front again, she saw Ruby serving T.J. a glass of iced tea. Ruby was a sweet girl, a little bit on the shy side, and very smart and pretty to boot. She was just the kind of girl T.J. ought to be dating, Wanda Nell decided. Maybe she'd suggest that to T.J., but she didn't want him getting annoyed with her like he was with his grandmother.

Wanda Nell surveyed the front dining room of the Kountry Kitchen. Most of the tables were occupied, though the lunchtime rush was past. She paused briefly to speak to Junior Farley, a mechanic from the garage next door who had always flirted with Fayetta.

"Sure is awful about Fayetta," Junior said, his fat

cheeks sagging. "I just can't believe it, Wanda Nell. You reckon Melvin done it?"

"No, I don't, Junior," Wanda Nell said. She raised her voice slightly, because she knew there were plenty of ears straining to hear her. "I don't think Melvin did it, and anybody that knows him knows it too. He wouldn't've done something like that, I don't care what anybody says or thinks. Somebody else did it, and before long that person's gonna be in jail, not Melvin."

Junior flushed bright red. "I don't believe he did it either," he mumbled. Wanda Nell reached over and patted his hand, which was more than twice the size of hers.

"Thanks, Junior," she said. "Melvin'll appreciate that."

Conversations resumed, and Wanda Nell stood and watched for a moment. Ovie Ashmore came in from the back dining room and motioned for Wanda Nell to join her.

Wanda Nell ambled back to her. None of the tables in the back room were occupied, so they had a bit of privacy.

"How's it going, Ovie?" Wanda Nell asked. "Any problems?"

"Everything's been fine. We been pretty busy," Ovie said. "That Ruby sure is a hard worker. I'd work with that girl anytime."

"Yeah, she sure is. I wish I had another one like her," Wanda Nell said. "You know anybody I can call about helping out afternoons and evenings?"

"There was a girl here about an hour ago looking for a job," Ovie said. "I told her to come back about two o'clock, that she'd have to talk to you."

"How'd she know we needed someone?"

Ovie shrugged. "She didn't, far as I know. Sounded like she'd been checking around, looking for work."

"What'd you think?"

"Seemed like a pretty sharp little gal," Ovie said after a moment's thought. "She was dressed real neat and clean, and she spoke nice to me. Said she's done a lot of waitressing and she could work any hours."

Wanda Nell checked her watch. It was nearly two. "Then I hope she shows up. She might just have herself a job. I can't afford to look around too long."

Ovie patted her arm. "I can help out now, don't you be fretting too much. We'll take care of business."

"Thanks, Ovie," Wanda Nell said, giving the older woman a quick hug. "You're a lifesaver."

Ovie went back to the front dining room and Wanda Nell drifted after her. Customers were trickling out and the slow part of the afternoon was starting.

Wanda Nell checked on T.J. He was having the day's special, chicken-fried steak, mashed potatoes, corn on the cob, and green beans, with blackberry cobbler for dessert. She shook her head.

"I don't know how you can eat that much and not get as big as the side of a barn," she told him.

He grinned up at her. "I work it off, Mama." He took a sip of his tea. "It sure is good. That cook you got is something else."

"I'll pass that along," Wanda Nell said. She picked up a pitcher of tea from the counter behind her and topped up his glass.

The door opened and in walked a young woman of about twenty-five, Wanda Nell reckoned. She approached the counter near the cash register and Wanda Nell walked forward to greet her.

"Afternoon," she said. "Can I help you?"

The young woman, who appeared older on closer inspection, smiled at her. "I sure hope so, ma'am. Are you the lady I need to talk to about a job?"

Wanda Nell nodded and introduced herself, coming around from behind the counter.

"My name's Katie Ann Hale," the young woman said, offering a hand. "Nice to meet you, Miz Culpepper."

"Why don't you come on back here and talk with me," Wanda Nell said, motioning toward the back dining room. "How about something to drink? Coffee, tea, a Coke?"

"I'm fine, thank you," she said. She followed Wanda Nell into the back room.

Wanda Nell indicated for her to take a seat, and she did. "Now, Miss Hale," Wanda Nell began, sitting down opposite her, "or is it Miz Hale?"

"It's Miss," she answered. "But, please, just call me Katie Ann." She flashed a smile that lit up her face.

Wanda Nell regarded her for a moment. She sure was a pretty girl, with short, curly reddish-brown hair, a perky little nose, and a beauty mark on her right cheek. The male customers would be flirting like crazy with her.

"Okay, Katie Ann," Wanda Nell said. "Tell me about yourself. How much restaurant work have you done?"

"I worked in restaurants ever since I was a kid," Katie Ann said. "My daddy used to run a restaurant in Goose Creek." Goose Creek was a small town about six miles south of Tullahoma. "I worked there all through high school and for a while after that, until my daddy died and the restaurant got sold. After that, I moved on. I worked in Memphis for a coupla years, then down in Jackson. I came back here about a year ago."

Wanda Nell had never conducted a job interview before, but she figured she knew what the most important questions were. "Where have you worked here in Tullahoma?"

Katie Ann wrinkled her nose. "I mostly been working at the hosiery mill, but I just don't like it. Being confined in that big old building with all them machines. I just got tired of it, so I been looking for something else."

"We do have an opening right now," Wanda Nell said. Should she explain why there was one? Might as well. "I have to tell you, one of our waitresses got murdered this weekend. And the owner is in jail right now." Katie Ann's eyes widened. Wanda Nell went on hastily. "But he didn't do it, I can promise you that. But until everything gets straightened out and they find out who really did it, I'm in charge."

"That's terrible," Katie Ann said. She looked down at her lap for a moment, then raised her eyes to meet Wanda Nell's. "I have to tell you, Miz Culpepper, that I knew Fayetta Sutton. We wasn't real close, but I did know her. And I heard about what happened to her." She bit her lip. "I know this sounds awful, me turning up here so quick, but I really need a new job, and I figured y'all might need someone."

Wanda Nell stared at her. She sure hadn't expected this. There was something slightly ghoulish about the girl turning up like this, but Wanda Nell knew what it was like to need a job. She couldn't blame Katie Ann, especially when there was a job available.

"Thanks for telling me that," Wanda Nell said finally. "I certainly understand. We do need someone to work afternoons and evenings. You'd be working with me." She explained the pay and the duties, and Katie Ann kept nodding.

"That's all fine with me," Katie Ann said. "When would you like me to start? I can start anytime."

"How about this afternoon?" Wanda Nell said, standing up.

"That's great," Katie Ann said. "Just put me to work." She stood up. "Am I dressed okay?"

"You're fine," Wanda Nell said. "Come on with me, and I'll show you where you can keep your purse." She led the way through the kitchen to the waitresses' closet. "Just find yourself an empty shelf and it's yours. Nobody'll bother your stuff." *Not with Fayetta gone,* she added grimly to herself. "Just come on out

110

front and I'll start showing you where everything is."

Katie Ann nodded. She found a place for her purse and turned back to Wanda Nell.

"Here's an apron," Wanda Nell said. Katie Ann put it on and tied the strings neatly at the front. "Come on, and I'll start showing you around and introduce to everybody."

They stopped in the kitchen for Katie Ann to meet Lurene and Elray, then Wanda Nell stepped out of the kitchen with Katie Ann right behind her.

Wanda Nell was about to introduce Ruby Garner when she noticed a man sitting at the counter near T.J. Her eyes widened in surprise.

What the heck was Deke Campbell doing in the Kountry Kitchen?

Nine

"Tell you what, Katie Ann," Wanda Nell said, her eyes fixed on Deke Campbell, "I need to take care of something. You go on and talk to Ovie—that's the older lady you spoke with this morning—and she'll get you started. I'll be along in a few minutes."

"Okay," Katie Ann said.

Wanda Nell barely heard her or felt her walk away. She was intent on Deke Campbell, wondering why he'd shown up here today when he came into the Kountry Kitchen maybe three times a year. Rich guys like him didn't frequent restaurants like this one.

Unless they were running for office, maybe.

Campbell was examining a menu as Wanda Nell approached him. "Afternoon, Mr. Campbell," she said. "What can I get you?"

He looked up from the menu, his shrewd dark eyes assessing her. Wanda Nell stared right back at him, refusing to let him intimidate her. She noted the long hair combed across a bald spot and slicked down with a strong-smelling gel. His face, florid and heavy, sported a beak of a nose with veins prominent all over it. She'd heard he was a heavy drinker, and his nose didn't lie.

"How about a cup of coffee?" he drawled in response. "And some of that there blackberry cobbler." He pointed to T.J. who was now working on his dessert.

"Coming right up," Wanda Nell said. She picked up a cup and saucer, along with utensils and a napkin and set them at his place. Then she poured him coffee. "Cream?"

"No, thanks," he said. "Gotta watch the old waist-line." He laughed, patting the belly hanging over his belt. "Got it out where I can see it now." He laughed again.

Wanda Nell smiled politely. "I'll be right back with your cobbler." She went to the kitchen and dished it out herself.

Back at the counter, she set down the bowl. "There you go. Let me know if you need anything else." She started to move away.

"You've worked here a long time, haven't you?" Campbell said.

Wanda Nell turned back. "Yeah, I have."

"And you're the one whose husband got killed a couple months ago." He spooned some cobbler and stuck it in his mouth, chewing noisily.

"Ex-husband," Wanda Nell corrected automatically.

"Ex-husband," Campbell repeated. "Whatever."

T.J. had given up any pretense of eating his dessert, and was watching his mother and Campbell closely. Wanda Nell caught his eye and moved her head slightly to one side. T.J. frowned, but got up from his stool and walked toward the back of the restaurant, in the direction of the men's room.

"Yeah, it was my ex-husband who got killed," Wanda Nell said when T.J. was out of earshot. None of the other stools near Campbell was occupied, so maybe now he'd get to the point.

"I heard you kinda stuck your nose into the sheriff's department bidness," Campbell said. "I heard they weren't too happy about that."

Wanda Nell shrugged. "I can't help what they thought. I wasn't going to stand around and let them arrest the wrong person. They put my son in jail, and I knew he didn't kill his daddy."

"I reckon you're dang lucky you didn't get that pretty little nose of yours in a vise," Campbell said, his tone jovial, but his eyes indicated an entirely different mood. "It'd be a shame if something happened to it, you nosing around where you shouldn't. If you

113

were gonna do something like that again, that is."

"Why should I do that?" Wanda Nell asked, over-doing the innocent act. "They got somebody in jail already, if you're talking about what I think you're talking about." She shrugged. "And you couldn't possibly have any reason to be interested in that now, could you?"

Campbell grinned. "Nope, not me. Just curious, that's all. A man like me . . . well, in my position I like to know what's going on in town. The bank's got a right to know if its customers are in some kind of trouble." He wiped his mouth with his napkin. "Come to think of it, you've got a loan with my bank, don't you?"

"Yeah, I do," Wanda Nell said. She still had several years to go on her payments for her trailer, and the bank in Tullahoma held the note. "What's your point?"

"No point," Campbell said, leering at her. "Just want our customers to know we keep an eye out for them. We've got their best interests at heart, after all." He stood up, dropping his napkin on the counter. "How much I owe you?"

"Three-fifty," Wanda Nell said.

He dropped a ten-dollar bill on the counter. "Keep the change," he said, winking. He turned and walked out.

Wanda Nell picked up the ten, wishing she could crumple it up and throw it in his face instead. She didn't like being threatened, especially by smug bastards like Deke Campbell. Just because he ran the bank he thought he could tell people what to do and get away with it.

She rang up the ticket in the cash register and made change, tucking the tip into her apron pocket. What she wanted to know was why he'd shown up there so quickly to deliver his little message to her. How had he known she was involved in this?

It had to be somebody in the sheriff's department, she reckoned. The story about her sneaking up behind Fayetta's house was probably all over the department half an hour after it had happened, and someone had let Campbell know.

But why? Who knew he had a reason to be concerned about Fayetta's murder? This clinched it. He had to have been sleeping with Fayetta, otherwise he wouldn't have tried such a stunt.

"Mama, what was all that about?" T.J. asked, reclaiming his seat at the counter.

Wanda Nell stared at her son. "Oh, just some talk, honey. Don't pay him any attention. I'm not going to."

"Was he threatening you?" T.J.'s tone was gentle but insistent.

Shrugging, Wanda Nell said, "Maybe. I don't know. He sure is interested in what's going on, though. And if he don't have anything to do with it, why'd he show up here?"

T.J. shifted uneasily on his stool. "I don't like this, Mama. Him threatening you. He's got a lot of pull around here, and he could cause a lot of trouble."

"Yeah, he could," Wanda Nell said. Then she grinned. "I might cause a lot of trouble myself. I don't like some big shot coming in here and trying to tell me what to do."

T.J. shook his head. "You don't like anybody telling you what to do."

"No, I don't," Wanda Nell said. "And I for damn sure ain't gonna be pushed around by him, even if he is the president of the bank." Would he try to make trouble over her loan? For all her brave words, she knew Campbell could make her life difficult if he really wanted to.

"We just got to be careful, that's all there is to it," T.J. said. "You've got to trust Tuck to do his job, Mama."

"I do, honey," Wanda Nell said. "And don't you be worrying about me. I can take care of myself." The front door opened and she turned to greet the newcomer.

"Hi, Mama," Miranda said. She plopped down tiredly on the stool next to her brother. "Hey, T.J."

"Randa," T.J. said, "you look like you been run over by something."

Miranda glared at him, then turned the glare on her mother. "I feel like crap," she whined. "I didn't get much sleep, and then I had to get up and go to work. I just wanna go home and sleep for two days."

Wanda Nell regarded her with scant sympathy. "Then you should've come home last night when you said you would, instead of staying out late, running

116

around with your friends. You go on home and get some rest, but you need to look after Lavon some and let your sister have a break."

"Yes, Mama," Miranda said, her lower lip sticking out.

"Oh, stop pouting, Randa," T.J. chided her. "Come on. I gotta get back to work myself. I'm gonna take you home." He stood up, pulling money out of his pocket to pay for his lunch.

Wanda Nell waved his money away. "It's on me, remember? Thanks for all the driving around you're doing, honey. If you need some gas money, let me know."

"I'm fine, Mama," T.J. said. "Come *on,* Randa. Drag your rear end off that stool and come on."

"Keys." Wanda Nell held her hand out to her daughter. Sullenly, Miranda dug in her pocket and passed the keys over to her mother.

"Y'all be careful," Wanda Nell called to them as they went out the door.

Shaking her head over Miranda, Wanda Nell cleared the counter. She found Ruby and gave her a tip for waiting on T.J.

"Thanks, Wanda Nell," Ruby said. She glanced shyly at the older woman. "Your son sure is handsome."

Wanda Nell smiled. "He is, and he's a nice boy."

Ruby nodded. "Sure seemed like it." She hesitated. "Well, if you don't need me no more, I reckon I'll be going. I got a couple of classes this afternoon." She gazed expectantly at Wanda Nell.

"You go on," Wanda Nell said. "We'll be fine. Long as I can count on you and Ovie to handle the mornings, this new girl and I can handle the rest."

"Okay," Ruby said. "If you talk to Melvin, you tell him I asked about him. I don't believe he did it, Wanda Nell." She shook her head. "I can't believe it. That Fayetta was kinda mean and trashy, but I just can't believe somebody'd do something like that."

Wanda Nell patted her arm. Ruby looked like she was going to start crying. "I'll tell Melvin," she promised. "He'll appreciate it, honey. Now you go on to your classes and don't even think about it. Hear?"

Ruby nodded and left.

Wanda Nell surveyed the room. Only one table with customers left. She checked to see if they needed refills, then went to the back room to find Ovie and Katie Ann.

The two women were chatting as they moved from table to table, filling containers with packets of sugar and no-calorie sweetener and checking the salt and pepper shakers. Wanda Nell interrupted them. "Ovie, I'll take over from here. Why don't you go on home and I'll see you tomorrow."

Ovie handed over her tray with a smile. "Sounds good to me. I'm ready to rest these old feet of mine and maybe give 'em a soak in some hot water."

"Katie Ann, I'll be back in a minute," Wanda Nell said, setting the tray down on a table. Katie Ann nodded and continued her work.

Wanda Nell followed Ovie into the front room. "What do you think?" she asked in a low voice. "Think she'll be okay?"

Ovie nodded. "Yeah, she seems like a good worker. And she knows what to do. You don't have to tell her much."

"Good," Wanda Nell said, relieved. She gave Ovie a quick hug. "Thanks, Ovie. You're really saving my bacon, you know that?"

Ovie smiled and returned the hug. "I'm glad to do it, hon. I can always use the money, and it gets me out of the house. You just be careful you don't overdo."

"I'll be okay," Wanda Nell said. "You go on home."

Ovie went to the back to retrieve her purse, and Wanda Nell went to the cash register to take money from the last customers. When they and Ovie had gone, she returned to the back to find that Katie Ann had finished all the refills.

"Thanks," Wanda Nell said. Katie Ann just smiled.

In the front again, Wanda Nell directed Katie Ann to make a fresh pot of coffee and check that all the tables were cleared and wiped clean. "It's usually pretty slow in the afternoons till about four-thirty," she said. "And on Monday nights it's not too busy."

"That's fine," Katie Ann said. "You just tell me what you want me to do."

Wanda Nell left her to her tasks, explaining that she needed to take care of a couple things in the office. In the kitchen she paused to chat for a few minutes with Margaret, the cook working the evening shift that

119

week. Wanda Nell explained what was going on, Margaret expressed her sympathy for their boss, and Wanda Nell, feeling mighty relieved that everyone was sticking by Melvin, went on down the hall.

She needed to start checking supplies to make sure they'd have enough for the next couple days. As she walked down the hall, she paused for a moment by the closet. As far as she knew, no one had checked to see if Fayetta had left anything on her shelf. Wanda Nell decided to investigate.

All the waitresses kept a few odds and ends on their shelves, a few cosmetics for quick repair jobs, maybe a spare pair of hose, some perfume.

Wanda Nell bent to examine Fayetta's shelf. Not much to see—the expected packets of hose, a big bottle of cheap-smelling perfume, a couple different lipsticks, a small mirror. She was about to stand up again when something caught her eye. Getting down on her knees, she peered up at the underside of the shelf above Fayetta's. There, stuck in the back corner where the corners met and flat against the shelf, was a small book. Fingers trembling a little, Wanda Nell grasped it and pulled it loose.

She examined it. It was a savings account passbook from the bank, Deke Campbell's bank. She opened it. Fayetta's name and address were written in it. *Wonder why she kept it here?* Wanda Nell asked herself.

Eyes widening in surprise, Wanda Nell kept turning the pages. What the heck had Fayetta been up to?

Ten

The first entry in the savings account passbook was about three years old. Fayetta had opened the account with a deposit of five hundred dollars. From that point on she had made deposits at least once a month, sometimes twice. The smallest deposit she had made, as far as Wanda Nell could tell, was for three hundred and fifty dollars. There were a few withdrawals, but not many, and the most recent deposit had been made a week ago, on Monday.

Fayetta hadn't kept a running total, but Wanda Nell was pretty good at doing math in her head. She started at the beginning and worked her way through the book. "Good Lord," she whispered when she was done. Fayetta had about twenty-three thousand dollars in her account, not counting interest.

Where the heck had she been getting that kind of money? Wanda Nell shook her head. Fayetta sure hadn't made it working at the restaurant.

Had Fayetta been blackmailing somebody?

She must have been, Wanda Nell reasoned, to accumulate that kind of money in her savings account. Melvin had said he thought Fayetta was blackmailing someone, too. But who? Deke Campbell came quickly to mind. He had to be involved in this somehow.

Fayetta had been pretty clever, Wanda Nell thought. She'd never given any hint she had this kind of money in the bank. Instead, she was always grousing about how poor she was, how hard she had to work to take care of herself and her kids. She let it be known she wasn't getting any child support. But now that Wanda Nell thought about it, the few times she'd seen Fayetta's kids, they were always wearing clothes that were a lot better than what they sold at Budget Mart. She'd always figured maybe Fayetta's mama was helping her out, but after seeing the way Agnes Vance lived, she realized that was unlikely.

"Wanda Nell!"

The sound of her name brought Wanda Nell out of her reverie. Stuffing the passbook into her apron pocket, she stepped out of the closet to find Margaret hovering near the door.

"What is it, Margaret? Something wrong?"

"No, but they's somebody asking for you out front."

"Thanks," Wanda Nell said. She stepped around Margaret and hurried through the kitchen, wondering who could be looking for her.

When she saw who it was, she almost turned around and went right back into the kitchen. Instead, she paused for a deep breath, then said, "Well, this sure is an unexpected pleasure, Elmer Lee. What can I do for you? You want something to eat? I think maybe we've still got some of the chicken-fried steak from today's special left."

Elmer Lee regarded her with a sour expression. "No, I ain't come here looking for something to eat. I need to talk to you, Wanda Nell. Somewhere private."

Wanda Nell glanced around. Katie Ann was busy sorting silverware down at the other end of the counter, and there weren't any customers at the moment. "Come on back here," she said, jerking her head to the right. She walked down to the end of the counter, telling Katie Ann to mind the front.

"Sure," Katie Ann said, regarding her curiously. She smiled broadly at Elmer Lee before sashaying off to the front of the restaurant.

"Who's that?" Elmer Lee asked. "She's new around here, ain't she?"

"Name's Katie Ann Hale," Wanda Nell said. "I hired her to work the evening shift with me." She led the way to a table at the very back of the restaurant. "Now put your eyes back in your head and tell me what this is all about."

"She sure is good-looking," Elmer Lee said, sitting down with his back to the wall. He had a clear view of the front of the restaurant and Katie Ann.

"You wanna ask her out?" Wanda Nell said, getting increasingly annoyed with him. "She ain't said anything about being married, and maybe if she's desperate enough, you might have a chance."

Elmer Lee scowled at her. "Cut the crap, Wanda Nell. I don't need your help asking women out, thank you very much."

"Yeah, you having such nice manners and all." Wanda Nell couldn't resist another dig. She figured Elmer Lee owed her a few, the way he had treated her after her ex-husband was murdered.

"Ha-ha," Elmer Lee said. "Now if you're through fooling around, I need to talk to you about something serious."

Wanda Nell could feel Fayetta's passbook burning a hole in her apron pocket. She ought to show it to Elmer Lee, and she would. But first she was going to see what he had on his tiny little mind.

"Talk, then," she said.

Elmer Lee shifted in his chair and looked away from her. "This is a pretty touchy situation we got on our hands." He squirmed some more. "And I want you to think twice about butting in, Wanda Nell. I know you, and I know how dang hardheaded you are. I want you to take this as a friendly warning. You understand?"

Instead of getting angry at him, the way she normally would anytime he tried to tell her what to do, she calmly sat there and stared at him. What was going on here? She thought about it for a moment. Then she spoke. "You don't think Melvin did it, either. Do you?"

Elmer Lee wouldn't look at her. "I'm not saying that. I'm just saying it's a real complicated situation, and it'll be a helluva lot easier for me if you don't put your oar in and try to row the boat. Let me do it."

"Well, let's see," Wanda Nell said slowly. "Way I figure it is, there's somebody trying to throw his weight around in this *situation,* and it ain't you." She paused a moment. "No, not you. But maybe somebody like the president of a bank?"

Elmer Lee finally met her gaze. "What do you

124

mean? Bank president? Where'd you get a crazy idea like that?" His tone was mocking, but his eyes had registered the truth. He knew what she was talking about alright.

"I can't help but hear things around here, Elmer Lee," Wanda Nell said. "You pick up a lot of talk about other people's business, one way or the other." She held up a hand when Elmer Lee started to speak. "That's all I'm gonna say. Don't push me. Besides, I got something to show you."

"What?"

She slid the passbook out of her apron and laid it on the table.

"What's this?" Elmer Lee stared at it with suspicion. "And where'd you get it?"

"I found it here in the closet where we all keep our stuff," Wanda Nell explained. "Just pick it up and look inside."

He picked it up and opened it. His eyes widened slightly as he began leafing through the pages. After a minute or so, he put the book back on the table and regarded Wanda Nell thoughtfully.

"Where the hell did she come by that kind of money?"

Wanda Nell shrugged. "She didn't make it here, I can tell you that. If we made that kind of money, I'd have done paid off my trailer and bought me a new car, that's for dang sure."

Elmer Lee picked up the book again and stuck it in his shirt pocket. "I may need you to come in and make a statement at some point about finding it," he said. He stood up. "I'd better get back. You think about what I said, Wanda Nell."

She stood up and looked him straight in the face. "Thanks for the warning, Elmer Lee. I appreciate your concern." She said it without sarcasm. For once, she really meant it. In his own rough way, he was doing what he thought was a good thing. It didn't matter that she didn't trust him as far as she could throw him.

He nodded. "I'd feel a lot better if I knew you was going to do what I asked." He sighed heavily. "But I ain't counting on it."

Wanda Nell laughed. "You're softening up in your old age."

He snorted and started walking away from her.

"Hang on a second, Elmer Lee," she called after him.

He turned back to look at her. "What is it?"

"Y'all gonna let Miz Vance go into Fayetta's house to get what she needs for those kids?"

"I done told the lawyer she could do that. Tomorrow morning, in fact." Elmer Lee's eyes narrowed suspiciously. "What bidness is it of yours?"

"I'm going with her to help out," Wanda Nell said. "You didn't know that?"

"I for damn sure didn't," Elmer Lee said, "but I might've known." He rubbed a hand tiredly over his face. "In that case, I reckon I'm gonna be the one there at the house in the morning while y'all are poking around. Y'all be there at nine, alright?"

"I'll check with Miz Vance," Wanda Nell said, "and I'll let you know if she can't come then, for some reason."

"You do that." Elmer Lee turned and stalked off.

Wanda Nell watched him go. He stopped for a minute to chat with Katie Ann, who appeared to be quite happy to flirt with him. Wanda Nell had to admit that Elmer Lee was actually pretty good-looking, at least to other women. Katie Ann was welcome to him.

She headed for the front, and by the time she'd reached the kitchen door, Elmer Lee was gone. A couple of men came in, and Katie Ann greeted them. Wanda Nell left her to it and went back to Melvin's office to use the phone there.

After a quick call to check on her daughters and grandson, Wanda Nell called Tuck Tucker's office. The lawyer was out, so she left a message with Blanche for him to call her when he had a chance. Then she busied herself with making sure the restaurant was going to have the supplies it needed for the coming week.

None of the suppliers, all local, gave her any trouble about continuing deliveries. By now everyone in town probably knew that Melvin was in jail, but he'd done business with these places for so long, they were willing to give him the benefit of the doubt.

Wanda Nell had just finished talking with the last one when the phone rang.

"Wanda Nell, it's Tuck. What did you need to talk to me about?"

She filled him in on the savings account book she had found. She figured T.J. had probably already told him about Deke Campbell's visit.

Tuck whistled into the phone. "Mr. Campbell is looking better and better as an alternative suspect."

"He sure is," Wanda Nell agreed. "What are you gonna do about it?"

"Good question," Tuck said. "I've been making some discreet inquiries, and for now, I don't want to do anything too aggressive. Show my hand. You know what I mean."

"Yes," Wanda Nell replied. "I bet he's pretty mean when he's riled. Campbell, that is, and you don't wanna rattle his cage too much just yet."

"Exactly," Tuck said. "Thanks for calling. I appreciate the information."

Before finishing the call, Wanda Nell told him about the appointment to get into Fayetta's house. She didn't tell him that Elmer Lee was planning to be there himself.

She made one more call, to Agnes Vance.

"I talked to somebody in the sheriff's department, Miz Vance," she said, "and they said you could get into the house at nine tomorrow morning. That okay for you?"

"I think so," Mrs. Vance said. "I'll have to ask one of my neighbors to watch the children. You want to meet me there, or do you want to come by here first?"

"I'll just meet you there," Wanda Nell said. "And let me know if there's any problem. I'll be at the Kountry

128

Kitchen until closing tonight."

By now it was almost four-thirty, and business would soon start picking up a bit. Finished with her chores in the office, Wanda Nell went back out front.

The late afternoon regulars started trickling in, and Wanda Nell and Katie Ann stayed pretty busy. A lot of them were asking about Melvin, and Wanda Nell got real tired talking about it, but she tried to answer their questions in a friendly way.

The evening dinner crowd was larger than usual. Wanda Nell realized it was because of the murder, and though it irritated the heck out of her, she consoled herself with the fact the restaurant was making good money. She was, too, considering the tips the customers were leaving her.

About eight o'clock, a familiar voice greeted her while she was busy cleaning off a couple tables in the back dining room.

"Good evening, Wanda Nell. How are you?"

Wiping her hands on her apron, Wanda Nell turned around to smile at Jack Pemberton. An attractive man about her own age, he was her daughter Juliet's English teacher at Tullahoma County High School. They had been out a few times, and Wanda Nell liked him a lot. He was kind, thoughtful, and awfully sweet. The only trouble was, he had a master's degree, while she had barely finished high school. Wanda Nell felt that difference keenly every time she was around him, though he never did anything deliberately to make her feel inadequate.

"I'm doing okay, Jack. How are you?"

"Hungry," he said, grinning. The light glinted off his round, rimless glasses.

Wanda Nell stared at him for a moment. Dang, but he sure was cute. She wanted to wrap her arms around him and give him a big kiss. She was sure he wouldn't mind that, but the restaurant was pretty full. She wasn't going to put on a show and embarrass them both.

Smiling instead, she said, "Have a seat, then, and let's get you something to eat."

He pulled out a chair at the table she indicated. "I'll be right back with a menu and some tea."

"How about the usual?" he called after her.

"You got it," she said over her shoulder. He worked out at the high school gym and ran a lot, otherwise all the chicken-fried steak, gravy, and mashed potatoes he ate at the Kountry Kitchen would have made him overweight.

As she went to the kitchen to turn in his order and get him his tea, she wondered idly what he looked like when he was working out. She'd never seen him in anything but a jacket and tie, but she figured he must have a pretty decent-looking body underneath.

"Who's that hunk in the back dining room?"

Katie Ann caught her as she was coming out of the kitchen. Wanda Nell blushed bright red, as if the other woman had read her thoughts.

"He sure is hot," Katie Ann continued, her voice low. "And he went right past me the minute he saw

130

you. That your boyfriend?"

"Kinda," Wanda Nell said. "We've been out a few times. His name is Jack Pemberton, and he's a teacher over at the county high school."

"I wouldn't mind letting him teach me a few things," Katie Ann said archly.

Wanda Nell didn't find that particularly amusing, and Katie Ann could see that.

"Sorry," she apologized. "I should keep my big mouth shut."

"It's okay," Wanda Nell said, relenting with a slight smile. "It's not like we're going steady or anything."

Going steady. Wanda Nell winced inwardly. That sounded very high school. She was too old for that.

"You know what I mean," she said hurriedly.

"Yeah," Katie Ann said. "But considering I just started a new job, the last thing I'm gonna do is get the boss lady mad at me by making a pass at her boyfriend."

Wanda Nell just smiled, deciding not to answer. She brushed by Katie Ann and took Jack his tea. He seemed like he wanted to talk, but Wanda Nell had too much to do.

"If you can hang around a little while," she told him, "things oughta start slowing down before long."

"Sure," Jack said with a smile, pulling a book out of his jacket pocket. "I'm in no hurry."

An hour later only a few tables were still occupied. Katie Ann had proved to be a very capable waitress, and Wanda Nell felt considerably relieved. She sat down with Jack for a few minutes to have a glass of tea and eat a sandwich.

"You're not usually this busy on a Monday night," Jack said when she had finished the sandwich.

"No," Wanda Nell replied. "It's because of the murder."

"Murder?" Jack said, sitting up straight in his chair. "What murder?"

Wanda Nell stared at him, puzzled. "You must be the only person in Tullahoma who hasn't heard."

"Maybe so," Jack said, frowning. "I was in Cleveland all weekend, remember? I told you I was going over to visit a friend of mine who teaches in the history department at Delta State. I just got back late this afternoon."

"Oh, yeah," Wanda Nell said. "With everything that's been going on, I forgot, I guess." She leaned forward, resting her elbows on the table. "Well, Fayetta got herself murdered this weekend."

Jack stared at her, aghast. "You mean the woman who usually works evenings with you? I wondered why you had somebody new." He shook his head. "What happened?"

Wanda Nell explained. Jack's expression of concern grew more pronounced the longer she talked.

"But I know Melvin didn't do it," Wanda Nell concluded.

"I guess I know you well enough by now," Jack said, "to believe you when you say that. But if Melvin didn't do it, who did?" He dropped his voice. "Do you

132

seriously think the president of the bank is involved?"

Wanda Nell shrugged. "He's gotta be somehow, else why would he come by here and try to threaten me?" She told him what Campbell had said to her.

Jack's face flushed with anger. "The sonofabitch! Who the hell does he think he is?"

Wanda Nell almost grinned. She'd never heard Jack use such language. "Now don't be getting upset. He don't scare me a bit."

"Even so," Jack said, cooling off slightly, "he's got no business talking to you that way. He needs a good thrashing."

This was a side of Jack she'd not seen before. He was beginning to sound just a little too territorial to suit her.

"Hold on, cowboy," Wanda Nell said lightly, "before you saddle up and head over for a shootout."

Jack laughed, then held up a hand in apology. "You're right, Wanda Nell. I've got no right to act that way. Besides, I know you're more than capable of taking care of yourself."

"Yeah, I am," Wanda Nell said firmly. "But that don't mean I don't need a strong arm to rely on now and then."

"My arm is at your service, fair lady," Jack said, leaning forward in his chair and dipping his head, like a courtier bowing to a queen.

Wanda Nell glanced around. The back dining room was deserted now, except for her and Jack. Their table was shielded from view of the front room. She got up

133

from her chair and went around to his. Leaning down, she kissed him. His arms encircled her and pulled her down into his lap.

When the kiss ended, they were both a little breathless, and Jack's glasses had fogged over. He took off the glasses and stared into her eyes.

"I think you ought to know, Wanda Nell," he said, his voice husky with emotion, "I'm pretty sure I'm falling in love with you."

Eleven

Wanda Nell froze. This was the last thing she was expecting. They'd only really known each other for a couple months. She couldn't deny the physical attraction between them, and Jack was certainly the nicest man she'd met in a long, long time. That said, this was moving just a little too fast for her peace of mind.

The silence stretched on a beat too long.

"Sorry, Wanda Nell," Jack said, his face averted. "I shouldn't have blurted it out like that." He was going to say something else, but Wanda Nell laid a finger across his lips.

"No, Jack, don't apologize. I'm just a little surprised, that's all."

He put his glasses back on, then gently took her hand from his mouth. "I know, and here I am, acting like a teenager when I ought to know better."

Wanda Nell grinned at him. For a moment, he did

134

look a little like an eighteen-year-old, with his boyish face and the way his brown hair kept slipping down across his forehead. "I wouldn't be sitting here in a teenager's lap, honey."

Jack laughed, still slightly tense. "No, I guess not." He sighed. "But you're not really responding the way I guess I hoped you would."

Wanda Nell eased herself gently off his lap and back into her chair. "I'm gonna be honest with you, Jack. You're the nicest thing that's happened to me in a real long time. A man like you even looking twice at a woman like me . . . well, I still can't quite believe it."

Jack interrupted her, his voice indignant. "What do you mean, a woman like you? Why shouldn't I look at you? You're a strong, attractive, bright woman. Any man with sense would look at you and realize you're something special."

Unexpectedly, Wanda Nell felt the sting of tears in her eyes. "I don't know what to say," she said around the lump in her throat. "You're something pretty special yourself, you know."

Jack grinned. "Two people as special as we are, then, ought to be together, don't you think? We deserve each other."

Wanda Nell couldn't help but laugh. "Oh, Jack, I like you an awful lot, more than any man since . . . well, you know."

"Since Bobby Ray Culpepper," Jack said.

She nodded. "Yeah. And I loved him with all my heart, even after the way he treated me. After I kicked

135

him out, I started trying to work him out of my system, but when he died, I realized I hadn't done it real well." She paused a moment. "But I'm getting there. You're helping, I have to say. You're decent and kind and thoughtful, all the things he wasn't. Things he never really knew how to be."

"Sounds like a testimonial for a Boy Scout," Jack said ruefully.

Wanda Nell grinned. "Yeah, but one helluva sexy Boy Scout."

He laughed. "Then I guess I don't mind too much after all."

"You sure you want to get mixed up with a divorced mother of three? Not to mention a grandmother?" Wanda Nell said it lightly, but she was completely serious.

It was Jack's turn to grin. "Yeah, but one hell of a sexy grandmother." He reached for her hands. "Listen, Wanda Nell, you can try to discourage me as much as you want, but it's not going to change the way I feel."

"Then just be patient with me, okay? Give me a little time to finish working it all out."

"I'm a very patient man," he said. "And a pretty determined one. Maybe a little impulsive sometimes." He shrugged.

"Thanks," she said softly. She stood up. "I guess maybe I'd better get back to work."

He stood and drew her toward him. "I'll get out of your hair for now. But how about a good-night kiss?" He watched her face closely.

She didn't hesitate. Her lips lingered on his. Finally she pulled away. "I'd better send you home right now, mister," she said, her voice huskier than usual.

He laughed at that. "Then come on up front and take my money." He turned and headed toward the cash register.

She followed, slipping behind the counter to ring up his check. Their fingers touched as he handed her the money, and she felt the physical spark between them. He winked before he left, and she stood at the register, staring at the door longer after he had left. *Lord, but he is one attractive man.* She finally shook herself out of her reverie. She might be falling in love with him, too, but she just had too much on her mind at the moment. She'd think about it later.

From there, the rest of the evening was all downhill. Feeling oddly deflated now that Jack had gone, Wanda Nell tried to settle down to the business at hand. They had a few stragglers come in for a late bite to eat, but otherwise the restaurant was pretty quiet until closing time at ten. Between them, Wanda Nell and Katie Ann had the place in good shape to reopen the next morning at five, so they didn't have to hang around long after the last customer had left.

Wanda Nell bade good-bye to everyone as she locked the front door of the restaurant. Walking wearily to her car, she was very thankful she didn't have to go on to Budget Mart tonight for her regular shift. She was ready to crawl into bed the minute she got home.

The short drive to the Kozy Kove Trailer Park was uneventful. Wanda Nell was climbing out of her car when her neighbor's backdoor light came on. Mayrene Lancaster stuck her head out the door and said, "Hey, Wanda Nell. Why ain't you at Budget Mart? Something wrong with one of the girls or Lavon?"

"Hey, Mayrene," Wanda Nell said, shutting her car door. "Everybody's fine, far's I know. I'm taking some time off from Budget Mart this week. Somebody's got to run the Kountry Kitchen till they let Melvin out of jail." She yawned, covering her mouth with one hand the way her mama had always insisted she should.

"You feel like coming in for a minute?" Mayrene asked. "Tell me what's going on, girl. You know how nosy I am. I been about to bust till you got home, and here I thought I was gonna have to wait till tomorrow morning sometime."

Wanda Nell laughed. She was tired, but she was itching to tell Mayrene about Jack Pemberton. "All right. For a few minutes, then I got to get to bed."

Mayrene offered her something to drink before they sat down on the couch, but Wanda Nell declined. "Now, I'm gonna tell you some things," she said, "but you gotta swear to me not to breathe a word. Not a word down at the beauty parlor."

Mayrene pretended to pout. "Come on now, Wanda Nell, you know me better than that."

"Uh-huh," Wanda Nell said. "That's exactly why

138

I'm swearing you to secrecy." She grinned.

Mayrene put a hand across her heart. "I solemnly swear I won't blab any of this to a living soul." She laughed. "Most of them old girls down at Lucille's don't qualify for living souls anyway."

"Yeah, right," Wanda Nell said. "Now listen here." She quickly filled Mayrene in on all that had happened. Mayrene whistled when she heard about Fayetta's savings account.

"Damn, I never figured that girl was smart enough to come up with that kind of money," she said, shaking her head. "Just goes to show you. But I bet you anything she had some men about ready to strangle her. Not to mention their wives, if they knew."

"Exactly," Wanda Nell said. "Which is why I'm sure it wasn't Melvin that killed her."

"Yeah, you're probably right," Mayrene said. "What're you gonna do next?"

"In the morning I'm going with Fayetta's mama, Agnes Vance, to Fayetta's house. Miz Vance wants to get some things for the children."

Mayrene frowned. "What'd you think of Miz Vance? Didn't she use to sell Avon or something?"

Wanda Nell shrugged. "Maybe. I don't know about that. She's kinda hard to figure out. She belongs to one of them real conservative churches, and I'm sure Fayetta acting the way she did was a real trial to her mama. She sure didn't hold with the way Fayetta lived her life."

"And I bet you that's why Fayetta was the way she was. She didn't like nobody telling her she couldn't do something," Mayrene said. "I ain't condoning Fayetta, but if her mama was real strict on her, that's probably why she was kinda wild."

"Maybe so," Wanda Nell said. "But I guess that don't really matter no more." She paused. "Something else happened."

"What?" Mayrene said, her eyes avidly searching Wanda Nell's face. "Something good? Or something bad?"

Wanda Nell said, "Something good, I guess. But it sure does complicate things."

"Come on now, girl," Mayrene said impatiently. "Tell me."

Blushing slightly, Wanda Nell said, "Well, Jack Pemberton came by the Kountry Kitchen tonight."

"And?" Mayrene prompted her when she stopped.

"And he kinda told me he thinks he's falling in love with me." Wanda Nell watched Mayrene closely to gauge her reaction.

Mayrene's plump face nearly split in two, her smile was so big. "Honey, that's wonderful. He's a helluva nice guy, and pretty sexy, too. If you like 'em a bit on the scrawny side, that is." She laughed, a deep, rolling sound. "I like 'em big and kinda stupid; you know that. Jack's too smart for me, but you and him oughta get along real fine."

When Wanda Nell didn't say anything in response to that, Mayrene poked her in the ribs. "Okay, give.

What did you tell him?"

"Ow," Wanda Nell said, rubbing her side. "I told him the truth. I told him I really liked him a lot, but I was still trying to get my head straightened out over Bobby Ray and all that. And he was real nice about it, too."

"He's a good man, then," Mayrene said. "You just better make sure if he's what you want you don't dillydally around and let him get away."

"I know that," Wanda Nell said, slightly exasperated. "I may not be as smart as he is, but I ain't stupid, either."

"I don't recall saying you was," Mayrene said loftily. "You just need a little help making up your mind once in a while, that's all."

"Then I guess that's what I've got you for," Wanda Nell said.

"Damn right," Mayrene said, laughing again. This time Wanda Nell joined in.

"Now, how about you and this Mr. Padget?" Wanda Nell asked when the laughter had subsided.

Mayrene attempted to look coy. "Well, you know how they say still waters run deep." She grinned. "And honey, I like to swim."

"Yeah, and it sounds like you've done a few laps already," Wanda Nell observed wryly. "You gonna keep him around for a while?"

"Oh, yeah," Mayrene said smugly. "He's plenty deep enough, and he sure seems to like me pretty well. Yeah, I think he may be a keeper."

"Well, good for you," Wanda Nell said, squeezing her friend's hand. "You deserve a good man."

"Don't we all?" Mayrene said. "Sounds like things are looking up for both of us, honey."

"Sure would be nice," Wanda Nell said, standing up. "And now I think I'm gonna go home and hit the hay." She covered another yawn with her hand.

"Good night," Mayrene called as Wanda Nell headed out the door.

Wanda Nell opened her front door warily. She was hoping she wouldn't have to nag Miranda to get to bed so she could get up for work in the morning. Then she remembered that Miranda was off on Tuesdays. "Thank the Lord for small mercies," Wanda Nell murmured. She had worried for nothing, however. The trailer was quiet. She tiptoed down the hall to check on Miranda and Lavon, and they were both sound asleep. She closed the door softly and retraced her steps to the front door. Checking to make sure it was locked, she then went down the other hall to Juliet's room.

The door was slightly ajar and Wanda Nell pushed it open. Juliet was hunched over the computer T.J. had brought her, staring at the screen. As Wanda Nell watched for a moment, Juliet began tapping the keys.

"What are you doing still up?" Wanda Nell said softly.

"Hi, Mama," Juliet said, turning to look at her mother as she advanced into the room. "I'm just writing a little bit. I'm keeping my journal on the computer now. It's good practice to learn how to use it."

Wanda Nell brushed a stray lock of blonde hair from Juliet's face. "Okay, honey, but you need to be getting to bed. Don't stay up much longer."

"I won't, Mama," Juliet promised as Wanda Nell kissed the top of her head.

Before Wanda Nell could wish her good night, Juliet spoke again. "Mama, do you think we could afford to get some kind of Internet service? I don't think it would cost very much a month, and I promise I wouldn't misuse it."

"How much do you reckon it would cost?" Wanda Nell studied her daughter closely. She could tell this was something Juliet really wanted.

"There's some different options," Juliet said, "and there's one that only costs about ten dollars a month."

"That sounds fine, honey," Wanda Nell said, vastly relieved. "Why don't you talk it over with T.J.? He knows a lot about that kind of stuff now."

"I did," Juliet said, "and he said this is the one they use down at Mr. Tucker's office."

"Then I guess it's okay," Wanda Nell said. She yawned again. "But let's talk about it tomorrow, okay? I got to get to bed, and so do you."

"I will. Thank you, Mama," Juliet said. Her eyes were shining with excitement and gratitude.

Wanda Nell gave her another kiss, then went to her own room. She quickly changed into her nightgown and cleaned off her makeup, rubbing some moisturizing cream into her face afterward. She peered into the mirror for a moment. All those years of smoking had given her some tiny lines around the mouth, but her teeth were looking a lot better since she'd quit. She was about to turn forty-one in September, and she decided she didn't look too bad for forty-one.

At least Jack Pemberton thought she looked pretty good. Smiling at that thought, Wanda Nell switched off the light in the bathroom and went to bed.

Twelve

Wanda Nell had set her alarm for seven, and when the clock started buzzing, she emerged from a sound sleep and fumbled for the off button. She stretched in bed, yawning. She had slept pretty well and actually felt rested for once.

A few minutes later, she found Juliet and Lavon in the kitchen just finishing breakfast. "Morning, honey," Wanda Nell said, brushing Juliet's head with her hand. She bent to kiss Lavon and tickle his chin. He giggled happily.

"Morning, Mama," Juliet said, wiping away the last of his cereal from Lavon's cheeks.

"Miranda still in bed?" Wanda Nell asked as she poured herself some coffee.

"Yes'm," Juliet said, her voice neutral.

Wanda Nell just shook her head. Miranda was taking advantage of Juliet's good nature and her love for her nephew. With Miranda being off today, there wasn't any reason she couldn't get up and feed her son herself. She knew Juliet would do it. Wanda Nell decided she was going to have to sit Miranda down again and have another little come-to-Jesus talk. Her having a part-time job didn't mean she could ignore her responsibilities at home.

Wanda Nell sighed as she sipped her coffee. T.J. had finally grown up and started acting like a responsible human being, and admittedly he'd been worse than Miranda had ever dared to be. But when was Miranda going to grow up? Sometimes she despaired the girl ever would. Trouble was, Miranda was too much like her daddy had been, thought the world owed her a living. But Miranda didn't have her father's slick charm and was just plain whiny most of the time. Wanda Nell smiled sadly as she thought about her late ex-husband.

"Have you eaten yet, honey?" Wanda Nell came out of her reverie to question Juliet.

"No, ma'am," Juliet said.

"Then how about I scramble us some eggs and cook some bacon? You hungry enough?"

"Yes, ma'am," Juliet said emphatically.

Wanda Nell smiled. "Then I guess I'll get started. You go wake up your sister, and tell her I want her up and moving around by the time breakfast is done. Then you can come back and do the toast."

Juliet made a funny face at her mother, then departed on her errand. Wanda Nell spoke to her grandson. "We're gonna get that lazy ol' mama of

145

yours up, sweetie pie. She's gonna clean all the bath-rooms today. Yes, she is." Lavon giggled and gibbered at her.

Wanda Nell kept an eye on him while she started breakfast. Moments later she heard a bit of a ruckus from the back of the trailer. It lasted for a few seconds, and then it was over. Juliet came back into the kitchen with a big grin on her face.

"What was all that noise?" Wanda Nell asked, whip-ping the eggs in a bowl with a little milk.

"Just me getting Miranda out of bed like you asked, Mama," Juliet said, her face the picture of innocence.

Wanda Nell turned back to her eggs. She should probably fuss at Juliet for whatever it was she had done to Miranda, but she figured Miranda had it coming. Miranda shouldn't take advantage of Juliet the way she did, and her mother couldn't blame Juliet for getting her own back.

The eggs were heating up in one skillet and the bacon was popping and sizzling in another when Miranda came into the kitchen, muttering under her breath.

"Good morning, Miranda," Wanda Nell said. "Glad you could join us for breakfast."

"Mama, I swear I'm gonna snatch every hair out of Juliet's head if she ever does that again." Miranda stood, arms akimbo, her dark hair sticking up in all directions, a furious glare on her face.

"What did she do?" Wanda Nell asked in a mild tone.

146

"She like to broke every bone in my body, that's what she done," Miranda said, the familiar whiny note creeping into her voice. "She came in there and dumped me on the floor. I was asleep, and I didn't know what on earth was happening. I thought maybe we was having an earthquake or something."

"I called your name several times," Juliet said as she buttered some toast, "and I even poked you twice. But you refused to wake up. And Mama said get you out of bed, and that's what I did."

"Well, I'm tired, and I'm going right back to bed," Miranda said.

"I think you'd better sit down and have some breakfast," Wanda Nell said, spooning scrambled eggs onto three plates. "Right there." She pointed with her spatula.

"I'm not hungry." Miranda folded her arms across her chest and pouted.

"You'd better eat something," Wanda Nell advised her in a no-nonsense tone. "You're gonna have a busy morning, young lady."

"Whatta you mean?" Miranda moved slowly to sit in the chair her mother had indicated.

"I mean," Wanda Nell said, as patiently as she could, "since you don't have to work at Budget Mart today, it's time for you to catch up on some of the chores you're supposed to be doing around here."

"Like what?" Miranda eyed her mother suspiciously.

"Like cleaning the bathrooms," Wanda Nell said,

setting a plate of bacon and eggs in front of her. Juliet placed a plateful of toast in the center of the table, and Wanda Nell set another plate for her.

"Aw, Mama," Miranda said. She hated cleaning the bathrooms about as much as she hating washing her son's diapers.

"No arguments," Wanda Nell said. "I've been cutting you some slack because you're working part-time now, but the party's over, Miranda." She sat down at the table with her own plate and reached for some toast. "You've been taking advantage of your sister enough. You should've been up feeding Lavon yourself this morning. He's your responsibility when you're not working at Budget Mart, not Juliet's."

Miranda knew better than to argue with her mother at that point. The tone in Wanda Nell's voice was a warning. Her mouth set in a mulish line, Miranda stared down at her plate while her mother and sister ate. Finally, after a long and pointed silence, she picked up her fork and began to eat.

By the time Wanda Nell was ready to leave to meet Agnes Vance at Fayetta's house, Miranda had about stopped sulking. After they'd finished breakfast, Miranda had taken Lavon and given him his bath while Wanda Nell and Juliet cleared the table and tidied up the kitchen.

"I'll be back in an hour or so," Wanda Nell told them, checking to be sure she had her car keys. "And if you're through with the bathrooms by then, Miranda, I'll think about letting you have the car for a couple of hours. Okay?"

Miranda's face brightened at that thought, and she even gave her mother a kiss on the cheek before she left.

It was five minutes to nine when Wanda Nell pulled up at Fayetta Sutton's house. A car from the sheriff's department was already sitting in the driveway. As she was getting out of her car, Agnes Vance arrived, parking her ancient, rusting Buick behind Wanda Nell's Cavalier.

"Good morning," Wanda Nell said, waiting for the older woman on the sidewalk.

"Good morning, Miz Culpepper," Agnes Vance responded. "I sure do appreciate you helping me with this." A shadow passed over her face. "I surely don't want to have to go back in there after what happened, but I know the Lord will give me strength to do what I have to do. He has always done that."

"Yes, ma'am," Wanda Nell said, taking Mrs. Vance's arm as they made their way up the walk, the pavement crumbling and chunks missing in some places.

Wanda Nell knocked on the front door, and almost as she pulled her hand away, the door swung open.

"Good morning, Wanda Nell."

Wanda Nell tried hard not to frown. She'd hoped Elmer Lee would be too busy to come himself, despite what he'd said yesterday. Maybe for once he wouldn't be too annoying.

149

"Miz Vance," she said, "this is Deputy Johnson."

"We've met," Elmer Lee said, interrupting the introduction.

"Yes," Mrs. Vance said, turning her face aside slightly. "Deputy Johnson was the one who came to tell me."

"Oh." Wanda Nell didn't know what to say to that. "Then I guess we'd better get started."

Elmer Lee stood aside to let the women in the front door.

Unthinkingly, Wanda Nell breathed deeply, then wished she hadn't. Various smells, all of them unpleasant, assaulted her nose. The house had been closed up, with no air conditioning, and the heat had only made everything worse.

"Can't we open some of the windows?" Wanda Nell asked. "Or maybe turn on the air conditioner?"

"Yes," Mrs. Vance said, fanning herself with one hand. "It sure is mighty close in here."

"I reckon so," Elmer Lee said. "But I'll do it. Y'all wait here a minute, and don't touch anything until I get back. You got that, Wanda Nell?"

She just glared at him, not bothering to answer. While he went around the house opening windows, the two women stayed where they were. Wanda Nell glanced around the small living room. It looked like Fayetta had been spending a little money on furniture. The sofa and end table were new, as was one of the chairs. The other bits of furniture around the room seemed even shabbier in contrast.

150

Elmer Lee came back. "I got the windows open. Might as well let the place air out a bit first, and then I'll turn on the air conditioner if need be."

Mrs. Vance thanked him, then stood indecisively.

"What would you like to do first?" Wanda Nell asked her gently. "Maybe get the children's clothes?"

"Yes," Mrs. Vance said gratefully. "Let's start there."

The door to the children's bedroom opened right off the hall across from the living room. Wanda Nell followed Mrs. Vance into the room. She shook her head at what she saw, thinking of those poor kids having to live like this.

There were two sets of bunk beds in the room, one small closet, a desk, and two chests of drawers. The room itself wasn't much bigger than Wanda Nell's bedroom in the trailer. What would Fayetta have done when the children got too old for boys and girls to keep sharing a room? Maybe she'd been planning to find a bigger house with all that money she had.

Mrs. Vance reached into her purse and pulled out a roll of plastic bags. "We can just put everything in these bags," she said. "I didn't have any boxes or enough suitcases, so I figured this was the next best thing."

Elmer Lee kept a close watch on the two women as they began to empty the chests of drawers. Each of the two chests had eight drawers, four on a side, and Mrs. Vance explained that each child had four drawers. To keep things organized, she suggested they empty each child's drawers into one or two bags, as needed. Wanda Nell did as she asked, noting that most of the childrens' clothing was old and faded, some of it heavily mended. Each of them had several new pieces of clothing, though, all expensive brands.

The closet contained mostly shoes and toys, along with a few jackets and a couple blankets. All these went into four more plastic bags. They put the bags in the hall near the front door when they had finished in the childrens' room.

"Is there anything else you need from here?" Elmer Lee asked Mrs. Vance.

"I need to check the bathroom," she responded. "I could use the extra towels and things for the children. And I guess we ought to look in the kitchen, too. There might be some food, canned goods and the like."

"Alright," Elmer Lee said, nodding. "That sounds okay."

"How about you take the bathroom, Miz Vance?" Wanda Nell suggested. "I'll do the kitchen. You think maybe there's a box or two around anywhere?"

"There's a small pantry in the kitchen," Mrs. Vance replied. "There might be some boxes in there. Thank you, Miz Culpepper."

The one bathroom in the house was between the two bedrooms, and the kitchen was opposite Fayetta's bedroom at the back of the house. While Mrs. Vance tackled the bathroom, Wanda Nell started on the kitchen. Elmer Lee stayed with Mrs. Vance.

She found the pantry, and in it, several small boxes. There weren't many canned goods in the pantry, but Wanda Nell packed everything. Mrs. Vance could sort out later what she wanted and what she didn't. Some of the cans looked pretty old, judging from the amount of dust they'd accumulated.

The pantry taken care of, Wanda Nell started examining the kitchen cabinets. She found a few cleaning supplies under the sink, but she left those, figuring they would be needed more here when the time came to clean up Fayetta's bedroom. The milk in the refrigerator had spoiled, and Wanda Nell poured it down the sink, her nose wrinkling at the smell.

In one of the cabinets over the sink, Wanda Nell found two boxes of cereal. She packed those into one of the boxes, then rummaged through the rest of the cabinets. There was no point in packing up the dishes and the silverware, such as they were, at the moment. Those could wait for another time.

In one of the large drawers under the counter, Wanda Nell found the usual odds and ends: clothespins, a couple screwdrivers, a hammer, nails and screws, and a tape measure. At the bottom of the drawer lay something dark and shiny with gold lettering on it. Frowning, Wanda Nell pulled it out of the drawer.

It was a menu from the Kountry Kitchen. Wanda Nell opened it, and on either side, behind the protective clear plastic sleeves, lay menu pages. A few months ago, Melvin had decided to try to upgrade the image of the restaurant with a fancier-looking menu, and this had been the result. The menus had been printed on heavy, good-quality paper, and the front of the menu had been embossed with fancy gold letters.

What on earth had Fayetta been doing with a menu in her kitchen drawer?

Shaking her head over the oddity, Wanda Nell put the menu on the table and finished her search through the kitchen.

"Find anything interesting?"

Elmer Lee spoke from the doorway, startling her as she was peering into the corner behind the refrigerator.

"No. Did you?" Wanda Nell asked.

Elmer Lee shook his head. "Miz Vance is about ready to go. You wanna help us load the stuff in her car?" He stepped forward to pick up one of the boxes.

"Is it okay if I take this back to the Kountry Kitchen?" Wanda Nell picked up the menu and waved it in Elmer Lee's direction.

"What is it?" he said, the larger of the two boxes in his hands.

"Just a menu Fayetta brought home." Wanda Nell shrugged. "I can't imagine why she'd want one, but she did have trouble remembering prices half the time. Maybe she brought it home to study." It would have been just like Fayetta to bring one home, then stick it in a drawer and forget about it.

Elmer Lee stared at her for a moment. "I don't see why not. Take it back where it belongs." He carried the box out.

Wanda Nell stuck the menu on top of the other box. She followed Elmer Lee outside and put the box into Mrs. Vance's trunk. She took the menu and dropped it into the front seat of her car. Along with Mrs. Vance and the deputy, she carried out the bags of clothes and linens, until the back seat of Mrs. Vance's car was full.

"That everything?" Elmer Lee asked Mrs. Vance.

"Yes, I think so," Mrs. Vance said. "Thank you, Deputy."

"Then I guess I'll go lock up," Elmer Lee said. He walked back to the house.

"Would you like me to come home with you and help you unload?" Wanda Nell asked.

"No, thank you. That won't be necessary," Mrs. Vance said. "The children can help me." She stared at the house.

"Would you like to go back in?" Wanda Nell asked after a moment of silence.

"I forgot my purse," Mrs. Vance said suddenly. She started back up the walk to the house.

Wanda Nell followed her. Something about the way Mrs. Vance had looked at her was bothering her.

Elmer Lee was shutting the windows in the living room when the two women reentered the house.

"What is it?" he asked.

"I forgot my purse," Mrs. Vance said.

"Where is it?" Elmer Lee asked.

Mrs. Vance didn't answer. She had already headed down the hall. Wanda Nell was right behind her.

The purse was sitting on the sink in the bathroom. Mrs. Vance hooked it over her arm, then turned to see Wanda Nell standing uncertainly in the doorway.

Wanda Nell stood aside to let the older woman out of the bathroom. Mrs. Vance paused, staring at the closed and sealed door of Fayetta's bedroom. One hand reached out, faltered, then fell by her side.

"Are you okay?" Wanda Nell asked quietly.

Mrs. Vance turned to her, but though her eyes looked right at Wanda Nell, she seemed to be seeing something else.

" 'And the Lord will smite Egypt,' " Mrs. Vance quoted, " 'smiting and healing, and they will return to the Lord, and he will heed their supplications and heal them.' "

Wanda Nell didn't know what to say. She recognized it as a quotation from the Bible, but that was as close as she could get. Was Mrs. Vance talking about her daughter? Did she think Fayetta's murder had healed her and returned her to the Lord?

Wanda Nell shivered. Mrs. Vance finally seemed to see her. Absently patting Wanda Nell on the arm, she started down the hall toward the front door.

Wanda Nell trailed behind her and waited on the doorstep while Elmer Lee locked the front door.

"What's wrong with you? You're pale as a ghost," Elmer Lee observed.

"I'm okay," Wanda Nell said. She didn't want to tell him that Mrs. Vance had just creeped her out. There had been something cold about the way she had said those words. She headed down the walk toward her own car.

"Thank you again, Miz Culpepper," Mrs. Vance called. "I surely do appreciate your help." She stood at the door of her car.

"You're very welcome," Wanda Nell said. "And if there's anything else I can do, you just let me know."

Nodding, Mrs. Vance got into her car, cranked it, and pulled away from the curb. Wanda Nell stared after her for a moment.

Behind her, Elmer Lee was backing his car out of the driveway. Waving at her, he too drove off.

Slowly, Wanda Nell opened her door and sat down. She pulled her keys out of her pocket and stuck them in the ignition. Then her eye caught the glint of the morning sun off the gold lettering on the restaurant menu.

She picked it up and opened it. The sun hit the cream-colored paper behind the clear plastic, causing a bit of glare. Wanda Nell tilted the menu slightly as she read.

As Wanda Nell scanned the list of dishes, she frowned. When she looked closely, she could see some odd splotches that seemed to have bled through the paper.

Her fingers trembling slightly, Wanda Nell removed the paper from the left side of the menu. Turning it over, she saw that someone had written on the back.

Her eyes widened in shock as she began to realize what it meant.

Thirteen

As the significance of what she was reading sank in, Wanda Nell reached for her purse and dug in it for her cell phone. Her fingers closed on the phone, and she pulled it out. She had forgotten to turn it on before she left the trailer that morning, and she punched the on button.

While she waited for the phone to be ready to use, she stared at the back of the menu page. She recognized Fayetta's handwriting. She also recognized most of the names the dead woman had written there, though most of them were only first names followed by an initial. Like "Deke C." and "Billy Joe E."— Deke Campbell and Billy Joe Eccles. Those names weren't a surprise. Her eyes widened in shock as she saw "Hector P."

Why did Fayetta have the name of Mayrene's new beau on her list? Surely there couldn't be more than one "Hector P." in Tullahoma?

The names Wanda Nell recognized were all those of men prominent in Tullahoma. One of them was even a clergyman. She counted quickly. There were forty-seven names on the list. Wanda Nell blanched. Surely Fayetta hadn't been blackmailing forty-seven different men?

Beside each of the names Fayetta had written various figures. Some of them looked like dates, others like amounts of money. Some names had stars beside them, others didn't. A few names didn't have any other notation. The clergyman's name didn't, and Wanda Nell wondered what that meant. Did it mean Fayetta hadn't blackmailed him?

Wanda Nell pulled the paper out of the other side of the menu and turned it over. There were a few more names listed on this page, but only about a dozen. They were marked in similar ways.

Wanda Nell put the sheets inside the plastic menu covers and dropped the menu on the passenger seat. She picked up her cell phone, but instead of punching in a number, she sat staring out the window. Should she call Elmer Lee right away, or should she let Tuck see this first?

While she sat and mulled it over, she noticed that a car drove by a couple of times. It was a sleek, foreign-looking car, and a woman was driving. After the woman drove by a third time, Wanda Nell acted on a hunch. She started her car and drove off. She turned right at the next intersection and passed a couple blocks before turning right again. She drove a block and made another right turn. This put her on the street that ran by the side of Fayetta's house, the place where Mayrene had dropped her off the other day so she could sneak up on the house from the back.

She parked about half a block away and, locking the car and bringing her cell phone and keys with her, walked casually toward the house. Her steps slowed as she reached the corner, and she turned to see the woman's car sitting in Fayetta's driveway. *Pretty brazen,* Wanda Nell thought, pleased she had been right about the woman's intentions.

She didn't see the strange woman at the front of the house. Slowly, Wanda Nell walked down the sidewalk and glanced down the heavily tree-shaded space between Fayetta's house and the next-door neighbor's. She was just in time to see bright pink legs wriggling through a window into the house.

Wanda Nell stood irresolute for a moment. Should she call the sheriff's department and report a break-in? She knew it was the right thing to do, but curiosity got the better of her. She walked through the grass to the window the woman had entered. It was the children's bedroom.

Peering in the window, Wanda Nell could see the woman rummaging through the closet.

"What are you looking for?" Wanda Nell called.

The woman's head jerked up and hit the clothes rail. Swearing loudly, the intruder whirled around to face Wanda Nell. "What the hell do you mean creeping up on someone like that? Who the hell are you?"

"I'm not the one breaking in to a dead woman's house," Wanda Nell pointed out mildly. She brandished her cell phone. "Maybe I ought to call the sheriff's department and let them come check you out."

"Don't be ridiculous!" The woman moved a few steps nearer the window and stared at Wanda Nell.

"This is none of your business, and I'll thank you to keep your nose out of it."

Wanda Nell stared right back at her, not flinching. She didn't know who the woman was, but she could guess. She had to be the wife of one of Fayetta's playmates. She looked a bit familiar, so Wanda Nell figured she must have seen her picture in the paper at some point.

The woman continued to glare in defiance at Wanda Nell, and Wanda Nell cataloged her from head to toe. Her clothes, pink slacks and a lime-green blouse, were expensive and screamed it. She had on enough jewelry to choke a horse, and her skin had the appearance of old leather. She had spent way too many hours out by the pool or, judging from her build, out on the tennis court. Her blonde hair was puffed up and out to about three times the size of her head, giving her an oddly unbalanced look. Wanda Nell had never liked what she called the "pumped up to Jesus" style favored by some women. She was some rich man's wife, with the attitude to boot.

"Do you really want me to know who you are?" Wanda Nell asked. "I don't have to know your name, but I can imagine why you're here."

"And why is that?" The woman practically spat the words at her.

"Because your husband was stepping out on you with the woman that used to live here."

The woman paled a bit at that and seemed at a loss for words.

161

"If you're looking for something that might incriminate your husband, whoever he is," Wanda Nell continued blithely, "I figure you're a little too late. The sheriff's department has been all over this place, and I'm sure they found everything there was to find." She didn't feel the least bit guilty about the lie. She'd see that Elmer Lee got the menu pages when she was ready to turn them over. "Besides, you're in the children's room."

"Are you some kind of deputy?" the woman asked, suddenly nervous. Her right hand fidgeted with three of the heavy gold chains around her neck.

"No," Wanda Nell replied. "I knew the dead woman, though."

"Oh, you did, did you?" The woman's eyes narrowed. "Then you knew what a no-good bitch of a slut she was. Getting her claws into other women's men. She didn't have the decency to leave married men alone."

Wanda Nell couldn't argue much with this assessment of Fayetta, but something perverse in her made her point out, "Well, she couldn't do it by herself. The men had to cooperate."

With a cry of rage, the woman launched herself at Wanda Nell. Startled, Wanda Nell stepped away from the window. The woman came flying through it and landed on the ground, the breath knocked out of her.

Wanda Nell was so astonished, she just stood there for a moment. The woman groaned, and Wanda Nell

162

squatted beside her. "Are you okay? Do you need to go to the doctor?"

The woman's hand snaked out, aiming for Wanda Nell's face. But once again Wanda Nell was too quick for her. From her squatting position, she leaped backward out of the woman's reach, almost toppling over when she landed. Getting her balance, she stood and prepared to run, in case the woman got up from the ground.

"Listen, lady, you keep away from me," Wanda Nell said, her exertions causing her to breathe jerkily. She held up her cell phone. "I'll call the police right now if you try anything else."

Groaning slightly, the woman got up and brushed herself off. The knees and legs of her expensive slacks had green streaks on them and her hands were dirty from where they had sunk into the ground. She limped by Wanda Nell without saying another word.

Wanda Nell stood and watched her as she made it to her car. She opened the door and almost fell inside. Moments later, the engine roared and the woman slammed backward out of the driveway, almost taking the mailbox with her. She sped off, her tires squealing against the pavement.

Shaking her head at the stranger's bizarre behavior, Wanda Nell went back to the window. It suddenly dawned on her that Elmer Lee had forgotten to lock it when he had gone around the house earlier, closing all the windows. That wasn't like him, but maybe he'd been distracted by Mrs. Vance coming back for her purse. She couldn't imagine him leaving it unlocked deliberately.

For a moment she thought about crawling through the window herself and poking around a bit. But she quickly nixed that idea. So far none of the neighbors had appeared, wondering what was going on. Maybe they were all at work or else just too busy to notice. She decided she didn't want to take the risk of running into another crazy wife or an inquisitive neighbor. She pulled the window closed from the outside. Maybe no one else would try to break in before someone from the sheriff's department came back to lock it.

Cell phone in hand, she went around the back of the house and cut through the backyard to the other street. Once she was safely in her car again, she considered her next move.

With a sudden grin, she punched in the number of the sheriff's department. When the dispatcher answered, she gave her name and asked for Elmer Lee.

After a few moments on hold, Elmer Lee came on the line. "What do you want now, Wanda Nell?"

"I got some information for you, Elmer Lee," she said. "You wanna hear it?"

Sighing loudly into the phone, Elmer Lee said, "No, but I guess I'm going to anyway. What is it?"

Quickly Wanda Nell told him what had happened at Fayetta's house after he and Mrs. Vance left.

Elmer Lee groaned into the phone. "I can't believe I

left that window open. Damn! Who was she? Any idea?"

"I've seen her somewhere before," Wanda Nell said. "I'd say she was over fifty, but she looked older; her skin was tanned like cowhide. Big blonde hair, poofed out like you wouldn't believe, and lots of jewelry. And a little shorter than me."

Elmer Lee didn't say anything.

"Who is she, Elmer Lee?" Wanda Nell said.

"You need to keep your nose out of this," Elmer Lee said. "Trust me on this."

"Come on, now, tell me who she is," Wanda Nell said. "You know I'll find out sooner or later." She paused a moment, then laughed. "Besides, you don't want anybody there knowing you went off and left a window unlocked."

Elmer Lee said something vulgar in a low tone, but Wanda Nell ignored it. She waited.

"All right, damn it! It sounds like Retha Eccles, Billy Joe Eccles's wife."

"Thanks, Elmer Lee," she said. "Now, I gotta run, but if I come up with anything else, I'll let you know." *Eventually,* she added silently. She ended the call.

Dropping her cell phone in her purse, she eyed the menu again. She'd give it to Elmer Lee, but first she wanted Tuck Tucker to see it.

She headed for downtown Tullahoma, where Tuck had his office in one of the old buildings on the square. The drive took only a few minutes, and soon she was passing by the memorial to the Confederate

165

war dead. She parked across the street from it and entered the building. Waiting for the elevator, she clutched her purse and the menu close to her, feeling nervous about what she was doing.

On the second floor, she walked down the hall to Tuck's office and opened the door. She passed through the waiting room and opened a second door. At her desk Blanche Tillman, Tuck's secretary, was busy tapping the keys of her computer and listening to country music on the local radio station. She looked up as Wanda Nell opened the door.

"Hey, girl," she said, her face lighting up with a big smile. "What you doing here? You need to see Tuck?"

"Is he here?" Wanda Nell asked. "I've got something he needs to see."

"He's over at the courthouse right now. He oughta be back in half an hour or so. You wanna wait?"

Wanda Nell shook her head. "No, I can't. But maybe I could leave something for him?"

"Sure," Blanche said.

"Can you make some copies of something for me?"

"Sure," Blanche repeated. She got up from her desk and walked to the door that led to the inner chambers of the office. "Come on back here with me."

Wanda Nell followed her through the door and down a short hallway to a small room at the end of the hall. A copier stood in one corner of the room, while shelves of supplies and books occupied the rest of the space.

Blanche flipped a switch. "It's gotta warm up. Takes a few seconds. What do you need to copy?" She held out her hand.

Wanda Nell hesitated a moment, but then she decided it didn't matter if Blanche saw what was on the backs of the menus. She was Tuck's secretary, after all, and there probably wasn't much that went on in this office that she didn't know about. "The backs of these menus," Wanda Nell said.

Blanche glanced at them as she took them from Wanda Nell. Her eyes widened slightly, but she didn't say anything. She placed the first one facedown on the copier and pressed a button. A moment later a copy snaked out of the machine.

"Can you make a couple of copies of each page?" Wanda Nell asked suddenly.

"Sure," Blanche said. She pressed the button again, waited a moment, then switched the pages on the copier. She punched a different button, then hit the copy button. Two pages came out.

Blanche handed Wanda Nell the originals, then pulled the copies from the tray. Wanda Nell stuck the first two pages back into the menu, then looked at the copies. She handed a set to Blanche and stuck the other set into the menu. "Give these to Tuck when he gets back from the courthouse, please. And ask him to call me. I'll be at home, and tell him I'll explain then. I've got to drop something off at the sheriff's department first, but then I'm going straight home."

"All right, honey," Blanche said. She led the way back to the reception area. "I'll make sure he sees this first thing."

"Thanks, Blanche," Wanda Nell said. "I appreciate it."

As she left, Blanche was tucking the two pages into a drawer in her desk. Wanda Nell gave her a little wave before shutting the door behind her.

In her car again, she stared at the menu. After a moment's hesitation, she pulled the copy Blanche had made out of the menu, folded the pages, and stuck them in her purse. She put the original pages back in the menu, but she put them in backward, so that Fayetta's lists were visible.

The sheriff's department was just across the square, on a side street heading north with the county courthouse across from it, facing the square. Wanda Nell drove her car to the sheriff's department and parked outside. She wanted to drop off the menu inside and make a quick getaway. She didn't really want to talk to Elmer Lee right now.

As she got out of her car, she glanced across the street. T.J.'s truck was parked on the side street by the courthouse, but she didn't see him. He was probably in the courthouse somewhere with Tuck.

Taking a deep breath to steady herself, she walked slowly to the front door of the sheriff's department. Inside, she waited a moment for her eyes to adjust to the dimmer light. She went to the desk and handed the menu to the deputy on duty.

"Could you see that Elmer Lee Johnson gets this?" she said. "He'll know what it's for."

The deputy, a black man with grizzled, close-cropped hair, glanced down at the menu. "Sure, ma'am. You wanna wait and give it to him yourself?"

"No, thanks," Wanda Nell said, starting to back away. "He'll know who it's from, and he knows how to get in touch with me."

Shrugging, the deputy placed the menu on the desk beside his phone. "Sure thing, ma'am. Have a nice day."

"Thank you," Wanda Nell said. She turned and hurried out the door.

The bright sunlight struck her right in the eyes. She stopped for a moment and shaded her eyes with her right hand.

Across the street, she caught a flash of movement. The driver's door to T.J.'s truck had just shut. Tuck Tucker stood beside it, talking to T.J. Wanda Nell could see the back of her son's head through the rear window of the truck.

Wanda Nell started to call out, but the words died in her throat.

Tuck had stuck his head into T.J.'s truck, and it looked like he and T.J. were kissing.

Fourteen

Without really thinking about what she was doing, Wanda Nell stumbled back inside the sheriff's department building. She stood blinking, her back against the door.

Dimly she became aware that someone was talking to her.

"Ma'am, are you all right? Ma'am?" The black deputy had left his desk and was approaching her.

"I'm fine," Wanda Nell said. "I, uh, I thought I dropped something on the way out." Pretending to scan the floor, she dipped her head. She took a couple of deep breaths. "It's not here, I guess." She looked up at the deputy and offered him a weak smile.

The deputy eyed her for a moment, then shrugged and turned away. "Have a good day."

"Thanks," Wanda Nell said. Her hand faltered on the door. Then, feeling more resolute, she pulled the door open and walked outside again.

She squinted into the light. T.J.'s truck was gone, and there was no sign of Tuck. She breathed a sigh of relief as she walked to her car and opened the door.

Sinking into the driver's seat, she closed the door and just sat there.

Had she really seen her son kissing another man? Her hands trembled as she gripped the stirring wheel.

It had all happened so quickly, maybe she hadn't

seen what she thought she'd seen. Maybe Tuck had stuck his head in the truck to be sure no one could overhear what he was saying.

Yes, that could be it.

But no one was anywhere nearby. *Except for me,* she told herself. *And I couldn't hear anything from across the street. They didn't even know I was there.*

So T.J. really had been kissing another man. His boss.

Wanda Nell's hands gripped the steering wheel even harder. What if Tuck was trying to force himself on T.J.?

She willed her hands to relax. She knew better than that. T.J. would have got out of the truck and beat the crap out of Tuck if that were the case. No, T.J. had been a willing participant; she realized that now.

She cranked the car and backed out of her parking space. She drove slowly around the square and back down Main Street on her way home.

As she drove, she felt almost dizzy from the speed of her thoughts. If T.J. liked men, that would explain a few things lately. Like him not wanting his grandmother pushing him off on all those girls she wanted him to meet.

And all the time he'd been spending with Tuck. The way he'd smile and his eyes would light up when he talked about Tuck.

She stared blindly at a traffic signal. Then there was the night he'd spent at Tuck's place, saying he'd had too much to drink and didn't want to drive home.

171

The light changed, and she pressed the accelerator too hard. Her car jumped forward into the intersection. She drove on auto-pilot.

On the rest of the short drive home, she searched her memory for other clues. Had it been there all the time, and she just hadn't seen it? Or hadn't she wanted to see it?

T.J. had never brought a girl home to meet her. Try as she might, she couldn't remember any time he'd mentioned a girl he really cared about. There'd been a couple of women he'd hung around with when he was seventeen or eighteen, but mostly he was running around with one of his buddies, like as not getting into trouble. He had been a wild teenager, and nothing she could say or do had seemed to get through to him. And his daddy sure hadn't been any help.

She could just imagine what Bobby Ray would've thought about this. She remembered some of the remarks he'd made about one of their high school classmates that everybody had said was queer. And the way they'd taunted an older man who ran a florist's shop.

Oh, Lord, was that what would happen to T.J. if people found out? Would some of his former buddies try to beat him up?

She felt like vomiting. She'd read about hate crimes, as they called them, and heard them talked about on the news. She didn't want her son to be the victim of one.

Vaguely she realized where she was. She had reached the turnoff from the highway to the lake road. She waited for a truck to pass, then turned.

T.J. had been saying he had something he needed to talk to her about. Wanda Nell had a feeling this was it.

What should she do? Call him and ask him to come over right now?

Or wait and let him tell her when he was ready?

What was she going to say to him?

She pulled her car into the driveway beside the trailer and switched off the engine. Before she could gather her wits enough to get out of the car, Miranda burst out the door and ran to the car.

"Mama, is it still okay for me to have the car for a couple hours?" She offered her mother a pleading smile.

Wanda Nell stared at her like she'd never seen her before.

"Mama? What is it? Is something wrong?"

Wanda Nell forced herself to smile and respond. "No, honey, I'm fine. Just thinking about something." She glanced at her watch—just about ten-forty-five. "Yeah, you can have the car for a while. Just make sure you're back here no later than one o'clock. Okay?"

"I promise, Mama," Miranda said. "And the bathrooms are clean, and I did some laundry, too. Juliet said she wouldn't mind watching Lavon while I'm gone."

"Thanks for doing all that, Miranda." Wanda Nell

clutched her purse and got out of the car. "Drive carefully."

Miranda hopped into the car as soon as her mother was out of the way. "I will." She cranked the car and started backing out before Wanda Nell could get around the car and into the trailer.

Wanda Nell stared after her a moment. What would Miranda say about T.J.? Would Juliet still idolize her big brother?

She glanced at her neighbor's trailer. And Mayrene? How would Mayrene feel about T.J.?

Thinking about Mayrene reminded her suddenly of something else. What would Mayrene say if she told her that Hector Padget's name was on Fayetta's list?

Suddenly feeling bone tired, Wanda Nell climbed the steps to her door and opened it.

She found Juliet in the kitchen with Lavon, having a mid-morning snack. She said hello and wandered to the refrigerator. Maybe some cold Coke would help her clear her head a little.

Wanda Nell pulled the two-liter bottle of Coke from the shelf and turned around to extract a glass from the cabinet.

"Mama, are you okay?"

"Hmm . . . yes, honey, I'm okay," Wanda Nell said as she finished filling her glass. She left the bottle of Coke on the counter and sat down at the table across from Juliet.

"Mama," Juliet said.

"Yes?"

"You put your purse in the fridge." Juliet frowned. "Are you sure you're okay, Mama?"

"I'm fine, honey. Just got a lot on my mind right now, what with the restaurant and everything," Wanda Nell said. She retrieved her purse and set it on the counter. Then she stood there, lost in thought.

She very badly wanted someone to talk to, but Juliet wasn't the one. Times like this she wished her own mama were still living. Her mama had been wise and kind, always thinking carefully before she spoke.

Her mama had never wavered in her love for her children, no matter what stupid or foolish things they did. Just the way she loved T.J., no matter what. The rest she'd have to figure out as it came.

With that realization, she felt calm. Time would sort everything out, one way or another. When T.J. finally talked to her about it, she'd do her best to understand.

Time to get on with some housework. She left Juliet with Lavon and checked on Miranda's cleaning efforts in the bathrooms. She was pleased with what she saw. Miranda had done a really good job.

She had also washed and dried Lavon's diapers and his clothes, but she hadn't folded them or put them away. Wanda Nell sighed as she began to fold. At least Miranda had taken a step or two forward.

By the time Miranda returned at seven minutes past one, Wanda Nell had fixed some lunch, changed clothes, and freshened her makeup. She was ready to go to work the minute Miranda returned the car.

"Y'all have a nice quiet evening planned?"

"Yes, Mama," Juliet said. "T.J. might come over later and take us to visit Grandma Culpepper awhile." She didn't sound too excited about the prospect. Miranda just rolled her eyes and sighed heavily.

"It's good for you to get to know her," Wanda Nell said gently. "She's an old woman, and you may not have much time to spend with her."

"We know, Mama," Miranda said. "And she's getting better. At least she calls us by the right names now. And she likes to hold Lavon in her lap." She brightened. "Maybe she'll leave him something in her will, and us, too."

That sounded exactly like something her daddy would've said. Wanda Nell shook her head and said she'd see them later.

Getting into her car, she glanced over at Mayrene's trailer. She'd had a lot of time to think about Fayetta's murder while she was doing housework, and she knew she was going to have to dig a bit deeper to be able to help Melvin get out of jail. They had to find somebody with a more compelling motive to murder Fayetta. Someone who had hated her enough to kill so savagely.

Should she tell Mayrene about Fayetta's list? How would Mayrene react? They'd been friends a long time, but Mayrene was funny when it came to her men. She didn't like anybody messing with them, or her.

Wanda Nell mulled over the problem on the way to work. As she parked at the Kountry Kitchen, she decided she had to tell Mayrene. If she was dating a man who was a possible suspect in Fayetta's murder, she ought to know that.

The lunch crowd had thinned out, but Ovie reported they'd had a busy morning when she and Wanda Nell conferred.

"I need to run to the bank to make a deposit, Ovie," Wanda Nell said. "Can you hang on here another half hour?"

"Sure thing, honey," Ovie said. "Take your time."

It took Wanda Nell about fifteen minutes to check the morning's receipts, recheck those from the previous day that she had stuffed in Melvin's office safe overnight, and prepare the deposit. With the bank bag tucked securely under her arm, she waved to Ovie and left the restaurant.

A little nervous over the amount of cash she had in the bag, Wanda Nell scurried to her car. The sooner she had it in the bank, the happier she'd be.

The bank was only a couple blocks away, and Wanda Nell pulled into the drive-through lane. Just one car ahead of her, she was relieved to see.

When her turn came, she handed over everything to the teller, a woman named Paulette Morgan whom she had gone to high school with.

Paulette didn't say a word about the murder, and Wanda Nell was grateful. They chatted about their kids, and then Paulette put the deposit slip in the drawer and Wanda Nell retrieved it.

Back at the restaurant, she met Katie Ann in the parking lot.

"Hey, Wanda Nell, how are you today?" Katie Ann's smile was bright and friendly.

"I'm doing fine, how about you?" Wanda Nell led the way to the door and opened it, motioning for the younger woman to go in ahead of her.

"Just peachy, thanks," Katie Ann said.

Wanda Nell paused to speak to someone at the counter, then continued on her way to Melvin's office to put away the deposit slip. As she passed the closet where they all stowed their purses and things, she saw Katie Ann on her knees, poking around some of the lower shelves.

"You lose something?"

Startled, Katie Ann turned around. "Oh, yeah, Wanda Nell. I think I heard something fall out of my purse." She ducked her head back down and continued looking. After a moment, she stood up and dusted off her knees. "Well, whatever it was, I can't find it." Flashing another smile, she pushed past Wanda Nell and walked down the hall toward the kitchen.

Shaking her head, Wanda Nell went on to Melvin's office and put the deposit slip in the desk. She didn't know why, but she had the feeling that Katie Ann had been lying to her.

But why would she lie about something so stupid? Had she been searching for something else?

Surely she hadn't been looking for Fayetta's savings account passbook. How would she even know about that?

Wanda Nell went back to the closet. When she'd found the passbook the other day, she had quit looking. Maybe there was something else there.

She began a systematic search of the shelves, but the more she looked, the more frustrated she got. There was nothing out of the ordinary that she could see.

She was about to give up when her fingers brushed across something plastic wedged at the back of the top shelf, behind a couple of large cans. Whatever it was, it was stuck into the join of the shelf. She'd need to get a bit higher before she could see it.

Testing one of the lower shelves carefully, Wanda Nell stepped onto it. It held, so she put her full weight on it and pulled herself up.

So far so good. Now her head was at the right height to see whatever was stuck behind the wood. She moved the cans out of the way, and she could now see that it was a bit of plastic about the size of a credit card.

Holding onto the shelf with her left hand, she reached with her right and pulled the card loose. Slowly she stepped back down from the shelf and examined her find.

Though it was the size of a credit card, Wanda Nell realized that it was actually a key card of the type that many hotels used. One side had two arrows on it, to show the user which way to insert the card.

She turned it over. There was a logo on the other

side. Stamped in plain, bold script were the words *The Deer Stand.*

Wanda Nell frowned. What the heck was this? She'd never heard of a hotel or motel called the Deer Stand. It seemed an odd name for a place to stay.

But maybe it was some kind of club. That made more sense.

Was this what Katie Ann had been searching for?

Wanda Nell decided she was just going to ask her, flat-out.

Clutching the card in her hand, she headed for the front of the restaurant. Katie Ann was chatting with Ruby Garner. Ovie was at the door, purse in hand. She waved bye when she spotted Wanda Nell, and Wanda Nell waved back.

She waited until Ruby had also gone, then called for Katie Ann to come with her to the back dining room. It was empty, and she could question the younger woman without worrying about anyone overhearing them.

Katie Ann sauntered back to where Wanda Nell stood. "What is it, Wanda Nell?"

Wanda Nell held up the card so Katie Ann could see the writing on it.

"Was this what you were looking for?"

Fifteen

Katie Ann paled, but she didn't say anything. She stared at Wanda Nell, her eyes round with innocence.

"Nothing fell out of your purse," Wanda Nell said flatly. "I checked. But you were looking for something, and this is the only thing I found that didn't belong in that storeroom."

Katie Ann frowned. "I don't like being called a liar." She tossed her head. "Why should I be looking for that thing? I don't even know what it is."

"Are you sure?" Wanda Nell demanded. "You've never seen it before, or one like it?"

"Looks like one of them key cards," Katie Ann said, after a moment's hesitation. "It's not a credit card."

"If it's not yours," Wanda Nell said slowly, "then who does it belong to?"

"How should I know?" Katie Ann said, her voice sharp. "I told you it's not mine."

Wanda Nell stared at her for a moment. She'd swear on a stack of bibles that Katie Ann was lying to her. The girl knew what the card was, all right. But how was she going to make her admit it?

"Maybe it belonged to Fayetta," Wanda Nell said. "In that case, I reckon I better turn it over to the sheriff's department. It may have something to do with her getting killed."

"Don't do that!" Katie Ann slapped a hand over her

mouth as soon as the words were out. She stared at Wanda Nell in dismay.

Wanda Nell waited.

"Oh, hell," Katie Ann said. She licked her lips. "Yeah, I was looking for it. I knew Fayetta had one, and I thought she might've left it here."

"Why would she leave it here?"

"She didn't want her mama finding it," Katie Ann said. "Her mama was always going through her stuff at home. Fayetta couldn't hide anything from her. That old woman is nosey like you wouldn't believe."

"Would Miz Vance even know what this is?"

"Maybe not." Katie Ann shrugged. "But Fayetta had a hard time standing up to her sometimes."

"Sounds to me you knew Fayetta a lot better than you let on," Wanda Nell said harshly.

"Yeah," Katie Ann said. She moved over to a table and sat down.

Wanda Nell checked the front. Junior Farley had come in while she and Katie Ann had been talking, but he just helped himself to coffee the way he usually did when they were busy. He waved at Wanda Nell.

"You need anything else, Junior?" she called.

"A date for Saturday night," he called back.

"Can't help you there," she said. She should've known. That was his standard response anytime one of the waitresses asked him that question.

She made a dismissive gesture with her left hand, then turned her attention back to Katie Ann.

"I guess I knew Fayetta pretty well," Katie Ann said. She sighed. "She didn't have too many women friends."

"No, I reckon not," Wanda Nell said.

"She knew I liked kids," Katie Ann continued. "I'd babysit for her sometimes to keep old pruneface from doing it. That's what she called her mama." She shook her head. "I was there one time watching the kids when the old lady came by. She about had a hissy fit when she found me there instead of Fayetta. She made the kids go home with her, and Fayetta like to had a stroke when she found out."

"Why didn't she want her mama looking after the kids?"

"Oh, come on, Wanda Nell," Katie Ann said. "Miz Vance was trying to get those kids taken away from her. She thought Fayetta was an unfit mother, and she kept saying she was gonna take Fayetta to court over it." She shivered. "You know, I almost think she hated Fayetta."

Wanda Nell felt a deep and unexpected sympathy for Fayetta. She knew what it was like to be threatened with losing her children. Old Mrs. Culpepper had tried to do it to her. But she was a lot more stable than Fayetta had been. She had to admit she could see Mrs. Vance's point. She had a right to be concerned.

Now that Fayetta was dead, Mrs. Vance could probably keep the kids, unless any of their daddies wanted to try to get custody of them. That didn't seem too likely, though, since none of their daddies had had anything to do with them, as far as Wanda Nell knew.

Wanda Nell decided it was time to get the conversation back on track. "Tell me what this thing is. What's this Deer Stand?" She laid the card on the table.

"Oh, it's just a club," Katie Ann said, very casual. "You know, hunters."

"Seems kinda fancy for a hunting club," Wanda Nell said, her fingers tapping the card. "Why would they need something like this for some old deer stand?" She thought about the one her own daddy and her brother had built. It was nothing fancy, just about big enough for the two of them and maybe one other hunter.

"It's real private," Katie Ann said. "From what Fayetta told me," she added hastily. "Not many people know about it, just the members."

"Where is it?"

Katie Ann shrugged. "In the woods somewhere."

Wanda Nell wanted to pinch her. A good part of Tullahoma County was wooded. "You can't be more specific than that?"

The younger woman shrugged again. "Fayetta never said."

There was something Katie Ann wasn't telling her; Wanda Nell could feel it. Maybe if she asked the right question. But what was it? She sighed.

"What was Fayetta doing at a men's hunting club? Surely she wasn't a member?"

Katie Ann shifted in her seat. She didn't look at Wanda Nell. "They kinda like to have a couple of women around. You know, cooking and waiting on them."

Wanda Nell didn't believe that for a minute. She knew why the club members had wanted Fayetta around, and the knowledge chilled her.

"Do you know any of the other women who worked at this club?"

"Fayetta didn't mention any names," Katie Ann said.

Wanda Nell stared at her for a moment, then at the key card. "I think the sheriff's department oughta know about this. It might have something to do with Fayetta's death." She stood up, and Katie Ann reached out and grabbed her arm.

"You can't do that!"

Wanda Nell shook off the other woman's hand. "Why not?"

Katie Ann was frightened, Wanda Nell could see it in her eyes and in the way she sat so rigidly in her chair.

Slowly Wanda Nell sat down. "What are you afraid of?"

"You don't know what you're messing with," Katie Ann said. "The men in that club ain't gonna like you talking to the sheriff's department."

"So what?"

"You don't understand, Wanda Nell," Katie Ann said, her voice pleading. "Those men are the kind of men you don't mess around with."

Wanda Nell suddenly put two and two together. That

185

list Fayetta had kept on the backs of the menu pages. She'd bet anything those men were members of the club. They were the men Fayetta had been black-mailing.

She swallowed hard. Katie Ann wasn't lying. Those men were some of the wealthiest and most powerful in Tullahoma. If they had some kind of private sex club going, they wouldn't like it if anyone came poking around. Hell, the sheriff himself might even be a member.

Wanda Nell dredged her memory for those names. Had the sheriff's name been on the list? She couldn't recall seeing it, and surely if she had seen it, she would have remembered.

She relaxed a bit. No, Jesse Shaw's name wasn't on that list. But it didn't mean he didn't know about it. Nobody knew more about what was going on in town or in the whole county than the sheriff. He turned a blind eye to some things, and maybe this was one of them.

"Wanda Nell! You got customers up here that need you."

Junior Farley's bellow startled both women. "I'm coming," Wanda Nell yelled back at him. She stood up, sticking the key card in the pocket of her polyester slacks.

"What are you gonna do?" Katie Ann whispered to her as they moved up front.

"I don't know yet," Wanda Nell said in an under-tone. She motioned for Katie Ann to see to the new

186

customers while she went to check on Junior.

While she got him the dish of blackberry cobbler he requested from the kitchen, she thought about what Katie Ann had told her. The girl was still holding out on her; Wanda Nell was sure of that. Maybe because she was one of the women who worked at the club with Fayetta?

Wanda Nell set the cobbler down with a thump. Katie Ann didn't look the type to be doing something like that. She sure wasn't like Fayetta, but Wanda Nell knew from long experience that you could never tell everything about a person from the way they looked.

Would Katie Ann admit it if Wanda Nell challenged her with that question?

After a moment's reflection, Wanda Nell decided it didn't matter, at least for the moment. Right now she had to figure out what she was going to do with the damn key card. This whole mess had suddenly gotten a lot more complicated, and she had to consider what she was doing very carefully.

If she turned the card over to Elmer Lee and explained what it was—if he didn't know already, and he just might—then she could be stirring up a real hornets' nest. Really big and really mean hornets at that.

But if she turned it in, could Elmer Lee keep her name out of it? Would he? He might not, just to dump her in the shit that would surely hit the fan. She never could tell with Elmer Lee.

"I said, I need some coffee."

Junior's petulant voice broke into Wanda Nell's

thoughts. Muttering an apology, she fetched the coffeepot and refilled Junior's cup.

"What's with you today, Wanda Nell?" Junior demanded, frowning. Normally, he was jovial, but today he looked downright peeved with her.

"Sorry, Junior," Wanda Nell said, setting the coffeepot down on the counter. "I got a lot on my mind right now. I should be paying more attention, though."

Mollified, Junior said, "That's okay. I understand." He leaned over the counter, as far as his large belly would let him. "You think Melvin really did it?" he asked in a low voice.

Wanda Nell regarded his chubby face, burned red by long hours in the sun. "No, I don't. And I bet you don't either. You know Melvin. You really think he could do something like that?"

Junior shook his head and settled back on his stool. "Not over Fayetta," he said. "He'd'a had to get in line. A real long line."

"Oh?"

"Yep," Junior said, his face solemn. "You probably don't know my cousin Eli Farley. He works down at the John Deere place out on the highway. He's a mechanic, and he's pretty tight with his money, so he don't eat out that much."

"No, can't say as I do," Wanda Nell said, hoping Junior would get to the point eventually.

"Well, Eli, he lives on the same street as Fayetta. In the next block, across and catty-corner from her. I stopped by there last night to see him; he's doing some work on my truck. I pay him real good, but he don't charge me as much as they would down at the Dodge place. And I owed him some money, so I stopped off there, and we got to talking." He paused for a sip of his coffee.

"About what?" Wanda Nell said, trying not to let the frustration creep into her voice.

"About Fayetta," Junior said, a puzzled look on his face. "What'd you think I was talking about? Anyway, me and Eli got to talking, and he was telling me how he saw men coming and going sometimes from Fayetta's house. Now, Eli can see the side of her house and her backyard from his front window, on account of his house being across the intersection and catty-corner. So he's got a real good view." He paused for more coffee. "Now, that don't mean he spends all his time spying on his neighbors. He's a good Christian man, and I reckon that's why Fayetta being his neighbor bothered him."

"Uh-huh," Wanda Nell said. She thought about taking his coffee away from him until he got to the point, but she knew she'd just have to be patient.

"Yeah, ol' Fayetta had men slipping in and out of her house. They reckoned they was being real smart by sneaking in from the side and coming through the yard with the trees for cover, but Eli could see 'em." Junior nodded briskly. "Yeah, he sure could. He thought about calling somebody about those kids of hers, but it seemed like their grandma was always coming and taking them away. Anyway, that's about it." He stared down into his coffee. "Oh, yeah. Eli said sometimes the house would be dark all weekend. Fayetta'd be gone, and so would her kids."

The weekends Fayetta was working at the club? Wanda Nell mulled that over. Could be.

Junior's rambling really didn't tell her much new. Except that Fayetta had been even busier than Wanda Nell had thought.

She tuned back, because Junior was still talking. ". . . talked to her mama a time or two, and Eli said she's a pretty sharp old lady, but kinda mean where them kids are concerned. He was out working in his yard a coupla times when she came by to get 'em, and he said she was reciting Bible verses at 'em while she was putting 'em in the car." He shook his head. "Ain't nothing wrong with kids learning the Bible, but Eli said it was all verses about the wages of sin being death and all that. I don't think it's right to say that to kids all the time. You need to tell 'em good things."

"You're right about that," Wanda Nell said, feeling a bit guilty. She hadn't been very good about seeing that her own children went to church on a regular basis. She really should make more of an effort to get there herself and set a good example. Maybe she'd try going to Mrs. Culpepper's church, since T.J. was going there with his grandmother.

What would the church say about T.J. if they knew?

The thought hit her suddenly, and she felt a headache coming on. *I'll think about that later. I've got more'n I can handle right now*. She put it firmly out of her mind.

Junior didn't have anything more to say, and Wanda Nell filled his coffee cup one more time. She cleared away the remains of his blackberry cobbler and went to wait on someone who'd just walked in.

As she worked, she thought about what she should do with the key card she'd found. She knew she should give it to Elmer Lee, but those nagging doubts just wouldn't leave her alone. She didn't want the members of that club coming after her or her family if Elmer Lee had loose lips.

No, she just wasn't sure she could trust Elmer Lee enough. So, for the moment, she had to do something else.

She could talk to Tuck about it. In fact, she should, because he needed to know about this. But she felt funny about Tuck now, after what she saw outside the courthouse. How could she talk to him, or to T.J. for that matter, and not let on that she knew something?

She glanced toward the door, hearing it open. The decision had been made for her.

Tuck Tucker had just walked in.

Sixteen

"Afternoon, Wanda Nell," Tuck said, sliding onto a stool at the counter.

"Afternoon, Tuck," Wanda Nell replied. "What can I get you?" She wiped down the counter near him, trying to avoid looking into his face.

"Got any decaf coffee?"

Wanda Nell nodded and turned away to get him some. She set the coffee down in front of him. "How about something to eat? We've got some blackberry cobbler, made fresh this morning."

"That sounds good," Tuck said. "But I'll have to run a couple of extra miles." He laughed.

Wanda Nell smiled vaguely in his direction as she left to fetch a serving of cobbler.

Don't be such a wuss, she scolded herself. *Just look at the man or he'll know something's wrong for sure.* She carried the bowl back out and placed it in front of Tuck.

"Dig in," she said brightly. "It's real good."

Tuck picked up a spoon and tasted the cobbler. "Mmm. Very good, and worth a couple of extra miles." He smiled at her.

"Thanks."

Tuck turned his stool slightly and surveyed the room. The nearest customers were sitting more than a dozen feet away, involved in an animated discussion.

He shifted back and regarded Wanda Nell.

"That was an interesting list you gave me," he said in a quiet tone. "Where did you find it?"

Keeping her voice low, Wanda Nell said, "In a menu Fayetta had stuck in a drawer at her house. I found it this morning when I went over there with Miz Vance."

"I see." Tuck had another spoonful of cobbler. He chewed thoughtfully. "Judging from the contents of that list, she was playing with a pretty interesting crowd."

"Yeah," Wanda Nell said. She slipped a hand in her pocket and fingered the key card. Should she show it to him now? She pulled her hand out of her pocket.

"Has anybody else seen that list?"

"I gave it to Elmer Lee Johnson," Wanda Nell said. "I made copies of it at your office, then I took it to the sheriff's department."

"I thought I saw your car parked there," Tuck said. He ate a bit more cobbler. "T.J. and I were at the courthouse this morning," he added in a casual tone.

"Oh, really?" Wanda Nell tried to keep her voice cool.

Tuck put his spoon down and fixed her with his brown eyes. Wanda Nell couldn't tear her own gaze away from them. She remembered thinking how attractive he was the first time she had met him, when she had gone to consult him about representing T.J. She blushed at those thoughts now.

"Yeah," Tuck said. "I thought I saw you ducking into the sheriff's department when I was talking to T.J.

in his truck." He watched her closely.

Wanda Nell tried to keep her breathing even. What should she say? That she saw them? Or deny it?

The silence stretched on a little too long.

"I reckon you must have seen us," Tuck said. He smiled slightly. "What you think matters a great deal to T.J. He's worked hard to turn his life around so you'll be proud of him, Wanda Nell."

"I know that," she said softly. "And I am *very* proud of him." She paused for a deep breath. "I just want what's best for him, and I don't want him getting hurt."

Tuck's hand trembled a bit as he played with his spoon. He set the spoon down on the counter. "I don't want him to get hurt either. Can you believe that?"

"Yes." And she did. She had never seen Tuck look the least bit vulnerable, but suddenly he did. She knew that one wrong word from her could cause damage not easily repaired, but she felt that things were moving way too fast. She needed more time to think and to understand.

"As long as we both want what's best for T.J.," she said softly, "then I guess somehow it'll all be okay."

"Good," Tuck said. "Just . . . wait till he's ready to tell you himself. Can you do that?" His eyes pleaded with her.

Wanda Nell nodded.

Tuck stood up and pulled some money from his pocket, suddenly in a hurry. He dropped a five-dollar bill on the counter. "I'd better be getting back to the office. I need to follow up on some things."

He was out the door by the time she remembered the key card. She could have run after him, but she didn't. All she wanted right now was to go someplace quiet so she could sit and think. The murder, T.J. and Tuck—everything was piling up on her, and she was starting to feel like she was suffocating.

"He sure is one good-looking man," Katie Ann said as she sauntered up to Wanda Nell. "I've seen him around town. What's his name?"

Jolted out of her reverie, Wanda Nell scowled. "Trust me, I don't think you're his type."

"Oh, really," Katie Ann said. "And you are?" She said it playfully, but Wanda Nell detected a note of spite in there somewhere.

"I'm not either," Wanda Nell said shortly. She started to push by Katie Ann.

"Isn't he a lawyer?"

Wanda Nell stopped and turned back. "Yeah, he is. If you must know, his name's Hamilton Tucker, and my son works for him. Are you satisfied now?"

"Well, thank you, Wanda Nell. I appreciate the information," Katie Ann said. "You never know when you might be needing a lawyer, and I might as well have me one that's as good-looking as him."

Wanda Nell didn't stay for another word from her. She stomped off through the kitchen and back to Melvin's office. They weren't that busy and Katie Ann could hold the fort for a little while. She wanted a few minutes of quiet.

She sat down behind the desk and stared at the calculator Melvin kept there, as if it could answer her questions. She had just told Tuck she wouldn't say anything to T.J. about what she had seen. She would wait and let T.J. come to her when he was ready. Part of her wanted to get it over with, to talk to T.J. right this minute. But another part of her just didn't want to know. Knowing meant having to acknowledge it completely, and she wasn't sure she was ready to deal with all that.

Instead, she steered her thoughts back to Fayetta's murder. What was she going to do with that dang key card? If she hung onto it much longer, she might find herself with some problems. She needed to get rid of it, make it someone else's responsibility. But whose?

She pushed that question away for the moment. What about Katie Ann? Wanda Nell was beginning to think that the younger woman was a lot more involved in everything than she let on. She had tried to mislead Wanda Nell about how well she had known Fayetta. That was one thing. The other was her snooping around here at the restaurant. Had someone put her up to that? Or was she doing it on her own?

If she was acting on her own, then why? Could she have killed Fayetta?

That didn't make much sense. Why would Katie Ann want to kill Fayetta? Was she jealous of all the men, and all the money, that Fayetta had? Did she want that for herself?

Even though she was sure Katie Ann was lying to her, Wanda Nell still couldn't picture her as a calculating, cold-blooded murderer.

No, Katie Ann must be in cahoots with someone, probably some member of that damn club. But who? The murderer?

Wanda Nell needed to know more about Katie Ann, but how could she find out? After a moment's thought, she reached for the phone. She punched in a number, and after only one ring, a familiar voice answered.

"Lucille's Style Shop. How can I help you?"

"Hey, Roberta," Wanda Nell said. She and Roberta had known each other forever, and Roberta had worked at her mother's beauty shop since she was sixteen. "Is Mayrene where she can talk?"

"Hey, there, Wanda Nell," Roberta said, cheerful as always. "Hang on a minute and I'll see." She put the receiver down and Wanda Nell could hear the sounds of women's voices mixed with hair dryers.

Nearly a minute later, Mayrene spoke into the phone. "Hey, girl, what's up?"

"I need a favor," Wanda Nell said.

"Shoot."

"Can you find out if anybody there knows anything about this new waitress I hired? Her name's Katie Ann Hale." Wanda Nell gave a brief description of her.

"I guess so," Mayrene said. "What's going on?"

"I'm not sure," Wanda Nell said, "but I think it's got something to do with Fayetta's murder. Can you ask around, real careful-like?"

"Of course, honey," Mayrene said. "I'll see what I can turn up. You gonna be working the afternoons and evenings at the restaurant all week?"

"Yeah, until Melvin gets out of jail. Which I hope won't be too much longer. Maybe they'll let him out on bail soon." That was something she should ask Tuck about, she realized.

"If I hear anything, I'll call you," Mayrene said. "I better get back to Miz Tribble. I left her looking like a lopsided poodle."

"Mayrene," Wanda Nell said, as another thought struck her. "You got any plans tonight?"

"No, honey," Mayrene said. "Mr. Padget is busy tonight. They've got a viewing at the funeral home, and he has to be there."

"How about coming by the Kountry Kitchen after you get off work?"

"Sure, I can do that," Mayrene said, sounding slightly puzzled. "Something wrong?"

"Just something I need to talk to you about," Wanda Nell said.

"Hang on, I'm coming," Mayrene called out to someone at the beauty shop. "I gotta go, Wanda Nell. See you later." The phone clicked in Wanda Nell's ear.

She put the receiver on its cradle and sat staring at the phone. She needed to talk to Mayrene about Hector Padget, but she wasn't sure how Mayrene would react. She couldn't put it off, though. This whole club thing was very serious, and if he was a member, well, Mayrene ought to know about it. Espe-

198

cially since it might have something to do with Fayetta's murder.

Wanda Nell rubbed her eyes tiredly. Lord, but she could use a cigarette about now. She started poking around in Melvin's desk. He usually kept a few packs here.

She found some in one of the drawers, and her hand reached out for one.

What are you doing? she asked herself. *Don't blow it, you fool, not after this long without one.* She slammed the drawer shut and got the heck out of Melvin's office.

It was time she got her rear end out front. She needed to keep a close eye on Katie Ann. She didn't think anybody from that club would show up here after Deke Campbell had put in an appearance, but you never knew.

Wanda Nell checked her purse first, to make sure that Katie Ann hadn't been snooping in it. The list was still there. She folded the two pages into a small rectangle and shoved it into her pocket. She didn't trust Katie Ann not to go through her purse.

For a moment, Wanda Nell was tempted to go through Katie Ann's. Her hand reached for it, but she stopped. No, she wasn't going to do that just yet. Surely Katie Ann was smart enough not to carry anything incriminating on her.

Business was slow for a while in the afternoon, but things started picking up around four-thirty, as usual. Wanda Nell and Katie Ann kept pretty busy, but there was a lull around six-thirty when Mayrene walked in.

Wanda Nell glanced at her watch in surprise. She'd lost track of time. The beauty shop usually closed at five. What had kept Mayrene?

Mayrene wandered through the front of the restaurant, stopping to chat a time or two with some of the men she knew. Wanda Nell waited until she had found a table in the back room before heading her way with a glass of water and a menu.

"Thanks for coming by," Wanda Nell said. Only a couple other tables in the back room were occupied. Mayrene had chosen one well away from them.

"No problem, honey," Mayrene said. "Can you sit down a second?"

Wanda Nell checked the front. All her customers had their food, and Katie Ann would be okay for a few minutes. She sat down.

"Did you find out anything yet?"

Mayrene shook her head. "Not yet. Nobody knew her. But we got a busy morning tomorrow, and maybe somebody'll know something. I'll keep trying."

"Thanks," Wanda Nell said. "I really appreciate it."

"So what's up with this girl?" Mayrene asked. "She sure is pretty, but why are you so curious about her all of a sudden? Don't she have any references?"

"I wasn't in much position to check around," Wanda Nell said. "She showed up looking for a job, and I needed somebody right away. She's a good worker; I'll say that for her."

"But?" Mayrene prompted.

Wanda Nell glanced over her shoulder. Katie Ann was up near the cash register. She turned back to Mayrene. "But she knew Fayetta pretty well—a little too well, I'm beginning to think."

"She know something about the murder?"

"She knows something," Wanda Nell said. "I haven't got it all out of her yet. There's something pretty strange going on." She hesitated. "Have you ever heard anything about a club called the Deer Stand?"

Mayrene pondered that a moment. "No, can't say's I have. What is it? Some kind of hunting club?"

Wanda Nell nodded. "Yeah, but I think they do more than hunt there, if you get my drift."

Mayrene snorted. "Honey, it don't surprise me none, what some of them hunters get up to. You should'a heard the way my daddy and his brothers used to talk. Half the time, they was so drunk, it's a wonder they didn't kill each other." She laughed, a deep, rolling sound. "Hell, my uncle Dub shot off three of his own fingers."

"Fayetta worked at this club," Wanda Nell said, putting a slight emphasis on the word *worked*.

Mayrene snorted again. "Probably flat on her back, knowing that girl."

"Probably," Wanda Nell said. "I think it had something to do with her getting killed."

"Who belongs to this club? Or do you know?" Mayrene picked up her glass of water and drank.

"I got a pretty good idea," Wanda Nell said. "Mostly

201

men you don't want to get mad at you." She took a deep breath. There was no easy way to do this, so she just plunged right in. "Mayrene, how much do you know about this Mr. Padget you're seeing?"

Mayrene's eyes narrowed. "What do you mean, how much do I know? Why are you asking about him?"

"I found his name on a list," Wanda Nell said.

"Damn it, I don't believe it," Mayrene said, fire in her eyes. "I meet the first man in months that seems like a decent guy, and here you are telling me he could be mixed up in this?"

"Mayrene, please, keep your voice down," Wanda Nell pleaded. "We don't need nobody else hearing all this."

"We sure as hell don't," Mayrene said, snatching up her purse and stood. "I don't want to hear any more myself." She stalked off, Wanda Nell staring helplessly after her.

Seventeen

Wanda Nell knew better than to try to stop Mayrene when she went stomping off like that. Better to let her cool off and try to talk to her later.

Besides, Wanda Nell figured, Mayrene wasn't really mad at her, or she would have come right out and said something. Mayrene would get right up in your face if you pissed her off.

Wanda Nell got up from the table and went back to

work. More customers started coming in, and before she knew it, it was almost eight o'clock.

Katie Ann caught her coming out of the kitchen with a tray full of desserts for one of her tables. "Wanda Nell, I need to run to the bathroom a minute, and maybe freshen up my makeup. Okay?"

"Sure," Wanda Nell said, scanning the room. "I can handle it for a few minutes."

"Thanks." Katie Ann whipped by her and into the kitchen.

Mindful of her resolve to keep an eye on Katie Ann, Wanda Nell watched as closely as she could and still handle her customers. It seemed like it took Katie Ann a little longer to touch up her makeup than it should have. She was gone nearly five minutes, and Wanda Nell wondered whether the girl had been snooping again when she popped through the kitchen door.

Katie Ann flashed a smile as she ducked into the hallway where the restrooms were. She was out in a couple of minutes. "Thanks," she said as she walked by Wanda Nell.

Wanda Nell nodded. From what she could see, Katie Ann hadn't done much to her face, except maybe touch up her lipstick.

What had the girl been up to?

Wanda Nell resisted the impulse to head for the storeroom and snoop around herself. She didn't want Katie Ann to think she was any more suspicious than she already was.

Half an hour later, Wanda Nell took advantage of a brief lull to use the bathroom herself. When she came out, she told Katie Ann she needed to check something in the office.

Katie Ann nodded, seemingly uninterested in anything except the good-looking young mechanic in greasy overalls she'd been flirting with when Wanda Nell stopped to speak to her.

Wanda Nell scanned the storeroom and Melvin's office, but she couldn't see that anything had been disturbed. What had Katie Ann been doing back here so long?

Shaking her head in annoyance, Wanda Nell went back to work.

The rest of the evening passed quickly, and when the last customer departed at nine-forty-five, Wanda Nell started closing up. She was ready to get home and get to bed. Katie Ann looked just as tired as Wanda Nell felt.

By ten the front door was locked and they were all heading for their cars. After Katie Ann and the others had driven off, Wanda Nell was about to do the same when her cell phone rang. Putting the car back into park, she pulled her phone from her purse.

The caller ID told her it was Tuck calling from his office.

"Hello," Wanda Nell said. "You're working mighty late tonight. Something wrong?"

"You might say that," Tuck answered. "Have you closed the Kountry Kitchen yet?"

"Yeah, I was just on my way home," Wanda Nell said, her stomach clenching. "Is it T.J.? Is he okay?"

"T.J.'s fine," Tuck assured her. "No, it's something else. I'd rather not go into it over the phone. I know it's late, but can we get together and talk?"

"Sure, if it's that important," Wanda Nell said. "You want me to come to your office?"

"No, I think we'd better meet somewhere else." He hesitated for a moment. "Is there a back way into the Kountry Kitchen? Some way you can get in and nobody can see you?"

"Yeah," Wanda Nell said slowly. "There's an alley that comes out on the street behind, right between the store and the old building next to it."

"That's good," Tuck said. "Drive off like you're going home, then circle back and wait for me back there. I'm coming right now."

His phone clicked in her ear, and Wanda Nell punched the end button on her cell phone. This was strange and more than a bit upsetting. What was going on?

She started her car and backed out of the parking lot. There was no traffic around as she pulled into the street. She drove a couple blocks east of the Kountry Kitchen, then circled back. The alley she'd told Tuck about was dark, and she shut off her lights as soon as she reached the back of the restaurant. She left her car running, just in case.

The minutes ticked slowly by, but Tuck was there seven minutes after he had hung up his phone. His sleek, dark Mercedes pulled up behind Wanda Nell's Cavalier, and he quickly shut off his lights. There was very little light from the moon through the clouds and the nearest streetlight was too far away to provide much illumination in the alley.

A dark shape loomed outside Wanda Nell's window. She rolled it down, and Tuck squatted so his face was level with hers. "Can we get into the restaurant from back here?" Tuck said, his voice quiet.

"Yeah," Wanda Nell said. She rolled up the window, and Tuck stepped back to allow her space to get out of her car. He followed close on her heels as she moved carefully through the alley to the back door of the Kountry Kitchen.

Fumbling with the keys, it took her a moment to get the door open. Her hands were shaking a bit. This whole situation was unnerving her, and she wanted an explanation.

Tuck made sure the door was locked behind them, then said quietly, "Is there somewhere we can talk where no light can be seen from the street?"

There were no windows on this side of the building, not even in Melvin's office, and Wanda Nell grasped Tuck's arm to lead him to the office. She knew every inch of the building, and navigating in the dark posed little problem for her.

She hit the light switch when they reached the office, and she blinked at the sudden burst of illumination. She set her purse on Melvin's desk and moved around to sit in the chair behind it. She motioned for

Tuck to take the only other chair, an old dining room chair with a wobbly back.

"What the heck is going on?" Wanda Nell demanded. "Why all this secrecy?"

"Sorry if I've frightened you," Tuck said, "but I thought it might be for the best. To tell you the truth, I'm a little spooked."

Now that Wanda Nell could see his face, she noticed the lines of strain in his forehead and around his mouth. "So what's going on?"

"I had a little visit this evening at the office," Tuck said. "I was working late. I'd sent Blanche and T.J. home, and I was by myself. The phone rang, and I answered, thinking it might be T.J. calling about something. But it wasn't T.J." He grimaced.

"Who was it?"

"Billy Joe Eccles," Tuck said. "He wanted to come by and talk to me, he said, and I told him to come on over. He must have been downstairs the whole time, because by the time I made it out to the front of the office to unlock the door, he was there. And he wasn't alone."

Wanda Nell's chest constricted. "Who was with him?" Her voice came out in a whisper.

"Hector Padget, the guy that runs the funeral home on Main Street, just down from Mrs. Culpepper's house. Do you know him?"

Wanda Nell shook her head. "I've heard of him, but I don't know him."

"And there was another guy, a real mean-looking

207

cuss. Nobody introduced him, and I don't remember seeing him before."

"What did he look like?"

Tuck thought for a moment. "He was a bit shorter than I am, say six foot, blond hair, very muscular, probably about thirty-five or forty. Oh, and he had a couple of tattoos, one on each forearm."

Wanda Nell blanched.

"You know who he is?" Tuck asked.

She nodded. "Tommy Eccles, Billy Joe's half-brother. I've heard about him, and I've seen his picture in the paper. You're right, he is one mean sonofabitch." Damn, but she wanted a cigarette. She clasped her hands in her lap to keep them from trembling. "People say he killed his mama and daddy, but nobody could ever prove it. He's beat some people up, too, but most of 'em won't testify against him. Billy Joe always takes up for him, even pays people off if he has to, to keep Tommy out of jail."

"Damn," Tuck said.

"What did they say to you?" Wanda Nell wasn't sure she wanted to hear the answer.

"Billy Joe and Hector came by, as they said, to let me know they were interested in Melvin's case." Tuck's lips twisted in a sneer. "Said what a shame it was that a respected businessman should go nuts like that and murder a woman. That it would be better for everybody if he just owned up to it and did his time."

"That's crazy," Wanda Nell burst out.

Tuck shrugged. "I thought about telling them I

didn't believe my client was guilty, but I could see it didn't really matter to them. They want Melvin to confess to the murder, and if he does, they'll make sure his mother and his two sisters are taken care of."

"That's bullshit," Wanda Nell said hotly. "Melvin didn't do it."

"Whether he did or not," Tuck said, "I don't like those men trying to bully me or my client. The whole time they were in my office, the goon you called Tommy just stood there, staring at me. I tried to ignore him, but he made my skin crawl."

"Did they threaten you?"

"Not in so many words. But it was pretty plain they expected me to go along with them. Eccles talked about how influence in the right places in town could make a real difference for someone like me. Crap like that. And Padget just kept nodding, like a puppet with someone's hand up his you-know-what."

"What did you say?"

"I didn't like the odds right then," Tuck said wryly, "so I just told them I would carefully consider everything they had to say. That I would confer with my client and get back to them." He shrugged. "Made me feel about three inches tall not to stand up to them."

"You did the right thing," Wanda Nell said.

"Maybe," Tuck said, "but I can't hold them off for long. They're going to want an answer, and if I don't give them the answer they want, well . . ." He shrugged again.

"We can always go to the sheriff," Wanda Nell said,

"and tell him about it. I don't think he'd stand for something like this."

"We could," Tuck said, "but how long do you think it would be before some kind of 'accident' occurred?" He laughed bitterly. "That was just one of the nice things Billy Joe mentioned before they left. How they hated to see accidents happen to people. If the sheriff did anything it would be after the fact, and that would be too late, at least for me."

Wanda Nell went cold all over. She was terrified, but at the same time she was getting madder and madder. She'd be damned if she'd let those sons of bitches get the better of her, or Tuck.

"What I'm wondering," Tuck said, "is why they're so interested in this case in the first place. It must have something to do with that list of names you gave me. Could Fayetta have been blackmailing all of them? But I don't see how she could. It just doesn't make sense."

"Yeah, it does," Wanda Nell said. She stood up and reached in her pocket for the key card she had found. She leaned over and handed it to Tuck. He examined it curiously.

"What is this?" he asked. "And what's the Deer Stand?"

"It's a private club, and I think that's what all this is about," Wanda Nell said. She told Tuck everything that Katie Ann had told her while Tuck sat there open-mouthed.

"You have got to be kidding me," he said when she

had finished. "Don't that beat all." Then he frowned. "Hang on a minute." He looked down at the card again. "So that's what they meant."

"What did who mean?" Wanda Nell asked when Tuck fell silent.

Tuck looked up at her and opened his mouth to speak, but before a word came out, they both heard a sound coming from outside, from somewhere near the back door.

Tuck switched off the light, and they both sat very still, listening intently in the darkened office.

Eighteen

Wanda Nell held her breath, feeling her pulse racing. Had someone followed Tuck here?

The sound coming from outside had stopped.

She could hear Tuck breathing shallowly, not far from her. Slowly she started to reach out her hand to find the phone on Melvin's desk. She couldn't see anything, so she tried to remember exactly where everything was.

Her hand touched the receiver. The sound came again. She listened intently for a moment, then relaxed.

Almost laughing with relief, she told Tuck in normal tones to turn the light back on.

"Are you sure?" he hissed the question at her.

"Yeah, it's just the cat."

Tuck flipped the switch, and they blinked at each other. "Cat? What cat?"

"Come on and I'll show you." She got up from the desk and walked down the hall to the back door. Tuck followed slowly.

Wanda Nell opened the door, and a small dark shape slipped inside. She reached down and scooped the cat up into her arms, pushing the door closed with her shoulder. "Hey, buddy," she said softly, scratching the cat under the ears. "You just about scared the life out of us, you know that?"

The cat purred and rubbed his head against Wanda Nell's hand.

"Where'd he come from?" Tuck asked.

"He's been hanging around back here for months now," Wanda Nell said. Carrying the cat, she moved toward the kitchen. Tuck came along. "He might belong to one of the houses nearby, but I think somebody threw him out. He's real friendly, and I've been thinking about taking him home. Poor little guy."

She stopped in front of the big walk-in refrigerator. Opening the door, she stepped in and hunted through the shelves until she found some left-over chicken. With her free hand, she pulled some meat from it, then asked Tuck to shut the door behind them.

With the cat in one hand and the chicken in the other, Wanda Nell walked back to Melvin's office. She put the cat and the chicken down on top of the desk and sat down. The cat started gobbling the food right away.

Tuck reclaimed his seat across from her.

"Thank the Lord it was only a cat," he said, "and not that goon Tommy Eccles. I didn't think anyone had followed me here, but when we heard that noise, I was afraid maybe I hadn't been careful enough."

"No kidding," Wanda Nell answered. Finished with his meal, the cat sat on his haunches and began to groom himself. Wanda Nell rubbed his back and he started purring.

"If you don't take him home," Tuck said suddenly, "I will. If he'll go with me, that is. My cat died a month ago and I miss having one."

Wanda Nell smiled. "Then he's all yours. I'd take him, but I'm not sure how good he and my grandson would get along. Maybe when Lavon's a little older."

Tuck reached out tentatively to touch the cat, and the cat allowed himself to be stroked by this strange hand.

"I think he likes you," Wanda Nell said.

"Good." Tuck continued to rub the cat and the purring got louder.

"Now, before this little guy scared us to death, you were saying something about that card I handed you," Wanda Nell said. "What'd you do with it?"

"Oh," Tuck said, looking puzzled for a moment. He stuck his hand into the inside pocket of his jacket. "Here it is." He held it in his hand and examined it again. "I remembered being approached by two men at a Rotary Club meeting. It was a couple of months ago now, I guess. They started quizzing me, asking me all about hunting. Asked me if I liked to hunt. Told me

213

they had a club I might want to join. When I told them I didn't hunt, as politely as I could, they backed off. And now I'm wondering if this was the club they were talking about. I think both their names were on that list you gave me."

"I'm glad you don't hunt," Wanda Nell said. The cat, now that he was no longer receiving attention, curled up on the desk and went to sleep.

"I don't hunt, and I certainly wouldn't have been interested in their little extracurricular activities, either." He grimaced.

Wanda Nell didn't know what that one word meant, but she got the gist of it. Then she felt cold again. She could just imagine what they would have done with Tuck if he had joined and then wouldn't play along.

"Exactly," Tuck said when she looked at him. He had read her mind easily.

"How do you keep people from finding out?" Wanda Nell said suddenly. Then she felt embarrassed, but went doggedly on. "I mean, do people know? Do you tell them?"

"I'm pretty open about it," Tuck said. "But it's not a topic that comes up in day-to-day conversation. If it does, it does." He laughed. "And you know how it is, the way we Southerners do things. If you don't flaunt it and throw it in everybody's faces, they'll leave you alone as often as not."

"I guess so," Wanda Nell said doubtfully. She recognized the truth of what he said, but she still worried.

"Wanda Nell, I'm not going to live my life in fear,"

Tuck said gently. "I'm not going out asking for trouble, but I'm not going to turn my back on it if it comes my way. My parents taught me to stand up for what I believe in, and I do my best to do that."

"What about your parents?" Wanda Nell knew she was prying, but if T.J. really cared for Tuck, then she felt she had a right to know something about his family.

"You mean do they know I'm gay?"

Wanda Nell winced slightly at hearing the word aloud. She nodded.

"Yes, they know," Tuck said. "It was a shock at first, but they handled it pretty well. One of my cousins is also gay, and she came out long before I did. They had a little time to get used to having a gay person in the family before I told them about myself."

"The only person I ever really knew was gay was this one guy I went to high school with," Wanda Nell said, "and I remember what a hard time he had. All the guys always picking on him. Soon as he finished high school, he left here and never came back. Last I heard, he was living in Memphis."

"That happens to a lot of gays and lesbians in small towns," Tuck said. "It's easier for some to find acceptance in big cities where they can blend in, find a lot more people like them." He paused. "But there are still plenty of us who don't leave, who stay in the small towns and get on with our lives. It's harder sometimes, but I'd much rather live here than in a big city."

"I don't want T.J. to go away and live in some big city," Wanda Nell said. "But if he'd be safer there . . ."

"I didn't say it was any safer, Wanda Nell," Tuck said. "Just easier to blend in. No matter where you go, there's always going to be someone who hates you for what you are. You can't get away from that." He rubbed his forehead, and Wanda Nell could see the exhaustion setting in.

"No, I guess you can't," she said. "And I wouldn't think much of you, or T.J., if you just tucked tail and ran."

"You're a pretty tough lady, you know that?" Tuck smiled at her.

"I've had to be," Wanda Nell said honestly. "And I'm damned if I'm going to let anybody run over me."

"Me either," Tuck said. He stood up. "I'll hold those men off as long as I can, but hopefully something will break soon. I'll see if I can't find out something more about this club without them finding out about it. Surely somebody'll be willing to talk."

"I'll see what I can find out, too," Wanda Nell said. "Maybe I can get Katie Ann to talk to me. I know she's holding back on me." She too stood up. "And I think I may just go see Miz Vance in the morning. Maybe I can get her to talking. I bet she knows more about what Fayetta was up to than she lets on."

Tuck moved close to the desk and rubbed the cat's head. The cat sat up and stretched, then yawned. Tuck picked him up, and the cat nestled in his arms.

"Guess I'll take him home with me," he said. "What shall I call him?"

"How about Lucky?" Wanda Nell said. "Maybe he's a good sign."

"Lucky it is," Tuck said, laughing. "What do you think, little guy? Are you going to bring us luck?" The cat meowed as if to say yes.

Wanda Nell waited until Tuck had made it to the back door before she turned off the office light. They slipped outside, and she made sure the door was locked.

"What will you do with that key card?" she asked. The night was dark and cool around them.

"I'm not sure yet," Tuck said. "I'll probably turn it over to Elmer Lee Johnson."

"Do you have to tell him how you found it?" All her worries about Elmer Lee's trustworthiness came flooding back.

"Maybe not. But don't worry, Wanda Nell. Elmer Lee's not such a bad guy. I know you two don't get along, but he's a pretty decent guy."

"I hope so," she said fervently. "I sure hope so."

They walked to their cars. Wanda Nell explained that the alley came out into the front parking lot of the Kountry Kitchen. "That way you don't have to back all the way out."

"Drive carefully," Tuck said, before he and Lucky got inside the Mercedes. "I'll talk to you tomorrow."

Wanda Nell drove slowly to the end of the alley. She didn't see any sign of traffic on the highway just up ahead, and she pulled slowly into the parking lot. All clear.

She drove through the parking lot and out onto the street, then turned onto the highway. She glanced back to see Tuck's car coming out of the alley. She breathed a sigh of relief as she hit the accelerator and sped toward home.

The next morning she was up at seven-thirty after a restless night. Peering at herself in the mirror, she grimaced at the bags under her eyes. She splashed her face with cold water and that helped.

Miranda was evidently still in bed, but Juliet and Lavon were in the kitchen eating breakfast. Wanda Nell was gearing herself up to roust Miranda when Juliet told her it was okay.

"She traded with somebody, Mama. Some other girl wanted to take tomorrow off, and Miranda switched with her. So it's okay."

Relieved, Wanda Nell poured herself some coffee and sat down at the table. She didn't relish another scene with Miranda, and not having to make arrangements for sharing the car today would make things easier for her.

The hot coffee helped her wake up, but she knew she'd pay for the lack of sleep later on. She had thought a lot about T.J. and Tuck, and when she wasn't worrying over that, she was worrying about the murder and those awful men. How could she protect herself and her family against them?

218

All that worrying did was make her more determined than ever to get this thing over with as quickly as possible. That meant she didn't have any time to waste.

Last night when she came home, she had really wanted to talk to Mayrene. Her best friend's trailer had been dark, and Wanda Nell didn't want to wake her. She got up from the table now and peered out the kitchen window at Mayrene's trailer. She had already left for work.

Wanda Nell had been debating about calling Agnes Vance this morning to suggest that she come over and help her. With what, she wasn't exactly sure. The more she thought about it, the more she figured she'd just show up at the woman's door. That way Mrs. Vance couldn't put her off, and Wanda Nell didn't think she'd get the door slammed in her face.

After she talked with Agnes Vance, she'd swing by the beauty shop and talk to Mayrene. She'd find some way to tell her friend what they knew and what they suspected. Mayrene would certainly be upset about her new beau, but she needed to know that he very well could be mixed up in the murder.

Her plans made, Wanda Nell had some breakfast, then showered and dressed. "I've got some errands to run this morning, honey," she told Juliet. "If y'all need me, just call. Tell Miranda she may not get to use the car today. Depends on how long it takes me to do what I need to do." She gave Lavon a hug and a kiss before she headed out the door.

219

The air was close and sticky today, and dark clouds were gathering. Sure enough, by the time Wanda Nell turned onto the highway toward town, rain had started falling hard and fast.

The trip to Agnes Vance's house took a few minutes longer than it ordinarily would. Wanda Nell hated driving in heavy rain, and she kept her speed down, just in case.

When she reached her destination, she sat in the car for a few minutes, waiting for the rain to slack off. Deciding that wasn't going to happen soon enough, Wanda Nell grabbed a decrepit umbrella from the back seat and stepped out into the rain.

She ran up to Mrs. Vance's front door, thankful for the shelter of the porch. She shook out the umbrella, then folded it up and set it down by the door. She knocked and waited.

Just as she was about to knock again, the door swung open, and Agnes Vance regarded her without expression.

"Good morning, Miz Vance," Wanda Nell said, slightly taken aback that the woman hadn't said anything. "I'm sorry for dropping by like this without calling you first, but I was running some errands. I thought I'd just check on you and see if there was anything I could help you with."

Mrs. Vance stepped back from the door. "Come on in, Miz Culpepper."

Wanda Nell stepped inside, feeling damp and slightly chilled from the rain. As Mrs. Vance closed the door behind her, Wanda Nell glanced to her left into the living room. Fayetta's four children were sitting on the sofa, staring curiously at her. They were arranged in a row by age, the youngest at one end, the eldest at the other. The oldest and the youngest were boys, and the two middle children were girls.

"The children and I were having Bible study," Mrs. Vance said. The way she said it, Wanda Nell felt like she should apologize again for interrupting them.

"Say good morning to Miz Culpepper, children," Mrs. Vance instructed.

"Good morning, Miz Culpepper," the children chorused in response.

"Good morning," Wanda Nell responded. Her heart went out to them. Fayetta may not have been the world's best mother, but she had loved them. They were all neatly dressed and clean, but their eyes had a sadness in them that made Wanda Nell want to cry.

Impulsively she walked forward until she was in front of them, then she squatted so that she was at eye level with them. "I worked with your mama. Do you remember coming by the Kountry Kitchen? I saw you there a few times."

The older two nodded.

"I sure am sorry about your mama," Wanda Nell said softly.

"We been praying so Mama can get into heaven," said the younger girl, who was about six, Wanda Nell thought.

The youngest, who seemed about four, started to whimper. Wanda Nell reached out to stroke his hand.

"Stop that crying, Elijah," Mrs. Vance said sharply. "Miz Culpepper, I think it would be better if we let the children get on with their studying." She handed the Bible to the oldest. "Here, Jeremiah, you read to the others."

Jeremiah took the Bible, but muttered something under his breath.

Wanda Nell stood up slowly and turned to Mrs. Vance with surprise. "I thought his name was Shawn."

Mrs. Vance's lips tightened. "I don't hold with those heathen names. Now come into the kitchen with me. There is something I need to talk to you about."

She turned away and headed for the kitchen. Wanda Nell glanced back at the sofa. Jeremiah had his tongue stuck out at his grandmother's back, as did the other boy when he saw what his big brother was doing. The two girls just looked scared.

Wanda Nell wished she could take these poor kids home with her, but she knew that was impossible. With a heavy heart, she followed Mrs. Vance into the kitchen.

Taking the seat indicated, Wanda Nell regarded the older woman. She was glad Mrs. Vance wanted to talk to her about something. That might make it easier for her to ask some questions.

"What is it you'd like to talk about, Miz Vance?" Wanda Nell said after she had turned down the offer of something to drink.

"I want you to start minding your own business, and leave me and mine alone."

Nineteen

Wanda Nell sat and stared at Mrs. Vance. Talk about strange! First the woman offered her something to drink, then she told her to mind her own business.

Stone-faced, Mrs. Vance ignored her lack of response. "It's not that I don't appreciate the help you've given me. I do. But I can't have anybody interfering with the children. I wrestled Satan for their mother's soul, and I lost. I'm not going to let those children grow up godless heathens like their mother."

Wanda Nell found her voice. "I don't recall doing anything to interfere with the children, Miz Vance. If you think me telling those poor kids I was sorry about their mama was some kind of interference, then you've got another think coming. I don't know what else I could've done to make you think I'm interfering."

Mrs. Vance's eyes narrowed. "I had a woman from the welfare department here yesterday because they received some kind of complaint. The only person I could figure might've done that was you. I don't appreciate other folks poking their noses into my business, and those children are my business."

"I didn't call them," Wanda Nell said. *I'm starting to wish I had, though,* she added silently. "Somebody else did that, not me."

"Then I apologize," Mrs. Vance said stiffly. "It's

223

none of those people's business either. What do they know about raising children? Those children need a firm Christian hand, and I'm the one who can give them that. 'Folly is bound up in the heart of a child, but the rod of discipline drives it far from him.'" For a moment, she looked like she was going to cry.

"I'm sure it will all be okay," Wanda Nell said, not knowing what else to say.

"They've got no right coming into a person's home and asking all those personal questions," Mrs. Vance continued as if Wanda Nell hadn't spoken. "She didn't even ask to see the children. I offered to let her see them, but she said that wasn't necessary."

"That's a little odd," Wanda Nell said, frowning. "Where were the children?"

"They were in their room taking their naps. They'd just had lunch, and I believe children should rest for an hour after they eat."

Wanda Nell wondered if Mrs. Vance ever let the children go outside to play. Surely she didn't keep them inside all the time. "Rest is good, but they need exercise, too. When do they play?"

"They play outside twice a day," Mrs. Vance said, frowning. "You know, that woman didn't ask me that. Come to think of it, she didn't ask me much about the children at all."

"What did she ask you then?" Wanda Nell said, hoping Mrs. Vance wouldn't be offended by the question.

"She tried to quiz me about my daughter and her

work. Wanted to know what all I knew about her job, and that kind of thing. She was a fool, if you ask me."

"Sounds like it," Wanda Nell said, though privately she wondered just what the social worker had been after. "What did you tell her?"

"Just that my daughter worked at that restaurant." Mrs. Vance didn't meet Wanda Nell's eyes as she spoke.

Knowing she had to tread carefully, Wanda Nell thought before she asked her next question. "But didn't Fayetta have money coming from somewhere else? I know what she made at the Kountry Kitchen, and it was okay, but not enough for the kind of money she spent on the kids' clothes and such."

A pained look flashed across Mrs. Vance's face. Her reluctance was obvious when she finally spoke. "Fayetta did sometimes work an extra job."

"Where was that?"

"Some private club," Mrs. Vance said. "That's all she told me. Just said she made good money wait-ressing and cleaning up at this place."

"Did you tell the social worker about that?"

"No, I did not," Mrs. Vance said. "I didn't like her attitude. She kept on asking me, but I told her, far as I knew, Fayetta only had the one job. I didn't like the way she kept pushing at it, and I pray the Lord will forgive me for lying. But it was none of her business."

Wanda Nell's suspicions had been completely aroused by now. This woman didn't sound like a proper social worker. Why hadn't she asked to see the children? Surely that would have been the appropriate procedure.

"Did this woman show you anything to prove she was who she said she was?"

"No, she introduced herself and said she was from the welfare department, and she needed to ask me some questions." Mrs. Vance thought for a moment. "As soon as she told me somebody had complained about the way I'm taking care of the children, I reckon I was so angry I didn't even think about any of that. Until now."

"What did she look like?"

"She had long black hair and was about your height, I guess. Maybe twenty-five or thirty. She wore glasses, and she had a mole on one cheek." Mrs. Vance paused. "She wasn't dressed the way I would've expected, either. She was wearing jeans and a blouse with a dark jacket. And tennis shoes. Not very professional, if you ask me."

Wanda Nell was more and more convinced that the so-called social worker was bogus. It was somebody trying to find out how much Agnes Vance might know about that blasted private club. But who? It didn't sound like anybody she knew.

"Did she give you a name?"

"I know she told me something," Mrs. Vance said, her face clouding. "But what was it? I think she said Hallie something. Now what was the last name?" She tapped a finger to her lips while she tried to remember.

Wanda Nell waited patiently. She didn't know anybody named Hallie, but she figured it was a false name anyway.

"Hallie Carter?" Mrs. Vance said. "No, that wasn't it." The finger tapped a few times more. "I tell you, I was so rattled and then so mad, it's a wonder I remember that much. Hallie Bates? No, that wasn't it either." She concentrated fiercely. "I've got it, Hallie Cates, that was it."

The name meant nothing to Wanda Nell, but she would remember it. Maybe Tuck could check to find out whether a woman by that name worked for the welfare department.

"I don't know her," Wanda Nell said. She debated whether to tell Mrs. Vance that she was sure the woman had been an impostor, but she decided it would only frighten her. The phony social worker probably wouldn't come back anyway, since Mrs. Vance hadn't told what she knew about Fayetta's other job.

"I don't think you have anything to worry about," Wanda Nell continued. "I don't imagine she'll come back anytime soon."

Mrs. Vance had been awfully confiding, but Wanda Nell wondered whether she could get her to open up a little more. It was worth a try.

"Miz Vance, I'm gonna be real honest with you. I'm real concerned about Melvin Arbuckle. I don't believe he murdered your daughter, and I'm trying to help him any way I can." Wanda Nell paused to gauge the other woman's reaction. So far so good. She went on. "I need to ask you something. Did Fayetta ever tell you anything about that other job of hers? Anything at all?"

Mrs. Vance turned stone-faced again.

"Please, Miz Vance. If you know anything, it could help get an innocent man out of jail. You wouldn't want him to go to prison for something he didn't do, would you?"

At first, Wanda Nell thought her plea had fallen on deaf ears. She was about to get up and walk out when Mrs. Vance finally spoke.

"'Blessed are the merciful, for they shall obtain mercy.'" Mrs. Vance fixed Wanda Nell with her piercing gaze. "If he is truly innocent, then I pray the Lord will be merciful to him. My daughter was wanton, and she knew I disapproved of what she was doing. She wouldn't tell me much. She did say one time that everybody in town would be shocked if they knew what some of our most upstanding citizens got up to." She turned her head away. "Knowing my daughter as I did, I had little trouble in figuring out what she meant."

"Did she ever mention any names?"

"No, though I scolded her for her wickedness. I begged her to stay away from that place, but she said she was going to make enough money so that she and the children could leave town."

"But somebody stopped her," Wanda Nell said softly.

"Yes," Mrs. Vance said sadly. "Her wickedness condemned her. 'But let justice roll down like waters, and righteousness like an ever-flowing stream.' I pray the Lord will punish those men for their lewdness and fornication."

"Somehow I believe He will," Wanda Nell said. "Thank you, Miz Vance. I appreciate you talking to me like this. I know it's hard for you, but like the Bible says, 'and you will know the truth, and the truth will make you free.'"

Mrs. Vance, not to be outdone, responded, "'Oh send out thy light and thy truth; let them lead me, let them bring me to thy holy hill and to thy dwelling!'"

Wanda Nell smiled faintly. She stood up. "I'd better be going now. I promise you I'm going to find out the truth, one way or another."

Mrs. Vance didn't speak again. Wanda Nell left her sitting at the table. The children were still in the living room where Shawn—Wanda Nell refused to think of him as Jeremiah—was struggling as he read aloud. Sighing, Wanda Nell let herself out.

Picking up her umbrella and opening it, she made a dash for the car. The rain had slackened into a slow drizzle, and the sun was trying to peek from behind the clouds.

Wanda Nell headed for Lucille's Style Shop. She hoped she would be able to talk to Mayrene for a few minutes, though the beauty shop wasn't the ideal setting for a heart-to-heart. But the sooner Mayrene knew about Hector Padget, the better, as far as Wanda Nell was concerned.

Lucille's place was in a house on the old state highway, not far from the county high school. There were several cars in the ersatz parking lot, otherwise known as the lawn, when Wanda Nell arrived. She made sure she wasn't blocking anyone before she locked her car and went inside.

"Hey, Wanda Nell, how are you?" Roberta, the receptionist and manicurist, glanced up from her desk when Wanda Nell walked in.

"I'm doing fine, Roberta. How're you?" The smell of chemicals hit her nose, reminding her of the main reason she didn't like getting her hair done. She hated those smells, especially hair spray.

"Doing great." Roberta glanced down at the appointment book. "Did you have an appointment today? I don't remember one."

"No," Wanda Nell said. "I don't have one. I was just stopping by for a minute. I wanted to talk to Mayrene, if I could." Craning her neck, Wanda Nell glanced into one of the side rooms where Mayrene and two other women had their stations.

Her friend was busy working on someone's head and talking a mile a minute. She had her back to Wanda Nell.

Roberta shrugged. "Just go on in. She's about done with Miz Bramble. You know Mayrene, she can talk and do hair at the same time."

Grinning, Wanda Nell said, "She sure can." She walked into the other room and sat down in one of the unoccupied dryer chairs.

Mayrene caught a glimpse of her in the mirror as she turned Mrs. Bramble's chair sideways. "Morning, Wanda Nell," she said. "To what do I owe the pleasure?"

Mayrene was still a bit huffy, Wanda Nell deduced. "I just thought I'd stop by and say hello. Thought I'd see if maybe you could work me in this morning."

Mayrene had never done Wanda Nell's hair, but she had been trying to for years. She was always telling Wanda Nell that she could do a lot for her, if she'd only let her have a go.

Mayrene's eyes gleamed. "Well, you're in luck today, honey. Miz Gilmore canceled on me, so soon as I'm done with Miz Bramble here, you're next."

Wanda Nell's heart sank. She should've kept her mouth shut, but now she had no choice. She'd have to go through with it. At least it would put Mayrene in a good mood.

Mayrene futzed around, putting the finishing touches on Mrs. Bramble's upswept red hair. "How's that new girl working out down at the Kountry Kitchen, Wanda Nell?" She leaned down close to Mrs. Bramble. "You look wonderful, honey. Mr. Bramble won't be able to keep his hands off of you." She picked up a can of hair spray and started spraying.

Over Mrs. Bramble's giggling, Wanda Nell said, "Oh, she's working out fine. She's a hard worker." She picked up a magazine from the table beside her chair and started fanning, hoping to keep the spray from drifting her way.

231

"What's her name?" Roberta had come into the room. She was a bigger gossip than Mayrene, and she hated not knowing anything.

"Katie Ann Hale," Wanda Nell said. "You know her?"

Roberta frowned. "I don't think so. She from Tullahoma?"

"No, she said she's from Goose Creek. Said her daddy had a restaurant there. Then she lived in Memphis and Jackson after her daddy died. She's been in Tullahoma about a year, working at the hosiery mill."

"Nope, I don't know her," Roberta said, sounding disappointed.

Mayrene turned Mrs. Bramble's chair around so that it was facing away from her station. She removed the protective cape from her client and folded it. "There you go, honey."

"Thanks, Mayrene," Mrs. Bramble said. "Would you hand me my purse?"

Mayrene pulled the purse from somewhere behind her and handed it to Mrs. Bramble. She dug into it and pulled out some money, folded it, and stuck it into Mayrene's hand.

"Thank you," Mayrene said.

"See you next week." Mrs. Bramble beamed as she walked to the desk, Roberta trailing behind her.

Mayrene tucked the money away in a drawer. Turning back, she regarded Wanda Nell with a smile. "Come on, honey, climb aboard."

Wanda Nell sighed as she sat down in Mayrene's

chair. "Just don't go crazy, okay?"

"You can trust me," Mayrene cooed. "You know that, Wanda Nell."

"Uh-huh," Wanda Nell said. "It could use a trim."

"How about some highlights?" Mayrene asked, fingering one of Wanda Nell's shoulder-length blonde strands.

"No," Wanda Nell said firmly. "I don't need no highlights. Maybe when I start going gray, I'll let you do it."

Mayrene chuckled. "I got news for you. It's highlight time."

Wanda Nell jerked up straight in the chair. "Where do you see any gray?"

"Relax, honey," Mayrene said. "It's only a couple of hairs. Nobody'll even notice. The highlights can wait, if you're sure you don't want me to do 'em today."

"I'm sure," Wanda Nell said. "Just give me a good cut."

Mayrene's large hands were surprisingly gentle. Wanda Nell usually just trimmed her hair herself at the bathroom mirror in an effort to save money. There was something soothing about the way Mayrene touched her head, though. She might have to reconsider having someone else do her hair.

Mayrene massaged her scalp. "You have beautiful hair, Wanda Nell. You really oughta take better care of it."

"I know," Wanda Nell said. "You're always telling me that."

233

"I think you need a good shampooing before we do anything else. This hair needs conditioning."

Wanda Nell started to protest that she had washed her hair that morning, but she knew better than to argue at this point.

The other stylists were busy chatting loudly with their customers as Mayrene led Wanda Nell into the room where they gave shampoos. She put Wanda Nell into position, tucked a towel around her neck, then turned on the water. At least no one could hear them in here, Wanda Nell hoped.

"Mayrene," Wanda Nell said, looking up into her friend's face. "About last night."

"What about it?" Mayrene asked, her hands busy wetting Wanda Nell's head, then working in the shampoo.

"What I said about your new boyfriend," Wanda Nell answered. Mayrene's hands stilled for a moment, then continued their work.

"You said something about a list," Mayrene said softly. "What kind of list was you talking about?"

"You gotta trust me," Wanda Nell said. "If it wasn't important, I wouldn't be trying to tell you something about him. Not something as serious as this. Promise you won't get mad at me."

"I promise," Mayrene said, sounding resigned. "I've known you a lot longer than I've known him. So go ahead. Tell me."

While Mayrene shampooed, rinsed, and then added conditioner to Wanda Nell's hair, Wanda Nell quickly

234

filled Mayrene in on what she knew about the club and its members.

"So his name is on that list?" Mayrene stared grimly down at Wanda Nell.

"Yeah, it is." Wanda Nell felt Mayrene's hands squeezing excess water from her hair.

Mayrene started toweling Wanda Nell's hair lightly. "That don't mean he's involved in everything the rest of 'em are doing."

Wanda Nell sat up, taking the towel from Mayrene. "You're rubbing too hard. And I'm afraid he *is* involved in everything. There's one more thing I haven't told you. He came with Billy Joe Eccles and his brother Tommy to Tuck's office last night. They were trying to put pressure on him. They want Melvin to say he did it, and they want Tuck to go along with it."

"Go along with what?"

Surprised, Wanda Nell turned to find Roberta standing in the doorway, her face alight with curiosity.

How much had she heard?

Twenty

"Go along with what?" Roberta repeated her question. "What are y'all talking about?" She walked into the room.

"Go along on a fishing trip," Wanda Nell said, watching Roberta's face closely. "Talking about my

235

son and his boss. They like to fish."

"Oh." Roberta looked mighty disappointed. "Where they gonna go? Somewhere out on the lake? There's some real good fishing spots out there, if you know where to look."

"They'll find something," Wanda Nell said. She eyed Roberta speculatively. Roberta did know a lot about what went on around town. Wanda Nell wasn't sure how she did it, but Roberta always knew the latest.

"They've been talking about hunting, too," Wanda Nell said. "I'm not much for hunting, but you know how men are."

Roberta laughed. "Ain't that the truth. One of my uncles thinks more of his hunting dogs than he does of his wife and kids. Course, knowing my aunt, I don't blame him."

"I heard somebody talking about a fancy hunting club not too long ago," Mayrene said. She exchanged a swift glance with Wanda Nell. "Sounded like it might be a pretty good club to join. You know anything about it, Roberta?"

"Well, I don't know," Roberta said doubtfully. "I know about several clubs. Which one is it?"

Mayrene shrugged. "I'm not sure what the name is, but only the big shots in town belong. It's real exclusive."

Roberta thought for a moment. "I bet I know the one you mean. My cousin Clarence told me about it. Nobody's supposed to know about it, but Clarence,

236

he's an electrician, and he did some of the wiring for it. They paid him real good and told him to keep his mouth shut about it."

Considering he's a cousin of yours, it didn't do much good to tell Clarence to keep his mouth shut, Wanda Nell thought. "I wonder where it is?" she said aloud.

"Clarence said it was out by the lake, over on the east side. You know, near where the state park is." Roberta grinned, pleased with herself for knowing so much about it. "Clarence said it's kinda hard to find. He missed the road twice the first time he went out there to work, but he finally found it. Once you know what to look for, it's real easy. There's this big old oak tree that got hit by lightning, and the road's right by it."

Wanda Nell blessed Clarence, wherever he was, for being as chatty as his cousin was nosey. If she needed to find that club, now she figured she could.

"Sounds like it's pretty expensive, if you have to be a big shot to belong to it," Mayrene said.

"I reckon," Roberta said. "Clarence didn't see any of the members when he was there. The guy that hired him, though, he's the brother of one of the big shots. You know Tommy Eccles?"

Wanda Nell nodded. "I know of him. I've never met him."

Roberta shivered. "He's pretty nasty. Clarence said Tommy was pretty mean about him talking to any-body, kept telling him he'd better keep his mouth shut."

Wanda Nell and Mayrene exchanged glances. Apparently even threats weren't enough to keep members of Roberta's family from talking.

Roberta observed them. "It's okay," she said, her tone defensive. "It ain't like Clarence has been running all over town talking. He told me about it, and he ain't even told his wife. I ain't told nobody but you. Nobody else's ever asked me before."

Wanda Nell considered warning Roberta not to talk to anyone else about it, but knowing Roberta, that would only make her more curious. Instead, she said, "Well, that club sounds like it's too expensive for my son and his boss to join. They'll just have to look somewhere else."

"Yeah," Mayrene said. "Come on, Wanda Nell, let's get to work on that hair."

Roberta preceded them into the other room and wandered back to her desk to answer the phone.

As Wanda Nell sat down in the chair and Mayrene placed a cape around her, she met Mayrene's eyes in the mirror.

"I'm sorry," she said.

Mayrene shrugged. She finished fastening the cape around Wanda Nell's neck. "It's okay, honey," she said as she picked up her comb and scissors. "I should've known he was too good to be true. I don't want no man who'll go off to some club like that and get up to all kinds of shenanigans. If I ain't woman enough for him, then I sure don't want him sniffing around other gals."

"When are you supposed to see him again?" Wanda Nell decided not to offer any more sympathy. Mayrene didn't waste any time feeling sorry for herself when she decided to move on.

"Tonight," Mayrene said shortly. "But I reckon I'm gonna have a real bad headache tonight and every night from now on."

"Would you consider not cutting him off completely, not yet anyway?" Wanda Nell said slowly.

Mayrene's hands paused. "Have you got some good reason why I shouldn't?"

"I know it's a lot to ask," Wanda Nell said, "and if you say no I'll sure understand. But maybe you could get him to talk."

"You think I could get him to confess to murder while we're basking in the afterglow?" Mayrene whispered fiercely as she bent near Wanda Nell's ear. "Girl, I'm good, but even I'm not *that* good. What to do you take me for, anyway?" She straightened up and went back to snipping hair.

"I didn't mean pillow talk," Wanda Nell said, mortified. "Get your mind out of the gutter. What I meant was just talking to him. I don't know. I'm just looking for ideas right now."

"Well, I don't think that one's gonna work," Mayrene said. "You sit still for a few minutes, and let me finish what I'm doing."

Wanda Nell kept her mouth shut and let Mayrene work on her hair. Her mind buzzed with all sorts of questions. There were way too many things she didn't know. All those men's names on that list. She had no way of checking up on all of them.

At that thought, she almost jerked out of the chair. Mayrene placed a steadying hand on her shoulder, and she sat still again.

She had given Elmer Lee that list yesterday. Had he done anything with it? She was surprised he hadn't called her to make some kind of smart remark about her trying to do his job for him. Surely he was curious about where she'd found it.

As soon as Mayrene had finished with her, she was going to call him and ask him. Make sure he knew what that list was. Seeing Tuck and T.J. yesterday had put it out of her mind for a while.

That set her mind going on another track. After the two talks she'd had with Tuck, she hoped T.J. would come talk to her soon. She wasn't sure how long she could pretend she didn't know anything. She didn't want to force him to talk to her before he was ready, but if he didn't do it soon, she might just have to sit him down and do it anyway.

"Wanda Nell, are you in there?"

She heard Mayrene talking to her, and she blinked. She'd been off in her thoughts and had completely forgotten where she was or what was going on.

"Sorry," she said. "I was thinking."

"I know," Mayrene said. "I could see the smoke coming out of your ears." She grinned. "I'm gonna blow-dry your hair a little, and then I'll let you see, okay?"

Wanda Nell nodded. Blow drying sounded okay—it was the teasing and spraying she had been worried about. She continued to sit patiently still while Mayrene finished with her.

At last Mayrene laid all her tools aside. She turned Wanda Nell around so the chair faced the mirror. "Ta da!" Mayrene announced.

Wanda Nell stared at herself in the mirror. "Damn," she finally said. "I look good." She grinned at Mayrene.

"You sure do, honey," Mayrene replied. "If I do say so myself. I took about five years off you with this cut. Don't you like it?"

"I love it," Wanda Nell said. She raised her right hand to touch her head. Before, her hair had hung long and straight down her back to just below the shoulder blades. Mayrene had cut it short and layered it, and her head felt ten pounds lighter. "Looks kind of like that skater, what was her name?"

"Dorothy Hamill," Mayrene said promptly. "Yeah, that's kind of what I had in mind. You've got a face kinda like hers, and that long straight hair just didn't flatter it. This is a lot better for you."

"The girls aren't gonna recognize me," Wanda Nell said.

"I bet you Jack will," Mayrene said playfully. "I bet you he's gonna love it."

"Maybe," Wanda Nell said. "We'll see. I still don't know what I'm going to do about him."

"Just take it slow," Mayrene advised. "Your heart

will tell you, one way or the other."

"I guess so."

Mayrene pulled the cape off and brushed Wanda Nell down for stray hairs. Wanda Nell, still marveling over her reflection in the mirror, wondered what kind of tip she was supposed to give her friend.

"Don't you dare think about giving me a tip," Mayrene said, as if she'd read Wanda Nell's mind. "Me finally getting to do something with that hair of yours, that's tip enough."

Slightly embarrassed, Wanda Nell hugged her. "Thank you."

"You're welcome." Mayrene hugged her back.

"Now, what we were talking about earlier." Wanda Nell stepped closer and spoke in a low tone.

"I won't do anything, or say anything, just yet," Mayrene promised, "but I am gonna have a headache tonight."

"Okay," Wanda Nell said. "I'll talk to you later."

She paid Roberta and let her *ooh* and *aah* over the new cut. Then she glanced at her watch. A few minutes past eleven. She'd better try to get hold of Elmer Lee.

"See y'all later," she said, waving at Mayrene. She got out the door before Roberta could start talking again.

Once in her car with the air conditioner going, Wanda Nell pulled out her cell phone and punched in the number for the sheriff's department. The way things were going, she reflected, she might as well put the number on speed dial.

She asked to speak to Elmer Lee and was told to wait. She sat there for nearly two minutes before she heard his voice at the other end.

"Oh, it's you," Elmer Lee said when Wanda Nell identified herself. "And what do you want today?"

"Did you get what I dropped off for you yesterday?"

"I did," he said. "And what the heck am I supposed to do with it? Where'd you find it?"

She answered the second question first. "I found it in a drawer at Fayetta's house when I was helping Miz Vance the other morning. I showed it to you then, and it wasn't until I got in the car and started looking at it real close that I realized there was writing on the other side."

"And what do you think the writing means?"

Wanda Nell wasn't sure if he was playing dumb just to get her reaction or if he really was that dense. She never could tell with him, one reason he drove her crazy.

"I think it's a list of the men Fayetta was black-mailing," she said as patiently as she could. "Remember that savings account passbook I found? Well, I think those are the men supplying the money. Some of those numbers sure looked like amounts of money to me."

"I reckon you could be onto something," Elmer Lee drawled. "But I reckon you also saw the names on this list. I can't exactly just march up to some of these men and ask 'em if they was being blackmailed, now can I?"

"I'm not saying you oughta do that," Wanda Nell snapped. "They'd just deny it anyway. But there's a connection you oughta know about, if you don't already."

"What's that?"

"I'm pretty sure they all belong to the same club."

"You mean like the Rotary?" Elmer Lee's tone couldn't have been more derisive. He snorted with laughter, and Wanda Nell was glad they weren't face to face, or she might have been tempted to scratch his eyes out.

"Now you stop that," she said, her patience gone. "Stop being a jackass and listen to me. All those men belong to a club, and it's one that Fayetta worked at. She was supposed to be a waitress, but I'll bet you what she was serving wasn't food, at least not most of the time. You get my drift?"

"How do you know that?"

"I got my sources," Wanda Nell said smugly. Then she remembered the key card. Had Tuck taken it to Elmer Lee yet?

"Has Tuck Tucker been by to see you today?" she asked.

"Yeah, he came by this morning," Elmer Lee said. "And he gave me that card you found, Wanda Nell. That's what all this is about, isn't it?"

"Yes, it is. That's the club I'm talking about. I don't know how much hunting they do, but according to what I heard, they do a lot more besides hunt."

Elmer Lee expelled a long breath into the phone.

"You can't just haul off and make accusations like that, especially about some of the men on that list. You could get in trouble if any of them ever find out you're talking about something like this."

"I know that," she snapped at him. "That's why I'm expecting you to do something about it, though I don't know why. Are you too scared of those men to investigate the way you should? Are you just gonna sit back and let Melvin be railroaded?"

"I am conducting this investigation," Elmer Lee said, his temper obviously beginning to get the better of him, "and you just better mind your own business, Wanda Nell. I'm tired of you interfering and telling me how to do my job. I know what I'm doing, even if you don't think so." He slammed the phone down.

Pissed off but satisfied, Wanda Nell clicked her own phone off. She didn't really think Elmer Lee would let all those big shots just walk all over him, but it didn't hurt to let him think she thought he would. The madder he was, the more likely he was to get something done.

What should she do now? Go home and relax for a couple hours before going to work?

No, she felt too restless for that. The girls would be fine on their own. She needed to do something. But what?

She looked at her watch again. She had plenty of time before she needed to be at the Kountry Kitchen. Maybe she'd take a little drive out around the lake, near the state park. See if she couldn't find a certain road.

Her mind made up, Wanda Nell set off.

Twenty-One

Wanda Nell turned on the radio and sang along with Faith Hill on her way out to the lake. She drove by the turnoff to the trailer park and kept going. Soon she was crossing the lake itself, over the dam erected back in the 1950s to help with flood control.

Having crossed the dam, she slowed down and began looking for an old oak tree damaged by lightning. This side of the lake was mostly woods. Part of the area belonged to a state park that skirted the lake to the east and south. Wanda Nell hadn't been on this side of the lake in years, but she knew the area was still largely undeveloped. Prime hunting ground, as a matter of fact. She would have figured the club was out here somewhere.

She had driven about three-quarters of a mile when she spotted the tree. An immense tree of great age, it was dying slowly from the lightning strike. To one side of it, Wanda Nell spotted a gravel road. She hesitated for a moment. There was no other traffic. More than likely no one would be out here this time of day, so she ought to be safe enough if she wanted to snoop around a little.

She turned onto the gravel road and drove slowly

down it. Trees and bushes crowded densely on either side of her car, and the sunlight, such as it was on this gloomy day, had difficulty penetrating the canopy of leaves above her. Once her eyes adjusted to the gloom, she felt better. She didn't want to have to turn on her lights, just in case.

After almost half a mile, she came to a gate and a fence. The fence stretched out on either side and disappeared into the woods. The gate sported a sign that read: PRIVATE PROPERTY. NO TRESPASSING. To her left was a gizmo situated on top of a post, about level with her car window. She pulled up and examined it. This seemed to be where they used the key cards to gain access to the club. For a moment, Wanda Nell wished she had held on to the key card. It would have made her snooping easier.

She sat in the car for a moment and decided what to do next. Should she just turn around and head back? She eyed the fence. It looked pretty ordinary, though it could be electrified. She figured she could probably squeeze under it if she wanted to.

But what could she do with her car? There was just enough room here, in the small clearing around the gate, for her to turn around and head back out. She hated to leave her car sitting here in case somebody came driving up the road. She thought about it a moment longer, then decided she'd take her chances. She turned the car around and left it unlocked, in case she needed to get into it in a hurry.

Opening the glove compartment, she pulled out a

flashlight she kept there for emergencies. She tested the batteries. They seemed strong enough. She wouldn't turn it on unless she had to, but it was big and heavy enough to use as a weapon if need be.

Approaching the fence and squatting beside it, she decided she could worm herself under it without too much trouble. She might get a bit grubby, but she'd deal with that later.

Wanda Nell found a spot where the ground dipped a little lower under the fence. She poked around with her flashlight. The last thing she wanted to do was roll over a snake. She shuddered at the thought: she was terrified of snakes.

Satisfied that no snake was lurking under this bit of fence, she got down on the ground and wriggled under. Up on her feet again, she brushed off her clothes and slowly walked beside the fence until she was in the road. As long as she stuck to the road, she thought, she was less likely to get in trouble.

The road led her up a small hill, the incline steep enough to leave her slightly short of breath. When she reached the top, she paused for a moment, looking ahead.

A building stood in a clearing about a hundred yards away. A large area had been paved, with parking spaces marked. Wanda Nell was relieved to see that none of them were occupied right now. The building itself was pretty ordinary, just a big block of concrete with two large double windows on either side of the front door. There was no sign indicating the name of the place, but Wanda Nell felt confident she was in the right place.

Wanda Nell approached the building cautiously. All around her the woods were quiet, except for the ordinary sounds of nature. Feeling a tad unnerved, Wanda Nell resisted the impulse to keep looking over her shoulder. There was no one watching her. She was simply jumpy.

She tried the front door but wasn't surprised to find it locked. Next she peered into the windows, flashing her light through them to see what she could.

Not that much, as it turned out. The windows on one side belonged to some kind of storeroom. Wanda Nell could make out the outlines of boxes and canned goods on the shelves. She flashed her light over the boxes, some of which were labeled. One had the logo of a popular brand of condoms. Evidently the club members bought them in large supply. Wanda Nell grimaced in distaste and moved on.

The windows on the other side belonged to what looked like a bedroom. Wanda Nell could see a bed, a table beside it, and a couple of chairs. That was all.

Suddenly she whirled around. *What was that sound?*

She didn't see anything.

Feeling foolish, she turned back to the windows. Probably just a rabbit, nothing more scary than that.

She moved along the side of the building, flashing her light through windows as she came to them, six in all. Most of the rooms appeared to be dormitory-style bedrooms, or rooms with beds, she corrected herself. Nobody lived here. Just slept here when they were hunting. Or used the rooms for other purposes. She pressed grimly on.

She had gone around the back of the building and had started up the other side when she came to a room that looked like someone was actually living in it. Clothes were strewn around, and she spotted a pile of beer cans on the floor. For some reason, this made her uneasy. She decided she'd found out all she was going to by coming out here. Time to get the heck out of Dodge and back where there were other people around.

She paused as she came to the edge of the building. She couldn't see anything in the clearing. Feeling a bit foolish, she ran across the clearing and down the hill toward the gate. She scooted under the fence as quickly as she could, not even stopping to check for snakes.

Back in her car, she dropped the heavy flashlight on the seat. She stuck her keys in the ignition, fired up the car, and drove as fast as she dared back through the woods.

She stopped to check for oncoming traffic when she came to the blacktop road. To her left the road curved sharply away from her, and she really couldn't tell whether anything was coming. To her right all was clear. She pulled onto the road to her right and stomped on the accelerator, relieved that she was getting away from the place. She wasn't sure she had learned anything helpful, but at least she knew where it was now.

Wanda Nell glanced into her rearview mirror. She frowned. A big pickup had come up behind her. He must have been coming around that curve when she was pulling out onto the road.

She sped up, but the guy in the truck hung right on her tail. She felt her heart begin to pound. The road ahead was straight and clear. Why didn't he just go around her if he was in that big a hurry?

Deliberately she slowed down to force him to pass. The big truck moved out into the other lane and started around her. Wanda Nell breathed a sigh of relief.

Her relief quickly turned to horror. The pickup didn't move ahead. Instead, the driver was keeping pace with her, pulling over into her lane, like he was trying to force her off the road. His right blinker was on.

She looked up. The driver was leaning over, pointing.

He wanted her to pull over.

She didn't want to. She had a bad feeling about this.

But if she didn't pull over, he might force her off the road into the ditch. She couldn't outrun him. His pickup was a lot more powerful than her faithful little Chevy.

Wanda Nell let her car coast to a stop on the edge of the road. The pickup stopped just ahead of her, out in the road blocking both lanes. The lake lay just ahead.

Damn! Now she couldn't drive around him when he got out of the truck. And even if she tried to turn around and go the other way he'd catch up to her before she got very far.

Her hands closed on the flashlight and pulled it into her lap. She waited for the driver to get out of the truck and approach her. If she had to, she could always try to knock him out with the flashlight.

With a shock, she recognized the man coming toward her. Tommy Eccles. She prayed that he didn't recognize her.

Her stomach knotted in fear. She felt the weight of the flashlight in her lap. If Eccles saw it, he'd know she'd been snooping.

Quickly she stuck it behind her back and pulled her purse over next to her. She spotted a large drink cup that Miranda had left in the car and grabbed it.

Eccles planted himself by her door and leaned over. "Hey there, little lady. Did you know that was private property you was trespassing on back there?"

Wanda Nell decided to do her best dizzy blonde routine. "Oh, you mean that road back there? Was that private?" She giggled. "I had to pull off the road somewhere, and that looked okay." She giggled again and held up the drink cup. "I just didn't think I could make it any further. I had too much Coke this morning." She batted her eyelashes at him. "I know I don't have to tell you what I mean." She gave him a big smile, praying that he'd be taken in by her dumb act.

Evidently it worked. He grinned at her. "That's okay, honey. When you gotta go, you gotta go." He crossed his arms and propped them on the window. "What's a purty gal like you doing all the way out here anyways?"

"I been over in Oxford visiting my cousin, and I was on my way home this morning."

Eccles frowned. "This is kinda out of the way, ain't it? You took the long way round if you was coming from Oxford."

She giggled again. "I know, but I kinda got lost somewhere. I get so turned around I don't know which way I'm going. I ended up on this road, and I stuck to it. Ain't that the lake there?"

He got a patronizing look on his face. "You women drivers. It's a wonder you can find your way out of a paper bag." He laughed, and Wanda Nell wanted to smash him in the face with her flashlight.

"Well, at least I know where I am now," she said, forcing herself to giggle again. As long as he thought she was stupid, she'd be safe. "I better get going, though. My boyfriend's expecting me."

"You sure you don't wanna come back with me and have a little party?" Eccles leered at her in what he probably thought was a seductive manner. "I got a nice private place back there, and ain't nobody gonna bother us. You and me could have us a real good time."

"I bet you know how to give a girl a good time," Wanda Nell cooed. "But my boyfriend, he's a real

253

jealous type, and if I don't show up soon, he'll be real mad, and I'll never hear the end of it."

Eccles didn't like that. Wanda Nell was afraid he was going to try to force her to go with him. "Tell you what, stud, you just give me a call, and soon as I can get away from my boyfriend, you can show me that good time you're talking about."

She wanted to gag, but if it meant she could get away from him, she had to keep up the act.

Eccles grinned at her. "Sure thing, sugar. What's your name?"

"Lila Jane Ledbetter," Wanda Nell said, pulling the name out of nowhere. "I'm in the book." Jeeze, she hoped there wasn't any Lila Jane Ledbetter in Tullahoma.

"Okay, Lila Jane, I'm'a gonna call you." Eccles stood up, tugged on his jeans, and swaggered back to his truck.

"Thank you, Lord," Wanda Nell whispered.

Eccles turned his truck around, headed back toward the club, and he waved at her as he went by. Wanda Nell grabbed the steering wheel with shaky hands and headed back to town, resisting the urge to floor the accelerator.

She'd been very lucky, she realized. If Tommy Eccles had known who she was, things could have ended very differently. She had thought she'd be safe, coming out here in the daytime in the middle of the week. How was she supposed to know Tommy Eccles was actually living at the club?

It had been foolhardy to come out here by herself, and she vowed not to do anything like this ever again. And what had she learned, after all?

She thought about that. Was it significant that Tommy Eccles was living at the club? Why should they need someone living there, acting like a caretaker? Did they keep anything really valuable there?

She wondered how long he'd been living there. Maybe only for a few days, maybe longer. Having someone on the premises probably meant that the club members were worried about something. But what?

Maybe besides the big box of condoms there was evidence that a lot more than just hunting went on at the club. Fayetta's death would have made them nervous, and having Tommy Eccles there meant they'd be prepared if someone came to investigate.

That was the best answer she could come up with, and it would have to do for now.

She had reached the other end of the lake and was nearing the turnoff to the trailer park. Should she stop by and check on the girls? She glanced at her watch. It was nearly twelve-thirty. She had spent more time than she realized on her little snooping expedition.

At this point, she might as well just go on to work. She could do a little work in the office before it was time to relieve Ovie and Ruby.

The lunchtime rush was in full swing when she arrived at the Kountry Kitchen. Ovie and Ruby had their hands full. The front room was packed, and several tables in the back dining room were filled as well.

Wanda Nell frowned. Usually Melvin was here to take up the slack and run the register. If they were this busy, they might need temporary help. She might even need to work both shifts, and she would if she had to. She'd discuss it with Ovie when she had the chance.

Forgetting about the office work momentarily, she dumped her purse in the back and slipped on an apron. Out front, Ovie and Ruby were grateful for the extra pair of hands.

About an hour later, things had slowed down considerably, and Wanda Nell thought she might have a few minutes to do some office work before Ruby and Ovie left. She was about to head for the office when she happened to glance toward the front door.

At first she thought she was seeing things.

No, she wasn't. That really was Lucretia Culpepper, her former mother-in-law, standing there, looking around with a superior smirk on her face. What the heck was she doing here? Feeling a dull throb start behind her eyes, Wanda Nell went to find out.

Twenty-Two

The last thing Wanda Nell felt like right now was having to deal with Lucretia Culpepper. The old woman had never deigned to set foot in the Kountry Kitchen before, and Wanda Nell wasn't sure she wanted to know what had made her do it today.

Forcing a smile, she walked up to Mrs. Culpepper.

"Afternoon, Wanda Nell," Mrs. Culpepper said.

"Afternoon, Miz Culpepper," Wanda Nell answered. She examined the older woman. Since T.J. had been living with her, she was looking a lot better. She certainly wasn't hitting the Jack Daniels the way she had been when her only company at home was her elderly black maid, Charlesetta. She appeared altogether sharper and more with it than she had in years. T.J. had seen to that.

"What can I do for you?" Wanda Nell went on. "Let me show you to a table."

"I'm not here to eat anything," Mrs. Culpepper said in a haughty tone. "I wouldn't even be setting foot in a place like this if I didn't need to talk to you, Wanda Nell. Where can we talk that's halfway private?"

"Follow me," Wanda Nell said, her hands clenched at her sides. She wasn't going to let the old woman get to her. She was going to keep her temper. She kept telling herself that as she led the way to the back dining room.

"Is this private enough for you?" Wanda Nell asked, gesturing toward a table against the back wall.

Mrs. Culpepper sniffed. "It will have to do." She pulled out a chair and inspected it for dirt before she sat down in it. She plopped her handbag on the table. "Well, sit down, Wanda Nell; don't just stand there gawking at me like an idiot."

Sighing, Wanda Nell sat down across from her. "What was it you wanted to talk to me about?"

"You have got to talk to T.J., Wanda Nell. Maybe

he'll listen to you. I have talked to that boy until I'm blue in the face."

Yeah, blue to match your hair, Wanda Nell thought snidely. The old witch always brought out the worst in her.

"He just will not listen to reason, and I don't know what else to do to make him understand. He has a position to uphold, and I expect him to do it."

"Position? What position?" Wanda Nell said. "What are you talking about?"

"He is a Culpepper," Mrs. Culpepper said primly. "And it is up to him to carry on the name into the next generation."

"Miranda's already done that for you. You've got a great-grandchild with the Culpepper name." Mrs. Culpepper hated to be reminded that Lavon was illegitimate and bore his mother's last name.

"That's not the same thing," Mrs. Culpepper said sharply, "and you know it, Wanda Nell. You know what I mean. Lavon is a sweet boy, but he can't really represent the family the way T.J. and his own son can."

Mrs. Culpepper had a rude awakening coming, and Wanda Nell took a bit of malicious satisfaction from that. Once the old witch found out the truth about her grandson, she might just have a stroke and die right that minute.

Then Wanda Nell felt ashamed of herself. She knew how hard it was going to be for T.J. to face up to his grandmother and tell her the truth. He hadn't even been able to talk to his own mother yet. Mrs. Culpepper would probably kick him out of her house and take away the truck she'd bought him. This whole thing was such a mess. Why did T.J. have to be different?

"Now, you listen to me a minute, Miz Culpepper," Wanda Nell said, trying to get her thoughts in order. She had to be careful not to blurt out anything. "I don't think you need to be rushing T.J. into anything. He's only twenty-two. He's got plenty of time to think about things like a family and all that. He needs some time to figure out what he wants."

Mrs. Culpepper opened her mouth to speak, but Wanda Nell rushed on. "Now, you know what he was like there for a while. He was as wild as he could be, always causing me grief and worry. I never knew from one minute to the next if he was gonna get himself killed or end up in jail. I'm just so proud of the way he's turned himself around. It took a lot of guts for him to make a change like that, and I think we should all give him time. Just be thankful he's finally acting like an adult, and don't push him."

Mrs. Culpepper's mouth had snapped shut into a prim line, but now she relaxed a tad. "I guess there's some sense in what you're saying."

Pressing home her advantage, Wanda Nell continued in a softer tone. "He's trying so hard to please everybody. He loves you and appreciates everything you've done for him. I know that, and so do you. He's doing his best to take care of you. Do you really want to drive him away?"

She gazed earnestly at Mrs. Culpepper, and for a moment the old woman's vulnerability showed in her face. Then the mask was back on.

"I'll think about it," she said. "He is a good boy. You just didn't know how to handle him, Wanda Nell. If you had, he wouldn't have got into all that trouble as a teenager. I should have taken him in years ago."

Oh, yeah, that was just what T.J. needed all right, Wanda Nell thought, wishing she could say the words aloud. Instead, she held on to her temper.

"I'm not going to argue that with you, Miz Culpepper," she said. "It'd just be a waste of my time and yours. I need to be getting back to work, if you're done saying what you came to say."

"I'll give him some time," Mrs. Culpepper said as she stood up. "But I'm not going to forget about this. He needs to put down his roots."

Wanda Nell walked away from her. If she spoke to the old battle-ax again right now, she didn't know what she might say. She stopped near the counter in the front dining room and watched Mrs. Culpepper stalk away. When the old woman was out the door, Wanda Nell breathed a sigh of relief. Now she could get back to work and forget about the old biddy.

Except that she couldn't, she found while she was checking through the invoices on Melvin's desk. Why did the old witch have such a bee in her bonnet about T.J. meeting a girl, getting married, and having a baby? What was so dang important about it right now?

260

Could Mrs. Culpepper be dying? Was that it?

Wanda Nell considered this idea. The good Lord knew what kind of shape Mrs. Culpepper's liver was in. All those years of heavy drinking might have taken their toll.

Or she could have cancer. Wanda Nell seemed to remember that Mrs. Culpepper's only sister had died about twenty years ago from breast cancer.

If the old lady was dying, Wanda Nell could dredge up some sympathy for her. She had been bitter and lonely until T.J. had come back into her life. For years before he died, her son hadn't had much to do with her, and her late husband, old Judge Culpepper, had been a notorious skirt-chaser.

Frankly, Wanda Nell thought the old woman was just plain too mean to die. She'd live to be a hundred and drive them all crazy, one way or another. Even T.J. confessing the truth about himself probably wouldn't kill her.

Maybe that was it!

Startled by the thought, Wanda Nell leaned against Melvin's desk and considered it. What if Mrs. Culpepper had somehow sensed the truth behind T.J.'s reluctance to go out with any of the girls she had selected? Maybe she thought she could force him into getting married anyway and giving her the grandson she wanted. All for the sake of the grand name of Culpepper.

The more Wanda Nell considered that, the more she figured it was probably the truth. Mrs. Culpepper was a lot sharper than she acted sometimes, and T.J. might have been careless around her, let something slip or said something that clued the old lady in to the truth.

She still had no idea what she was gonna say to T.J. when he finally got up the nerve to talk to her. But he needed to clear the air, and soon. Not talking about it wasn't doing any good.

Wanda Nell forced herself to concentrate on the invoices. It was almost time for Ruby and Ovie to leave, and Katie Ann should be arriving pretty soon for the evening shift.

When she had finished with the invoices, Wanda Nell let herself think about Katie Ann. She needed to sit that girl down and have a talk with her. Maybe if she really pushed Katie Ann, she could get her to tell everything she knew about Fayetta and the club.

Wanda Nell stopped in the kitchen to chat with Margaret, the cook. She checked to make sure deliveries had been arriving properly and with the right items. Margaret had a complaint about some of the produce they'd been getting, and by the time Wanda Nell had discussed it with her and promised to take care of it, it was nearly two o'clock.

Ruby had already left so she could get to an afternoon class on time, and Ovie was nursing a glass of iced tea near the register. A couple of men occupied one table. Wanda Nell didn't see any other customers.

"No sign of Katie Ann yet?" she asked Ovie, frowning.

"Not yet," Ovie said. "She's been coming in on time up to now."

"Yeah, she has," Wanda Nell agreed. "Wonder why she's late today?"

"You want me to hang on for a while? I can stay till three or maybe four, if you need me to."

Wanda Nell appreciated the offer, but she knew Ovie was tired and ready to go home. She didn't know what she'd do, though, if Katie Ann didn't show up. Who was she gonna call? She wracked her brain for names.

"I'm sure Katie Ann'll show up in a few minutes, or at least maybe call," Wanda Nell said. "If you don't mind hanging around till I hear from Katie Ann, one way or another, I'd appreciate it. And if you can think of somebody I might could call, I'd appreciate that too."

"I'll think on it, honey," Ovie said. "And I'll hang on, just in case."

Wanda Nell went back to the office and dug out the card Katie Ann had filled out. She called the home phone number Katie Ann had written down. The phone rang eight or nine times, but no one answered. Frustrated, Wanda Nell hung up and went back out front.

The door opened, and Katie Ann rushed in. "Sorry I'm late, Wanda Nell," she said, a little out of breath. "My old car wouldn't start, and I had to call a friend to come give me a ride to work."

"That's okay," Wanda Nell said. "You could've

called me, and I'd've come and got you."

"I didn't think of that," Katie Ann said. "Next time I will, but my friend didn't mind."

"I reckon I'll be heading home," Ovie said. "Bye, y'all." Purse in hand, she departed.

"Let me just put my stuff away, and I'll be right back, Wanda Nell," Katie Ann said on her way to the back. She paused at the kitchen door. "That's a great haircut, by the way." She disappeared into the kitchen.

Ovie and Ruby had both admired her new look earlier, assuring her that it took at least five years off her age. She wondered what Jack Pemberton would think. He was used to seeing her with long hair. All of a sudden, she had a hankering to see him. What if she called him and asked him to come over for dinner?

But how would he interpret it? Would he make more out of it than just a friendly invitation?

Wanda Nell dithered a moment, then decided she didn't care.

The two men who had been taking their time with their lunch came up to the register then to pay. Wanda Nell took their money and thanked them. Katie Ann returned, and Wanda Nell told her she'd be back in a minute.

In the office, she picked up the phone and punched in Jack's home number. He was teaching summer school in the mornings, but in the afternoon he was usually at home writing. He was working on a true crime book, and he hoped to be finished with it by the time school started again in August.

Normally she wouldn't call and interrupt him when she knew he might be writing. If he didn't want to come to the phone, he'd let the machine take the call.

The phone rang three times, and Wanda Nell was mentally composing the message she would leave, when a woman's voice answered.

Slightly confused, Wanda Nell didn't respond at first. The woman repeated her hello.

"Uh, hello," Wanda Nell said uncertainly. "I'm trying to reach Jack Pemberton. Maybe I called the wrong number."

The woman laughed. "No, it's the right number. But he's out running an errand right now. Can I take a message?"

"Uh, no, that's okay." Wanda Nell was almost stuttering, she was so taken aback. "I'll call back later." She dropped the phone on the cradle.

What the hell was some woman doing at Jack's house in the middle of the day? Especially when he'd just told her he thought he was falling in love with her?

He had never mentioned having a maid, and Wanda Nell doubted the woman was a cleaning lady. She'd sounded too educated and refined for that.

Jack hadn't mentioned having a sister, either. The woman had sounded too young to be his mother, and anyway, she thought Jack had told her his mother was dead.

So who was she?

Twenty-Three

Damn it! She already had more crap to deal with than she needed, and now this. What did he mean, taking up with some hussy so fast? How dare he?

She was working herself into a good hissy fit when common sense began to prevail.

Just because she had told Jack she needed time didn't mean he'd run out and found himself the first available woman to console himself with.

Cool down, she told herself. Her temper had gotten the better of her for the moment.

Jack wasn't that kind of man; she was sure of it. She just had to trust him. There was probably some innocent explanation for why that woman was at his house in the middle of the day.

The irony of the situation hit her. Here she'd told Jack she needed time to think, and the minute she thought he'd taken up with some other woman, she was acting like a jealous harpy.

I guess that answers one question anyway, she thought.

If she was this jealous at the thought of Jack having another woman, it meant she really did care about him. She shied away from saying the *L* word yet. But she had to admit she did have strong feelings for him.

Haul your carcass back out there and get to work, she advised herself, *and stop thinking about it.*

She walked back out front. Katie Ann was going from table to table, refilling the napkin holders and gathering salt and pepper shakers that needed to be topped off.

She glanced up at Wanda Nell. "I sure do like that new haircut. Where'd you get it done?"

"Lucille's Style Shop, down by the county high school on the old state highway. I got a friend that works there, and I finally let her get me in the chair."

"You look a lot better, if you don't mind me saying so," Katie Ann said.

Wanda Nell did mind, but the phone ringing just then kept her from saying so. She walked to the cash register and picked up the phone sitting beside it.

"Kountry Kitchen," she said.

"Hey, Wanda Nell, it's Tuck," the voice announced. "Got some good news for you."

"I sure could use some about now," she said. "What is it?"

"Melvin's out on bond. Since he had no previous record, the magistrate didn't set bail as high as I thought he would. Melvin was able to post it. I just dropped him off at home, and he said he'll be at the Kountry Kitchen as soon as he has a shower and changes clothes."

"That's wonderful news," Wanda Nell said. "I completely forgot to ask you about that yesterday."

"I know," Tuck said. "So much was going on, I forgot to tell you last night that the hearing was set for this morning."

267

"Oh, I'm so glad. I know Melvin's real happy to get out of there."

"He sure is," Tuck said, "and now I just have to see to it that he doesn't have to go back."

"What did they say at the hearing?"

"Their case was mostly circumstantial, but it was enough to convince the judge to bind Melvin over for indictment by the grand jury. The good thing is that he was allowed to post bond."

"When's the grand jury due to meet?"

"Not for another couple of months, and I'm confident that in that time Melvin will be cleared, one way or another."

"Thank the Lord," Wanda Nell said fervently. "I just want all this to be over and done with, for Melvin's sake and everybody else's."

"Amen to that," Tuck said. "Gotta go, Wanda Nell. Talk to you later."

Wanda Nell put down the phone feeling lighter of heart than she had since Melvin first called her on Sunday morning.

"You look pretty happy," Katie Ann said. "Did I hear right? They're letting that guy out on bail?"

"Yes, they are," Wanda Nell said, "and it's about damn time."

"You don't think he did it?"

"No, I don't," Wanda Nell said sharply. "If you knew him, you'd know he couldn't have done it."

"I think I met him once, when I was at Fayetta's and he stopped by," Katie Ann said. She picked up her tray of supplies and moved on to the next table. "He was real good-looking, I thought, but he was kind of sharp with Fayetta."

"Yeah, well, she could do that to anybody," Wanda Nell said. "He's a good man. Are you saying you don't want to work here with him back?"

Katie Ann shrugged. "Not exactly. I don't know him like you do, and it makes me a little nervous, I guess. But if he didn't do it, who did?"

Wanda Nell wanted to say, *You tell me. I know you're not telling me everything you know.*

Instead, she said, "I don't know. But it seems to me, Fayetta made a lot of people angry, one way or another. Somebody from that club could've done it. Maybe she was threatening to tell somebody's wife about what went on there."

"Maybe," Katie Ann said doubtfully. "But I wouldn't be too sure about that. I'd look a little bit closer to home if it was up to me."

"What do you mean, closer to home? You think one of her kids did it?" Wanda Nell shook her head in disbelief.

"No, silly, that mama of hers." Katie Ann shivered. "She gives me the creeps. Always quoting the Bible at you, and talking about sin and hell and getting saved. She didn't approve of Fayetta and was always going on at her about those kids, and how she was ruining their lives." She shivered again. "Maybe she did it, because she sure wanted to take those kids away from Fayetta and raise them right."

269

Wanda Nell stared at her. The more she considered Katie Ann's theory, the more sense it made to her. Mrs. Vance was awfully fixated on raising those kids and making sure they didn't turn out like their mama. She might have done it, thinking she was saving the children.

But she was also very devout in her faith. How could she kill her own daughter? Could she justify that by saying that it was better to save the children, since her daughter refused to repent and give up her sinful life?

"Maybe she did," Wanda Nell said slowly. "I can see what you mean, but it's still pretty far-fetched. To think she'd kill her own daughter."

"Yeah," Katie Ann said, "but you should've heard how she talked to Fayetta sometimes. She talked to her like she was some dog off the street. They hated each other."

"Then why did Fayetta even have anything to do with her?"

"Well, she was Fayetta's mama. What was Fayetta gonna do, get a court order to make her stay away from them?" Katie Ann threw up her hands. "I don't know. Sometimes she didn't have much choice, I guess, when she needed somebody to look after those kids. Miz Vance is the only person I know of that those little hell-raisers are afraid of. They sure wouldn't mind me when I was looking after them."

"Pretty sad," Wanda Nell said, and it sure was. She thought about her relationship with her late mother

270

and how different it had been from that of Fayetta and Mrs. Vance. She had been really lucky.

Talking about Mrs. Vance and Fayetta recalled her conversation with Mrs. Vance from that morning. What about that so-called social worker? She had meant to ask Tuck to check into that. She reached for the phone to call him back, but her hand froze halfway to it.

She was looking at Katie Ann, and Mrs. Vance's words flashed through her mind. According to Mrs. Vance, the social worker had a mole on one cheek.

Katie Ann had a mole on her right cheek.

Mrs. Vance had also said the social worker was dressed pretty casually: blue jeans, sneakers, and a jacket over a blouse.

That sounded like what Katie Ann might have worn, if she was pretending to be a social worker.

Katie Ann's hair wasn't long and black, but she could have worn a wig.

"I went by to see Miz Vance this morning," Wanda Nell said slowly. "I just wanted to check and make sure she and the kids were doing okay."

"That was mighty nice of you," Katie Ann said. "I wouldn't go near that old witch if it was me." She turned away from Wanda Nell and started working at the next table.

"At first Miz Vance was kinda mad at me," Wanda Nell said.

"Why would she be mad at you?" Katie Ann still had her back to Wanda Nell.

271

"She thought I called the welfare department on her," Wanda Nell said. She laughed. "Can you beat that? Why she thought I'd do such a thing, I don't know. But she said some social worker showed up at her house yesterday around lunchtime, asking all kinds of personal questions."

She waited a moment, but Katie Ann didn't say anything.

"I don't even know anybody in Tullahoma who's a social worker," Wanda Nell said. "Do you? Now, what was the woman's name? I know Miz Vance told me."

Wanda Nell was watching Katie Ann's back closely. She thought it tensed up once or twice, but she wasn't sure.

"I know. Hallie Cates. That was it. You know anybody by that name?"

Katie Ann finally turned around. She laughed. "Now why should I know any social worker? What call would I have for a social worker?" She laughed again.

Wanda Nell knew she was lying. Katie Ann was trying too hard to sound casual.

"Just thought I'd ask," Wanda Nell said. "You never know." She was convinced that Katie Ann had pretended to be a social worker in order to question Agnes Vance. But what exactly was she trying to find out?

She probably just wanted to know how much Mrs. Vance knew about Fayetta's extra job. It was a good thing Mrs. Vance had claimed not to know anything, otherwise she could be in danger.

272

If Mrs. Vance wasn't the killer, that is.

Wanda Nell's head whirled with all the possibilities and all the unanswered questions. What was Katie Ann's role in all this? By now Wanda Nell was pretty sure that someone had planted Katie Ann here so she could report anything that happened. And Wanda Nell had given her a job because she was desperate for help.

Katie Ann had probably worked at that club with Fayetta, and that meant she knew the members as well as Fayetta had. The members were trying to protect themselves, and Katie Ann was just one of their tools. Cynically, Wanda Nell wondered how much they were paying her. She also wondered why they weren't worried Katie Ann would blackmail them, too, just like Fayetta had.

Who were they protecting? Had one of the members snapped and killed Fayetta, refusing to be blackmailed any longer?

Or had Tommy Eccles taken care of the problem for them? Her blood ran cold as Wanda Nell thought about her encounter with him that afternoon. He was rumored to be a killer, but his brother had always protected him. Pretty useful to have a brother who's not afraid to kill.

That seemed the most likely answer, Wanda Nell reasoned, but how the heck would anybody be able to prove it?

The door opened and three customers came in. Wanda Nell took their orders and went to get their drinks.

273

In the next half hour, several more customers trickled in, and Wanda Nell and Katie Ann took turns waiting on them. Wanda Nell was at the cash register, making change for one of the customers, when Melvin Arbuckle walked in.

Wanda Nell hastily finished making change, then walked around the counter to greet Melvin. She threw her arms around him and gave him a big hug. "I'm so glad to see you," she said.

She stood back and took a good look at him. Physically he looked fine, but Wanda Nell could see in his eyes that he was worried.

"Thanks, Wanda Nell," Melvin said, his voice gruff with emotion. "I appreciate you taking care of the restaurant for me. I don't know what I'd've done without you."

"You're my friend," Wanda Nell said simply. "You've done the same for me, remember?"

Melvin smiled. He really was a good-looking man, Wanda Nell thought, not for the first time.

"Who's that?" Melvin said, suddenly noticing Katie Ann.

"Your new waitress," Wanda Nell said. "Katie Ann Hale. She showed up here Monday morning looking for a job, and I hired her. She's a good worker."

"I've heard that name before," Melvin said. "And she looks kinda familiar."

"She and Fayetta were friends," Wanda Nell told him.

Melvin's lips tightened at the sound of Fayetta's

name. "Is she a whore, too?" He said it softly, but viciously.

Wanda Nell's heart ached for him. He had cared more about Fayetta than he'd let on, and Fayetta had treated him like dirt a lot of the time. Even so, she didn't think Melvin was a killer.

"Don't think about it," Wanda Nell said. "Why don't you come on back to the office with me for a few minutes and let me show you what I've done with the orders and all that stuff. I'll introduce you later."

Melvin nodded and followed her. He raised a hand to the customers, and they all acknowledged him. Wanda Nell breathed a sigh of relief.

In the kitchen, Margaret the cook and Elray the dishwasher greeted him warmly, telling him they were glad to see him. He thanked them and told them how much he appreciated their support. Wanda Nell was surprised to see him get a little teary-eyed. Normally he didn't let his emotions show much, but he'd been through some pretty traumatic experiences in the last few days.

Wanda Nell explained what she'd done with the paperwork, and he thanked her again. "If you have any questions, just ask. I talked to the produce company and the other suppliers, and they said they'd wait until next week. But all the invoices are there."

Leaving him to take care of the paperwork, Wanda Nell headed back out front with a lighter heart. She was happy to see him back where he belonged, plus she no longer had to be responsible for running the place. That was one less headache for her.

Katie Ann was talking to a couple sitting at the front table. They hadn't been there when she and Melvin had gone back to the office. Wanda Nell couldn't see them clearly, but something about the man's shoulder looked familiar.

Then Katie Ann moved, and Wanda Nell had a clear view. She felt her stomach knot up. Jack Pemberton and some woman she'd never seen before were sitting at the table.

Twenty-Four

Wanda Nell stood there for a moment, uncertainty rooting her to the spot. Then she scolded herself for acting foolish. She started forward.

Jack turned and, seeing her, got up from the table. "There you are," he said, smiling. "I've got somebody I want you to meet, and she wants to meet you." He held out a hand to her.

Two more steps, and she was able to grasp Jack's hand. "This is a nice surprise," she said, smiling back at him. Then she turned to look at the woman Jack had brought with him.

"Wanda Nell, this is my cousin, Lisa Pemberton. Lisa, this is Wanda Nell Culpepper."

Lisa extended a hand and Wanda Nell, loosing her hand from Jack's, took it. "Nice to meet you," she said, feeling relieved.

"Nice to meet you, too," Lisa Pemberton said with a shy glance. "Jack's been telling me all about you." Wanda Nell figured she was about thirty. She had a cap of blonde curls, like Shirley Temple, and a dusting of freckles across her face. A bit on the plain side, Wanda Nell thought, but she looked friendly.

"Sorry I missed your call earlier," Jack said. "I checked the caller ID, and I knew it must have been you. I was planning to bring Lisa by tonight to meet you anyway, and I figured we might as well come on by now."

"Would y'all like something to drink?" Wanda Nell asked.

"I took care of that already," Katie Ann announced from behind her. She was carrying a cup of coffee and a glass of iced tea. She set the tea down in front of Lisa and the coffee in front of Jack.

"Thanks," Jack said. "Do you have time to talk for a few minutes?"

"Sure, it's pretty quiet now," Wanda Nell said. Jack pulled out a chair for her, and she sat. He resumed his seat as Katie Ann walked off.

"Have you ever been to Tullahoma before, Lisa?" Wanda Nell asked.

"A couple of times since Jack moved here," Lisa said. "I live in Meridian now, but I grew up in Cleveland."

"Lisa's a nurse," Jack said, "and she was here for an interview at the hospital. She's been thinking about moving back closer to home, and the job here is a really good one."

"We always need good nurses, and I'm sure Jack would be happy to have some family here," Wanda Nell said. "When will you find out about the job?"

Lisa's face turned slightly pink. "Actually, they offered me the job at the interview."

"That's great," Wanda Nell said, impressed. "Are you going to take it?"

Lisa nodded. "I think so. Like Jack said, it's a really good job. My parents died a few years ago, and Jack's the only other family I have." She smiled at her cousin. "And it sure would be nice to be able to see him more often."

"I've been trying to talk her into it for months," Jack said, frowning. "She needs to get away from Meridian anyway. It's not a good place for her."

That made Wanda Nell curious, but she was too polite to come right out and ask.

Lisa, her head down, said, "It's okay. You can tell her."

Jack reached over and patted her hand. "It's going to be okay," he said firmly. He turned to Wanda Nell. "Some guy's been stalking her, and we think he might leave her alone if she leaves Meridian."

"That's awful," Wanda Nell said. No wonder the girl acted like a scared rabbit. "You poor thing. Has he tried to hurt you?"

Lisa shook her head. "No, but he calls me all the time, even though I've got an unlisted number. I've changed it three times, but somehow he manages to find out what it is. And he drives by my house all the time. He just won't leave me alone." She wiped away several tears.

"Can't the police do anything about it?" Wanda Nell asked.

"He's a cop," Jack said bitterly. "So they don't take her seriously when she complains. They dated for a couple months, then Lisa broke it off. Since then, he's made her life hell."

"Then you definitely need to move," Wanda Nell said. "And you'll be far enough away he'll have to stop."

"I hope," Lisa said, sounding very depressed. "He probably won't stop calling me, but at least he won't be able to follow me around."

"If he comes here and tries that crap," Wanda Nell said fiercely, "then we'll fix his little red wagon, believe you me."

"That sounds good to me," Lisa said, almost smiling again. "I just want it to be over."

"It will," Jack said firmly. "We'd better get going, though. We're going to look for a place for Lisa to live this afternoon. The sooner she can move here the better." He stood up and reached for his wallet.

"This one's on me," Wanda Nell said as she got up. Impulsively, she leaned down and gave Lisa a hug. "You just hang in there, sweetie."

Lisa smiled up at her through tears. She reached for a napkin to wipe her face. "Thanks."

"Why don't y'all come back tonight and have dinner here?" Wanda Nell said, escorting them to the door.

"We will," Jack said. He held Wanda Nell's hand for a moment and squeezed it. "Thanks."

Wanda Nell gave him a quick peck on the cheek. "Good luck house-hunting," she said as they went out the door.

Wanda Nell's heart went out to Lisa. She'd had to put up with a lot of crap from her ex-husband, Bobby Ray, but she'd never had to deal with a stalker. She hoped Jack was right, that once Lisa moved to Tullahoma the stalker might leave her alone.

There would be time to think about all that later, she decided. Right now she needed to get back to work, and to think about keeping Melvin from going back to jail.

Since business was still pretty slow at the moment, Wanda Nell headed back to the office to talk to Melvin again. He'd had a little time to settle in, and maybe now he'd feel like talking about Fayetta. Earlier she hadn't wanted to press him, but she had to know what he knew about Fayetta and her blackmail scheme.

She figured she'd better be a bit cagey about it. If Melvin didn't know about some of what Fayetta was up to, it was better he didn't find out from her. Then, if he got put on the witness stand, he could say truthfully he didn't know about it. She should have talked to Tuck about this, asked him what he'd told Melvin, but there was no time for that now.

Melvin was standing at the back door, smoking.

Wanda Nell had often found him this way in the past, and the normality of the scene comforted her. They had to keep him from going back to jail again.

"Hey, there," she said, coming to stand behind him.

He turned slightly. "Hey. You need me for something?" He exhaled a cloud of smoke, and Wanda Nell sniffed at it appreciatively.

"No, just to talk a minute," she said.

"You want one?" Melvin held his pack of cigarettes out to her.

"Yeah, I do," Wanda Nell said, "but I'm not gonna have one. I'm not falling off the wagon now."

"Suit yourself," Melvin said, stuffing the pack into his shirt pocket. He flicked his butt toward the Dumpster, but it fell short, landing on the pavement a few feet from its target.

Melvin walked back to his office, Wanda Nell right behind. He sat down at his desk, and Wanda Nell perched on the corner.

"So what you wanna talk about?"

Wanda Nell studied his face for a moment. Some of the strain had left him, now that he was back on familiar ground, but there was still something in his eyes that haunted her. She wanted to hug him again, to comfort him, but she was afraid he might misinterpret the gesture. Instead, she crossed her hands and let them rest on her lap.

"I don't want you to have to go back to jail," she began, and he laughed, a short, bitter bark. "I know, you don't wanna go back either, and I aim to see that you don't. I believe you didn't kill her."

He nodded, and she went on. "But somebody did. And if it wasn't you, then who was it? The best way to keep you out of jail is to prove somebody else did it."

"Yeah," he said. "You got any ideas about who?"

"You know much about Miz Vance?"

Melvin frowned. "More'n I wanna know, I reckon. She was always riding Fayetta about something, and she sure as hell don't like me. She's something else."

"You think she could have done it?"

Melvin's shock registered in his face. "Her mama? You gotta be kidding. Why would her mama want to kill her?"

"Didn't Miz Vance wanna take those kids away from Fayetta?"

"Yeah, but what's that . . ." Melvin paused, considering. "That's still crazy, though. Killing her daughter, so she could raise her grandchildren."

"I admit it sounds a bit crazy," Wanda Nell said, "but just think about it a minute. I only talked to her two or three times, but she made it real clear what she thought about the way Fayetta was raising those kids. She didn't like it one bit. And somebody told me she was gonna try to get Fayetta declared an unfit mother so she could get custody."

"Fayetta said something about that," Melvin said, frowning, "but she just kinda laughed about it. She didn't really think her mama could do it."

"I don't know if she could," Wanda Nell said.

"Maybe she found out she couldn't, or something, and that pushed her over the edge. Then she decided the only way she could get hold of those kids was to get rid of Fayetta."

Melvin shrugged. "I guess it's possible, but it still sounds pretty damn crazy to me."

"Depends on how crazy Miz Vance is," Wanda Nell said.

"I don't think she's crazy," Melvin said after a moment. "Just because she quotes the Bible a lot and talks about the wages of sin being death and all that, it don't mean she's crazy. She has her beliefs, and she sticks to 'em." He shook his head. "She's real religious, but just because you and me ain't that religious, it don't mean she's crazy."

"No," Wanda Nell said, "I know that. She's got a right to believe the way she wants to, and I can't argue with her about the way Fayetta was raising those kids. She wasn't setting much of an example for them."

"No, she wasn't," Melvin said, his face darkening. "And that's one of the things we was arguing about that night. She was getting worse and worse about running around. She always made sure somebody was watching the kids, but she should've been spending more time with 'em herself. They're getting old enough to start figuring out what was going on, and that ain't good for kids, to know their mama's behaving like that."

Wanda Nell looked down at her hands. "What all was she doing?"

"Well, first it was just going out with married men," Melvin said. "And she made sure any man she went out with had some money. They'd give her things, either stuff she could sell, or sometimes they'd just give her money. She liked that, used to flaunt it, tell me she could make a lot more money than I ever paid her."

Wanda Nell almost flinched at the bitter anger in his voice. "Why'd you put up with it? And her?"

Melvin wouldn't meet her eyes, and Wanda Nell understood something for the first time.

"You really loved her," she said slowly. She couldn't quite keep the surprise out of her voice. She wanted to ask him why, but she knew she couldn't.

"Yeah," he admitted, his voice low. "I loved her. I don't know why the hell I did, but I did." Tears trickled down his face. He rubbed them away wearily with his right hand. "Shows you what a damn fool I am."

"I never realized you cared about her that much," Wanda Nell said, trying to choose her words with care.

"I know," Melvin said tiredly, leaning back in his chair, his eyes closed. "It don't make much sense, does it? I knew better, but it just happened. I wanted to marry her and try to be a daddy to those kids. For a while, I thought maybe I could talk some sense into her." He sighed deeply. "But there was just something wild in her. Something I could never touch. I should've fired her and turned my back on her, but I

284

felt sorry for those kids."

"You're a good man, Melvin," Wanda Nell said softly, stretching out a hand to touch him lightly on the arm.

His eyes opened, and the bleak pain in them made her want to cry. "Didn't do me or her much good, did it?"

"I don't think anybody could help her," Wanda Nell said. "You know what they say: you gotta recognize the problem and ask for help yourself, before you can do anything about it. You can't save somebody that don't wanna be saved." She knew that well, from her own bitter experience with her ex-husband and her son. Bobby Ray had never really tried to grow up and face his responsibilities. T.J., thank the Lord, finally had, though Wanda Nell was more afraid for him now than she ever had been.

"I know you're right," Melvin said tiredly. "Sometimes I wondered why she just didn't put a gun to her head. Or why I didn't."

"Don't talk like that," Wanda Nell said sharply. "You did what you could, and that's a damn sight more than most men would've done. She wasn't worth killing yourself over."

Melvin shrugged. "I didn't really mean it. Spending that time in jail made me think a lot. I guess I've learned a few things about women. I ain't gonna be making a mistake like that again."

Wanda Nell felt some reassurance at those words. It was going to take him time to get over this, but he seemed to be headed in the right direction. She hated to have him rake over any more of Fayetta's life at this point, but she knew they had to do it.

"A little while ago, you said something like, 'At first she just went out with married men.' What else was there?"

"You know how she'd wanna take Friday night and Saturday off a couple times a month?"

Wanda Nell nodded.

"Well, she had some other job," Melvin said, frowning again. "She wouldn't tell me just what it was, but she did say it was working in a private club. That's all she'd say, except that she made about fifty times more on those weekends than she could a whole week here."

"And that's all she told you?"

Melvin fixed her with a sharp glance. "You know something about it I don't know?"

Wanda Nell hesitated. "Maybe. But if that's all you know, then that's all you need to know for now."

"You mean, if I knew everything, it might mean I had more of a reason to kill her."

"Something like that," Wanda Nell said, made uncomfortable by the hurt in his face.

Melvin rubbed his forehead. "Damn, but I feel like going on a three-day drunk. I can't take much more of this." He pulled his cigarettes out of his pocket, shook one out of the pack, and lit it with the lighter on his desk. He exhaled smoke, turning his head away from Wanda Nell. "All I know was she kept talking about

286

having more money, but I ain't got a clue what she was doing with it."

Wanda Nell almost told him, but she caught herself in time. If he didn't know about that savings account, he was better off not knowing for now. Instead, she shrugged.

"What happened to it, I wonder?" Melvin asked. "The way she talked, it was a lotta money, and I don't see where she was spending much, except on some clothes for her kids."

"Good point," Wanda Nell said.

Melvin's eyes narrowed as smoke drifted around his head. "Maybe somebody killed her for that money. You thought about that? Maybe it all came down to money."

Twenty-Five

"Could be," Wanda Nell said after a brief pause. "You have any idea how much money she had?"

"I'm not sure," Melvin admitted. "She liked to talk big. Hell, you know how she was. Course, she didn't talk about that kinda stuff in front of you. It was just me she was throwing it up to." His tone had turned bitter again. "But if I believed half of what she was telling me, she had to have at least ten grand, maybe more, put away somewhere."

"That's a lot of money," Wanda Nell said, "but what was she doing with it? Keeping it under her mattress?"

"I don't know," Melvin said. "Maybe she put it in

287

the bank. She wasn't fool enough to have that kind of money in the house." He scratched his head. "Yeah, she must've put it in the bank."

"In that case," Wanda Nell said, "how could someone get ahold of it by killing her? I guess it'd belong to her kids now, wouldn't it?"

"I guess so," Melvin said. His face darkened. "But I bet those kids won't ever see a dime of that money, if somebody ain't swiped it already."

"Who'd've swiped it?"

"Deke Campbell for one," Melvin said bluntly. "I know for a fact he was one of the men Fayetta went out with sometimes, and I bet you anything he was giving her money. And if she put it in his bank, I bet you by now it's gone. I wouldn't put anything past that bastard."

"But there'd still be some kind of record, wouldn't there?" This was giving her a headache, acting like she didn't know about Fayetta's savings account. From what she could tell, Melvin didn't know for sure that Fayetta had banked the money, and that was a point in his favor.

"Sure there would," Melvin agreed, "but with them computers, I bet you ol' Deke can do anything he wants with the records. He'd find some way of making that money disappear, and ain't nobody gonna find it."

"But Fayetta would've had some kind of paper records, surely," Wanda Nell said, pushing the point further.

"Yeah," Melvin said, shrugging, "I guess she would. But whoever went in there and killed her could've taken what records she had. I bet you the sheriff's department didn't find no records like that." He stubbed out his cigarette in the ashtray on his desk.

"That's possible," Wanda Nell said. She felt funny about continuing to deceive him, but it was for his own good. Still, she had to admit Melvin had a point. Deke Campbell could have decided the only way to stop Fayetta from bleeding him and the other members of the club completely dry was to kill her and then make sure the money and all trace of it disappeared. That way no one could link him or anyone else to Fayetta.

Too bad for him, Wanda Nell thought with a feeling of satisfaction. *I put a little kink in that plan when I turned over that passbook to Elmer Lee.*

Even if Deke Campbell managed to manipulate the bank's records somehow, there was at least some evidence that the account, and the money in it, had existed at some point. *I bet Deke Campbell would sure like to get his hands on that passbook,* Wanda Nell thought.

Why hadn't she thought of that before? For a moment forgetting where she was, Wanda Nell played with the idea of using her knowledge of the passbook to trick Deke Campbell into making some kind of move, one that would get the sheriff's department interested in him.

How could she make that work?

"Wanda Nell."

She came back abruptly from her thoughts at the sound of Elray, the dishwasher, calling her from the kitchen.

"What is it?" She stepped out into the hall.

Elray said, wiping his hands on his apron, "That new girl, she be calling for you. Looks like it getting busy out there."

"Thanks," Wanda Nell said. "I'll be right out." She turned briefly back to Melvin. "Back to work, I guess. You hang in there, you hear? We'll get it all sorted out, one way or another."

Melvin nodded as he reached for another cigarette. "I'll come out in a few minutes. I got a couple more things I need to do in here first."

Back out on the floor, Wanda Nell didn't have much time to think about Fayetta's murder for a while. The customers kept coming in a steady stream, and she and Katie Ann stayed very busy. Whatever suspicions Wanda Nell harbored over Katie Ann's involvement in the murder, she had to admit the girl was a top-notch waitress. She certainly didn't seem to mind hard work.

With Melvin back at his place at the cash register and helping bus tables, Wanda Nell could concentrate more on her customers. She enjoyed the people, for the most part, and usually they responded by leaving her generous tips. They got the occasional jerk who wasn't satisfied with anything, but Wanda Nell handled customers like that with a firm hold on her temper. She had never yet been rude to a customer, though she had been sorely tempted many a time.

Around seven o'clock, Jack Pemberton returned with his cousin Lisa. Wanda Nell didn't have much time to chat with them, but she did hear they had found a nice house for Lisa to rent. In the same neighborhood where Jack lived, it was only a short drive from the hospital where Lisa would be working.

"Sounds like everything's working out just fine," Wanda Nell told Lisa as she topped off her tea glass.

Lisa nodded shyly. "I can't wait to get moved. I just want to get away from Meridian."

"I don't blame you," Wanda Nell said. "We're not gonna let that guy bother you here." She laughed. "If he shows up here, I'll just get my friend Mayrene to have a little talk with him. Her and her shotgun. He'll leave you alone after that, or Mayrene'll have him singing soprano in the church choir."

Jack laughed. "If anyone can do it, Mayrene can."

Lisa looked dubious. "I don't want anyone to get in trouble because of me."

"Just wait till you meet Mayrene, honey," Wanda Nell said with a big grin. "She won't get in any trouble, and she'll enjoy every minute of it."

As Wanda Nell left them, Jack was telling Lisa all about Mayrene and the events of a couple months ago.

By nine-thirty most of the customers were gone, and business was winding down for the night. Katie Ann had gone to the office with Melvin for a talk, the first time they'd had to get acquainted since Melvin had returned.

When Katie Ann came back out front, she told Wanda Nell that Melvin wanted to see her.

"He sure is a nice guy," Katie Ann said. "Seems like a real good guy to work for."

"He is," Wanda Nell said, pausing on her way to the office. "You be square with him, and he'll be square with you. Can't ask for better than that."

"No, I guess not," Katie Ann said with a slight frown. "Are you sure he didn't kill Fayetta?"

"Yes, I'm sure," Wanda Nell said, her tone firm. "You just put that idea right out of your head. Somebody else did it. I don't know who, but it sure as hell wasn't Melvin." With that, she pushed through the swinging door into the kitchen, leaving Katie Ann to handle the front.

"What's up?" she asked Melvin when she reached his office.

He expelled a plume of smoke. "I got a little favor to ask."

"Sure," Wanda Nell said, waving a hand to stir the smoke around. "You're gonna have to air this place out, you keep smoking like that in here."

"Sorry," Melvin said.

"I'm not complaining," Wanda Nell said, grinning. "If I can't get it from smoking myself, I'll take it second-hand. I sure do miss it."

"You're better off giving it up," Melvin said, stubbing out his cigarette. "I oughta quit, too. Maybe tomorrow."

"Uh-huh," Wanda Nell said. Melvin talked about

quitting periodically, but he never did anything about it. "What's that favor you wanted?"

Melvin reached into the top drawer of his desk and pulled out an envelope. "Would you give this to Fayetta's mama?" He slid the envelope across the desk, and Wanda Nell picked it up.

Surprised by the thickness of it, Wanda Nell resisted the urge to peek inside. "What's this?"

"What I owe Fayetta," Melvin said. "And a little extra for those kids. I reckon Miz Vance can use it. Fayetta was always saying how her mama don't have much money."

"Don't you want to give it to her yourself?"

Melvin shook his head. "No. I figure it'll be better if you give it to her. She never did like me much, and I'd just as soon not see her if I don't have to."

"I don't mind taking it to her," Wanda Nell said. "And you're right, I'm sure she can use it. With four kids to feed, she's gonna need all the help she can get."

"Yeah," Melvin said. "And you can bet none of their daddies are gonna pitch in. They never did before. Even the one Fayetta was married to. That was Red Sutton, and he ran off right after Shawn was born."

Wanda Nell debated a moment before she asked, "You have any idea who the other daddies are?"

Melvin shrugged. "Not really. I can guess on a couple of 'em, but Fayetta never would talk about it."

"Why didn't she try to get child support from any of them?"

Melvin shot her a look.

"Oh, I get it," Wanda Nell said slowly. "You mean every one of them was a married man because she liked going out with married men."

"That's what I figure," Melvin said. "I know she got money out of some of 'em occasionally, but nothing real regular. She could've caused a big stink if she'd wanted to, but she never did."

"Until just recently," Wanda Nell said, tucking the envelope into her pocket. "Then she must've changed her mind for some reason. Decided she wanted money and didn't care how she got it."

"And somebody didn't want to play along and killed her," Melvin said.

"Yeah." Melvin would find out soon enough all the sordid details—the savings account, the blackmail list. As she thought the words, Wanda Nell realized she'd been overlooking some important evidence. She should have been paying more attention to the names on that list, although she also figured Elmer Lee Johnson should be following up on it. Things could be touchy, considering some of the names on the list, but that was his lookout.

When she got home tonight, she'd get that list out and go over it again. Try to identify all the names on it, for one thing, and then go from there. The killer was very likely one of the men on that list, or maybe several of them were involved in it together.

Whether it was a solo effort or a group enterprise, Wanda Nell felt like kicking herself for not paying

294

more attention to the list. Now that she had told Mayrene about Hector Padget's involvement, maybe she could enlist Mayrene's help with the names.

"Wanda Nell."

At the sound of her name, Wanda Nell blinked and focused on Melvin.

"Sorry," she said. "Just woolgathering, I guess."

"It's about time to start closing up," Melvin said. "I told Katie Ann she could go, soon as her friend gets here to pick her up. You don't mind staying and closing up with me, do you?" He got up from his chair.

"No, that's fine," Wanda Nell said. "I'd better go check, though, and see if she's ready to leave."

She headed for the kitchen, Melvin right behind her. Melvin stopped to talk with the cook and the dishwasher, and Wanda Nell advanced to the door and peered through the small window in it.

She had her hand on it and was about to push it open, when what she was seeing registered in her tired brain.

She recognized the guy talking with Katie Ann at the counter, just a few feet from the kitchen door.

Tommy Eccles.

Her stomach knotted in fear. What the hell was he doing here?

Twenty-Six

Wanda Nell jerked her head back from the window and stepped away from the door.

She couldn't let Tommy Eccles see her. She didn't want him to know where she worked, or who she really was.

She turned around to find Melvin watching her, a puzzled look on his face.

"What's wrong with you?"

"Don't ask now," Wanda Nell practically hissed at him. "You just go out there and get Katie Ann and her friend out of here. I'll explain when they're gone."

She brushed past him and ducked into the hallway. Her back against the wall, she made herself breathe slowly and evenly.

Peeking around the corner, she didn't see Melvin. He must have done as she asked. She leaned against the wall, trying to relax.

If Tommy Eccles was Katie Ann's friend, that definitely tied her in. Otherwise, why would she be hanging around with a goon like him? Then Wanda Nell started shaking her head, realizing she didn't need any more confirmation.

Katie Ann really had been a plant the whole time. Billy Joe Eccles and Deke Campbell and the whole damn lot of them had put Katie Ann up to coming to the Kountry Kitchen looking for a job. They all knew

Fayetta was dead, and they wanted somebody they could trust keeping an eye on things at the restaurant. Somebody who could help them make sure, if at all possible, Melvin was the one who went to jail, and not one of them.

Wanda Nell thought of a few choice names she'd like to call Katie Ann to her face, and hoped she would have the opportunity to, once she was sure that Melvin was safe from having to go back to jail. She'd laugh in Katie Ann's face when one of the men who'd put her up to this was in jail instead.

No wonder Katie Ann knows so much about Fayetta, she thought. *She was working at that damn club with her.* The realization made her sick at her stomach.

Katie Ann had seemed like a pretty nice girl. What did she want with working at a place like that? Especially when she could make a decent living as a waitress. She was single and didn't have any kids, as far as Wanda Nell knew. Why would she lower herself to take a job like that?

She hadn't lived Katie Ann's life, or Fayetta's, and it wasn't her place to say why they'd made the choice to prostitute themselves. *"Judge not, that you be not judged,"* Wanda Nell quoted to herself.

"What the heck was all that about?" Melvin's voice interrupted her thoughts.

"Are they gone?" Wanda Nell demanded.

"Yeah, they're gone, and so are Elray and Margaret, so it's just you and me," Melvin said. "What's going on?"

297

"Did you recognize that guy?"

Melvin frowned. "I've seen him around town, I guess. Why, do you know him?"

"That's Tommy Eccles, Billy Joe Eccles's brother," Wanda Nell said. Then, when Melvin didn't react, she continued, "You know, the one who's supposed to've killed his mama and daddy."

Melvin's face registered comprehension. "Oh, yeah, I heard about him." He shrugged. "But I don't get what you're so spooked about."

"For one thing," Wanda Nell said, "he saw me this afternoon when I was snooping around somewhere I probably shouldn't've been. Out at that so-called club of his brother's. I didn't want him to see me and connect me with you or the restaurant."

"Okay," Melvin said. "He didn't see you, far as I know."

"Good," Wanda Nell said, relieved. "But you realize what it means, don't you, him and Katie Ann being friends?"

Melvin shook his head.

Wanda Nell wanted to kick him. Ordinarily he wasn't this slow. Maybe he was just worn out from being in jail, and the strain was affecting his brain.

"It means," Wanda Nell said, as patiently as she could, "that Katie Ann is a plant. I bet you anything Billy Joe Eccles and that bunch put her up to asking for a job. With Fayetta dead, they knew we'd need someone, and with her here, they had their very own spy right in the Kountry Kitchen."

"Yeah, I get that," Melvin said, slightly testily. "But what is there for her to find out? I didn't kill Fayetta, and she ain't gonna find anything here to prove I did."

"No," Wanda Nell said, "but what if she finds something to prove you *didn't*?" She waited a moment for that to sink in. "I've caught her snooping around, and you better believe she was looking for something. And if she found something, *anything,* that might point the finger at somebody else, like a member of that damn club of theirs, you can bet it's long gone."

Melvin paled as the full implications of what she was saying finally sunk in. "That little bitch! I'll fire her ass. I don't want her back in here."

"You can't do that," Wanda Nell said, holding up a hand to focus his attention on her and stop him ranting. "I mean, you can do that, but I don't think you should, at least not yet."

"Why not?"

"Because if you fire her," Wanda Nell said, "they'll know you've figured out what she's up to. We don't want them to know that. Understand?"

Melvin nodded reluctantly.

"Now, I can't tell you exactly what," Wanda Nell said, "but I found what I think she was probably looking for." She held up a hand again when Melvin started to speak. "It ain't no use you asking me what it was. I'm not gonna tell you, for your sake. If you do have to go into court and answer questions about all this, it's better if you don't know about it beforehand." She paused for a breath. "If Tuck wants you to know, it's up to him to tell you. Okay?"

"Okay," Melvin said. Wanda Nell could tell he didn't like it, but she couldn't help that.

She felt like a secret agent in some really crappy movie, but she also believed she was doing the right thing.

"We just need to be real careful about anything we say in front of Katie Ann," Wanda Nell said.

"I don't plan on saying much to her at all," Melvin responded. "The sooner I can get rid of her, the better."

"It won't be long," Wanda Nell said. "It'll all be over soon." She prayed she was right, for all their sakes.

"I hope to God you're right," Melvin said. "Let's get out of here. I just wanna go home and sleep in my own bed."

"You gonna be okay on your own?"

"Why? You gonna come home with me and scare the bogeyman away?" Melvin grinned at that.

"Not exactly," Wanda Nell said, shaking her head at his attempt at humor. "I mean, you're welcome to come home and spend the night with me and the girls if you don't want to be by yourself tonight. Juliet can sleep with me, and you can have her room."

"Naw, I'll be fine," Melvin said, "but thanks for asking."

"Okay, then, just be careful."

"You think something might happen?"

Wanda Nell shrugged. "Probably not. But I just

don't trust these guys. They might try something, because they'll all be happier if it's you in jail and not one of them."

"I can look after myself," Melvin said, his face darkening. "They better not mess with me. I wasn't a Marine for nothing."

Wanda Nell had forgotten that. When it came to a fight, Melvin could look after himself pretty well. She just hoped it wouldn't come to that. But saying anything more about it to him right now wouldn't do a dang bit of good.

She and Melvin made sure everything was set for the night, then she waited until the front door was locked before heading to her car. "See you tomorrow," she called. Melvin waved to acknowledge he'd heard her as he got into his pickup.

There was very little traffic on the drive home, and Wanda Nell made it in record time. She was locking the car when she heard Mayrene hailing her from next door.

"Hey, Mayrene, what are you still doing up?"

"You got time to come on over and talk a bit?"

Wanda Nell glanced at her trailer. Everything seemed fine. Miranda's bedroom was dark, and so was Juliet's. "Sure," she said.

"How about something to drink?" Mayrene asked as she closed the door behind Wanda Nell.

"Not for me, thanks," Wanda Nell said as she made herself comfortable on Mayrene's leather sofa. "What you want to talk about?"

"Hang on a minute, honey," Mayrene called out as she headed into the kitchen. She came back with a bottle of beer and sat down on the sofa near Wanda Nell.

"It's that no-good skunk, Hector Padget," Mayrene said after downing nearly half of her beer.

"What's he done?" Wanda Nell asked, vaguely alarmed. Now that she looked closely, she could see Mayrene had had more than a couple beers already.

"That rat ain't done nothing," Mayrene said, "but try to play all lovey-dovey with me, telling me how much he cares about me, and what a fine-lookin' woman I am." She burped. "Hell, I know that. I got plenty of men telling me what a fine-lookin' woman I am, and I don't need some damn snake in the grass trying to cozy up to me." She shook her head dolefully, then downed the rest of her beer. She got up from the sofa and headed toward the kitchen. "Sure you don't want one?"

Wanda Nell shook her head, and Mayrene disappeared into the kitchen. She came back in a minute with another beer. "The last one," she said, brandishing the bottle. "Damn it! You got any over at your place?"

"No, Mayrene, I don't," Wanda Nell said, "and I don't think you need any more anyway. What's got into you? You don't drink like this."

Mayrene sniffled, then drank some beer. She burped. "That sonofabitch, Hector. I just can't get over him, talking all that sweet talk to me, and all the time, him being a part of that club and whooping it up with whores and who knows what else."

Wanda Nell had rarely seen her friend like this. Mayrene must have cared more for Hector Padget than she'd let on, or else it was just her pride smarting a bit. "He don't deserve a good woman like you," Wanda Nell said. "And you know it. Ain't no use you sitting around and crying in your beer over a jackass like that. You know better. Like you said, there's plenty other men out there, good men, who think you're a fine-looking woman. Don't waste your time on him."

"You're right," Mayrene sniffed. "I shouldn't let that jackass get to me." She set her half-full beer bottle down on the coffee table with a thump. "And no point wasting good beer on him either."

"That's the spirit," Wanda Nell said.

"Damn right." Mayrene burped again.

Wanda Nell stood up. "I think you ought to be getting to bed."

"Aw, now, sit down a minute and talk to me," Mayrene said, waving a hand in the air. "Tell me what's going on."

Wanda Nell sat back down. Considering the state Mayrene was in, Wanda Nell didn't want to start some long, drawn-out story about everything that had happened today. "Well, Melvin's out of jail, and he's back at the Kountry Kitchen. And we're still trying to figure out who really killed Fayetta."

"Gotta be somebody in that damn club Mr. Hector

Padget belongs to," Mayrene said. "Right?"

"Probably," Wanda Nell said. "But who? And how can we prove it?"

Mayrene sat there, silent, blinking at her. Figuring her friend was about ready to pass out, Wanda Nell stood up again. "Why don't you let me help you to bed?"

Mayrene flapped a hand at her. "Oh, I'm fine, honey. Just thinking. Not ready for bed yet."

"Well, I am," Wanda Nell said, unable to suppress a yawn. "So I'm going to bed."

"Okay, you do that," Mayrene said. She didn't get up from the sofa.

Shaking her head, Wanda Nell let herself out, closing the door carefully behind her. All was quiet in her own trailer, and she quickly got ready for bed. She slid into bed and was asleep almost as soon as her head hit the pillow.

She awoke sometime later to the ringing of the phone. Fumbling with the covers, she sat up in bed and switched on the bedside lamp. Squinting at the clock as she reached for the phone, she saw that it was a few minutes past midnight.

"Hello," she said, her heart racing.

"Hey, girl," Mayrene said. "Get on over here, right now. I need you."

The phone clicked in her ear. Alarmed, Wanda Nell scrambled out of bed, pulled on a robe over her nightgown, and slipped her feet into her house shoes.

What on earth could be wrong with Mayrene? When she'd left her over an hour ago, she'd seemed fine.

The ringing of the phone didn't seem to have disturbed either of the girls or the baby. Wanda Nell opened the door and made her way quickly across to Mayrene's trailer. Mayrene was just coming into the living room from the direction of her bedroom when Wanda Nell stepped inside. Fully clothed, Mayrene was carrying her shotgun.

"What's going on?" Wanda Nell said, thoroughly alarmed. "Did somebody try to break in?"

Mayrene laughed. "Come on, honey, I got something I want you to see." She turned and headed back toward her bedroom.

Her curiosity piqued, Wanda Nell followed. She couldn't imagine what Mayrene was up to.

Mayrene walked into the bedroom, turned, and with a flourish said, "He's all yours, honey."

Dumbfounded, Wanda Nell stood in the doorway and stared. Spread-eagle on Mayrene's bed, his arms and legs attached to the bed frame with rope, was a large, heavyset man, naked except for a leopard-print thong covering his private parts.

Twenty-Seven

"Who . . . who is he?" Wanda Nell finally managed to get the words out. She tore her eyes from the sight on the bed and stared hard at Mayrene.

"That's Hector Padget, honey." Mayrene guffawed. "Ain't he a sight?"

Padget cut loose with a few choice words, most of them describing Mayrene and various members of her family.

In response, Mayrene took her shotgun and nudged the leopard-skin thong with it. Hector Padget shut up immediately.

"When I want something out of you, jackass," Mayrene said, "I'll let you know. Till then, you just keep your mouth shut." She turned back to Wanda Nell.

"Are you nuts?" Wanda Nell practically hissed the words. "What are you doing?" She pointed in the direction of the man on the bed, trying not to look at him. After she had finally looked at his face, she had realized who it was.

"Just trying to help you and Melvin out," Mayrene said serenely. "I figured you could talk to ol' Hector here and get a few things straightened out. You ask him some questions, and me and ol' reliable here'll make sure he talks," she said, patting the shotgun.

Wanda Nell stared hard at Mayrene. As far as she could tell, her friend was stone-cold sober. Sober, but mad as a wet hen. Wanda Nell almost felt sorry for Hector Padget. She glanced back at the bed and the large amount of exposed pale white flesh on display. Padget glared at both of them, his eyes dark pebbles of hate.

Wanda Nell couldn't help herself. She was tired, and the whole situation was downright bizarre. She started laughing. The man just looked so ridiculous there on the bed.

Mayrene laughed with her till the tears ran down her face. After a couple of minutes of laughter, Hector Padget started talking again, telling them just what he planned to do to them when he got loose.

At first both women ignored him, but as the threats grew more vicious, they stopped laughing.

Mayrene rested her shotgun on his leg, the barrel pointing right at his thong. Padget shut up again.

"Now you listen up, Hector. I don't want no more smart talk out of you. None of them threats, because you ain't gonna do one damn thing to me or my friend here. And you know why?"

Padget didn't respond. Mayrene jiggled the shotgun. "Why?" he managed to croak out.

"Because," Mayrene said, "I got two brothers who make you look puny, Hector. And you ain't exactly petite. My brothers don't take kindly to no jackass threatening their sister, either. You know what they'd do if they was to get hold of you?"

Padget didn't say anything.

"Well, I reckon they'd take you on down to Louisiana to one of them bayous they got down there. My brothers kinda like those swamps. And they like hunting for gators. Reckon you'd like to be gator bait, Hector? Wouldn't be the first time they took care of some jerk who pissed me off."

For the first time, Padget looked frightened instead of angry. Mayrene's voice was dead cold, and Padget was buying every word of it.

Somehow Wanda Nell managed to keep a straight

face. She had met Mayrene's one and only brother, a short, skinny, mild-mannered guy who was manager of a grocery store in Tupelo. But Hector Padget didn't need to know that.

"I'm just asking for a little cooperation here, Hector. If you play nice and answer all our questions, then I'm gonna cut you loose. Then we're all gonna forget this happened. I won't tell anybody, and you won't either. But if you try anything, just think about being gator bait. I already told my brothers all about you, and they're just itching to go gator hunting."

"All right," Padget said, his voice raspy. "Ask your damn questions. I don't know what the hell you're up to, but you're just plain damn crazy, Mayrene. I don't ever wanna see you again, believe you me."

"Go ahead, honey," Mayrene said, nodding her head toward Padget. "Tell him what it is you want to know."

"Can't you at least cover him up a little bit?" Wanda Nell asked in an undertone. "It's kinda hard to think with him lying there like a beached whale."

Mayrene rolled her eyes, but she did twitch the bed-spread around until the thong and a large amount of white flesh were covered.

"Thank you," Wanda Nell muttered. She moved closer to the bed and rested her hands on the brass railings at the foot. "Better get this over with. Okay, Mr. Padget, what this is all about is the murder of Fayetta Sutton. You know who I'm talking about, I'm sure."

Padget's eyes had widened at the mention of

Fayetta's name. He didn't say anything for a moment. "Yeah, I know who she is," he finally admitted.

"And I bet you know that Melvin Arbuckle was arrested for her murder." Without waiting for a response, Wanda Nell went on. "The thing is, Melvin didn't do it. So we've got to figure out who did, and that's where you can help."

"How can I help?" Padget frowned.

"I'm getting to that," Wanda Nell said. "Now, Fayetta got up to some pretty interesting tricks, like working at a private club called the Deer Stand. I know you know all about that. You're one of the members, aren't you?"

Padget didn't say anything. Mayrene let him see her fondling her shotgun.

"Yeah, I'm a member," he said sullenly. "So what?"

"Well, I got a good idea what really goes on there," Wanda Nell said, not bothering to keep the distaste out of her voice. "And the kind of *work* Fayetta did there. Fayetta was making pretty good money, but not just from working there. She had a little extra thing going. Blackmail."

If anything, Padget turned even whiter at that last word. "You're outta your ever-lovin' mind, lady. She wasn't blackmailing anybody." His tone didn't sound convincing, and he realized it himself. He swallowed convulsively.

"She was," Wanda Nell said. "I know she was. I found the proof of it myself. I even know how much money she was getting."

"So this is a shakedown," Padget said. "You and this crazy bitch with the shotgun, you wanna take over from that whore Fayetta, don't you? How much do you want?"

Mayrene had bristled at the words *crazy bitch,* but Wanda Nell laid a restraining hand on her arm. "Neither one of us wants any money out of you," she said coldly. "Not from you, or from anybody else that belongs to that sorry excuse for a club. What we want is the truth. We wanna know which member of the club you're protecting. One of you killed Fayetta, and you're gonna have to turn him over to the sheriff's department."

Padget didn't say anything, just stared at her.

"Well, come on. Who did it? Or did y'all hire somebody to do it?" Wanda Nell didn't want to mention Tommy Eccles, but she figured he was probably the one they got to do their dirty work for them.

"You heard her," Mayrene said when Padget continued to remain silent. She poked him with the shotgun.

"I don't know," Padget said furiously. "I don't know who did it."

"You mean you don't know which member of the club did it?" Wanda Nell said, pressing the point home.

Reluctantly, Padget nodded.

"Who does know?" Wanda Nell asked.

"I'm not sure," Padget said. "They don't tell me much."

"Who's they?"

"Billy Joe and Deke," Padget answered grudgingly. "They're the ones that run everything. I'm just a member."

"Some hotshot you are," Mayrene commented. "Just a lot of big talk and hot air." Padget ignored her.

"So you think maybe one of them did it?" Wanda Nell kept pressing him, thinking he might knew more than he was willing to admit, despite his situation.

"I don't know." Padget shouted the words at her. "Jeez, woman, I've told you what I know. One of them could've done it. They're acting pretty strange right now. Billy Joe might've got that crazy brother of his to kill her for all I know." He shuddered. "That guy's a nutcase. You don't wanna get crossways of him."

Wanda Nell and Mayrene looked at each other. "What do you think?" Wanda Nell said.

"I reckon that's about all this peckerwood's gonna tell us. Probably all he can tell us. He's just a flunky." The scorn in Mayrene's voice caused Padget to start mumbling.

"You ain't loose yet," Mayrene told him. "So watch what you're saying there, jackass."

"I think you need to cut him loose now," Wanda Nell said quietly.

"Yeah, I guess so," Mayrene said. "I want to get the bastard out of my house for good." She handed Wanda Nell the shotgun. "You hang onto this, just in case."

Wanda Nell wasn't keen on handling the shotgun, but she took it. Padget might try something, despite

311

Mayrene's threats. She watched as Mayrene untied him.

When the final rope was loosed, Mayrene stood back and regarded Padget, sitting on the bed and rubbing his wrists in turn. "Now, if you're smart, the first thing you oughta do in the morning is hightail it to the sheriff's department and have a talk with them."

"What for?" Padget said, struggling to get dressed with some semblance of dignity.

"You're even dumber than I thought," Mayrene said in disgust. "Because they already know you're involved in that club, and sooner or later they're gonna come knocking on your door. If you go to them and tell them what you know, well, they'll take it easier on you."

"How do they know I'm involved?" Padget demanded as he buttoned his rumpled shirt.

"Because they have a list," Wanda Nell said. "They know who belongs to the club, and they also have a pretty good idea who was paying Fayetta hush money."

By now Padget was looking green around the gills. He was pretty well screwed, and he was beginning to realize just how bad it was.

He slumped down on the side of the bed, trying to get his shoes on. Wanda Nell watched him, almost feeling sorry for him. He'd gotten himself into a hell of a mess, but anybody who'd participate in that kind of club deserved whatever they got.

All traces of defiance gone, Padget stumbled toward the bedroom door. Mayrene and Wanda Nell stood out of his way. He turned to look back at them.

"Are you going to the sheriff's department?" Mayrene asked him.

Padget nodded. "First thing in the morning." He turned and walked down the hall.

Taking the shotgun from Wanda Nell, Mayrene followed him. Wanda Nell trailed behind. Mayrene stood at the door, watching until Padget's car was out of sight. She closed and locked the door, then laid her shotgun on the coffee table.

She and Wanda Nell sank down on the sofa at the same time and sat staring at each other.

"That's one way of getting somebody to talk," Wanda Nell said. "Maybe you oughta go to work for the sheriff's department."

Mayrene grinned. "You just have to know how to talk to 'em, honey."

"How'd you get him over here and tied up in bed like that?" Wanda Nell asked. She'd been dying of curiosity the whole time, but she hadn't dared ask before.

Mayrene laughed, a deep, rolling sound that made her body shake. "Oh, honey," she finally said. "That man's been so hot to trot, all I had to do was say a few little words, and he was standing on my doorstep, his tongue hanging out like an old dog that ain't had no water for months." She laughed again. "I told him how excited I'd get, having a big handsome hunk of man tied up in my bed, and he couldn't get tied up fast enough."

"You never cease to amaze me," Wanda Nell said.

"Sometimes a woman's gotta do what a woman's gotta do," Mayrene said. "And, Lord knows, I'm woman enough to get just about anything done."

"Amen to that." Wanda Nell laughed. "But why'd you decide to do something like this? Even for you, it's a little bit on the wild side."

"Oh, I was sitting here, feeling real sorry for myself," Mayrene said. "It was just the beer talking, but I decided I was gonna do something about it. Figured some good might as well come of the whole blamed mess. So I stirred up the pot a little."

"You dang sure did," Wanda Nell said, suppressing a yawn. "Maybe this'll be what the sheriff's department needs. If Padget goes and talks to them, they can't just ignore it."

"I sure as hell hope not," Mayrene said. "They damn well better do something about that so-called club, or I might just have go out there and accidentally set it on fire." She grinned wickedly.

She was probably kidding, Wanda Nell thought, but with Mayrene, you never could be sure. Right now she was too tired to worry about it. She leaned forward and gave her friend a big hug. "I'm going to bed, and I advise you to do the same," she said. "And make sure your door is locked, just in case."

"Don't worry about me," Mayrene said. "Ol' reliable and me are gonna be just fine. Ain't nobody gonna come around here and mess with us."

Shaking her head, Wanda Nell left Mayrene's trailer. Opening her own door, she slipped quietly inside. Everything seemed still as she tiptoed down the hall to her room.

She lay in bed for a while, slowly relaxing, trying to keep her mind from worrying too much about Hector Padget and Mayrene's rash behavior. *I'll think about it tomorrow,* she told herself. She snuggled down into the bed and drifted off to sleep.

When she woke later that morning, she sat up in bed and stretched. She had slept soundly, and she felt good. For a moment, what had taken place in Mayrene's trailer just hours ago seemed like a strange dream.

She glanced at the clock. It was nearly nine. Yawning, she pushed herself up from the bed and went into the bathroom. Emerging a few minutes later, she advanced into the living room and then the kitchen. She poured herself a cup of coffee from the pot that Juliet had probably made. There was no sign of either of her daughters or her grandson.

Miranda should be at work by now, and Wanda Nell hoped she was. But where were Juliet and Lavon? For a moment, Wanda Nell's heart skipped a beat.

Then, in the silence of the morning, she heard the sound of her grandson's laugh, coming from somewhere outside. Relaxing against the counter, she realized Juliet had taken him outside to play. From the sun streaming through the windows, it looked like a fine morning to be outside.

She sat down at the table and sipped at her coffee, her thoughts skipping around various subjects. She wondered if Hector Padget had lived up to his promise and gone to the sheriff's department yet. If he knew what was good for him, he had. Otherwise he'd have Mayrene breathing down his neck. Wanda Nell had to grin at that thought.

She heard a car pull up outside the trailer. Maybe it was T.J. coming to see her. Her stomach knotted up. She knew they needed to talk, but was she really ready for it?

Someone knocked on the door, and she hurried to answer it. She swung the door open.

Katie Ann stood there, her head down. Then she looked up into Wanda Nell's face, and Wanda Nell gasped in shock.

Twenty-Eight

"Good lord, girl, what happened to you?" Wanda Nell reached out to pull Katie Ann inside.

"I walked into a door," Katie Ann said bitterly. She touched one hand to her bruised left cheek and eye. Her hair hadn't been brushed, and she wore clothes that looked like she'd dug them out of a dirty clothes hamper.

Wanda Nell glanced over the girl's shoulder and spotted a pickup. It looked familiar. Where had she seen it before?

She was closing the door behind Katie Ann, ready to take her into the kitchen, when she remembered. That was Tommy Eccles's truck. But, thankfully, there was no sign of Tommy Eccles.

"Come on into the kitchen," Wanda Nell said, "and let's put some ice on that."

"It don't matter," Katie Ann said, allowing herself to be propelled along. "I don't care what it looks like, or how much it hurts." She burst into tears.

Not knowing what else to do, Wanda Nell wrapped her arms around the younger woman and put Katie Ann's head on her shoulder. She made soothing noises, and slowly the sobbing eased. Katie Ann pulled her tear-stained face away and rubbed her face tiredly.

"I'm sorry," she said, letting Wanda Nell lead her into the kitchen and sit her down in one of the chairs.

"About what?" Wanda Nell asked gently, taking a chair across from her.

"You've got every reason to hate me," Katie Ann said, "but I came here to tell you how sorry I am about everything."

"You mean about spying on me and Melvin at the Kountry Kitchen?"

Katie Ann nodded, evidently not surprised that Wanda Nell knew.

"Why'd you come to tell me that?" Wanda Nell said. "I mean, this morning, of all times. What's happened?"

"The shit's done hit the fan, that's what's happened," Katie Ann said bluntly. "Somebody's gone to the sheriff's department, talking all about that damn club, and now everybody's stirred up." She rubbed the left side of her face. "And that bastard tried to take it out on me."

"You mean Tommy Eccles?"

"Yeah," Katie Ann said. "But I fixed his little red wagon."

"What did you do?"

"Can I have a glass of water?" Katie Ann asked. "I didn't realize how thirsty I am."

Wanda Nell got up to fill a glass with water for her. She handed it to Katie Ann, who took a long swallow.

"Thanks," she said, setting the glass down on the table. "Well, I was sound asleep in my bed when it all started happening. My guard dog, that bastard Tommy, was in the other room." She broke off as she caught the look on Wanda Nell's face. "You thought he was my boyfriend."

Wanda Nell nodded.

"He makes my flesh crawl," Katie Ann said, shivering. "I was terrified he was going to do something to me. They had him watching me, making sure I did what they wanted. I didn't have any choice. Tommy made it clear what would happen if I didn't do what they wanted."

"You poor thing," Wanda Nell whispered. Katie Ann might be putting on a big act, but Wanda Nell didn't think so. Her fear and disgust seemed all too real.

"Anyway," Katie Ann said, "I was sound asleep, and

Tommy got a call from somebody. The next thing I know, he's in my room, screaming at me about something, and then he hit me. I don't know what he thinks I done, the bastard, but evidently somebody went to the sheriff's department and told 'em all about what was going on at the club."

Hector Padget had come through after all, but for the moment, Wanda Nell wasn't going to explain any of that to Katie Ann. Instead she asked, "How'd you get away from him? I mean, you're driving his truck. Where is he?"

Katie Ann laughed. "The dumb bastard. He made the mistake of turning his back on me after he hit me a couple of times. I picked up a real heavy lamp and whopped him upside the head. He never knew what hit him."

"So you just left him there? He's gonna come after you," Wanda Nell said nervously. "And I don't want him here, not with my daughter and my grandson here."

"Don't worry," Katie Ann said, laughing again. "He ain't going nowhere for quite some time."

"What do you mean?"

The look in Katie Ann's eyes chilled her. "I told you, I fixed his little red wagon. When I knocked him out, I tied him up with some clothesline. Then I got a baseball bat out of the closet. He ain't going nowhere."

The way she said it, she might just as well have said she wanted eggs for breakfast or was going shopping for a new dress. Wanda Nell didn't know what to do

319

or say. She didn't want to set Katie Ann off again. There was no telling what she might do. But should she try to call the sheriff's department? Had Katie Ann killed him? Was he lying there, badly injured, maybe dying?

"Don't worry about him," Katie Ann said, perhaps reading Wanda Nell's thoughts. I called the sheriff's department before I left. Somebody's done come and picked up what's left of him by now."

Wanda Nell didn't say anything, couldn't think of anything to say.

"I'm sorry," Katie Ann said quietly after a long moment of silence. "I'm sorry they made me spy on you."

"I can understand," Wanda Nell said. "They didn't give you any choice."

"No, they didn't," Katie Ann agreed. She drank the rest of the water in her glass, then held it out to Wanda Nell for more.

Slowly, Wanda Nell got out of her chair and refilled the glass from the tap. She stood sideways, a little worried about turning her back on Katie Ann, but the girl just sat there, staring off into space.

"Thank you," she said when Wanda Nell handed her the refilled glass. She drank about half of it, then set it aside.

"Can I ask you some questions?"

"Sure," Katie Ann said. "I owe you that much."

"What was it you were looking for?"

Katie Ann shrugged. "Well, one thing was that key

320

card you found. That was Fayetta's, and they didn't want nobody else finding it. They sure didn't like it when I told them you beat me to it on that one."

"Did anybody hurt you because of that?"

Katie Ann shook her head. "No, but when I told them about it, that's when they started having Tommy watch me all the time. Like I was gonna forget what they wanted."

"What else were you looking for?"

"Billy Joe told me Fayetta'd conned a lot of money out of him and some of the others. A hell of a lot more money than they were giving me, that's for damn sure," Katie Ann said bitterly. "I couldn't believe it when I found out. If somebody else hadn't killed the bitch already, I would've done it myself."

"You didn't kill her?"

"No, I didn't, I swear it," Katie Ann said, staring Wanda Nell earnestly in the face. "I've done a lot I'm ashamed of, but I didn't kill her." She broke off for a moment. "I didn't kill that bastard Tommy either, though I probably should've. If he finds me, he's sure enough gonna kill me."

"Not if you go to the sheriff's department," Wanda Nell said. "You need to go talk to them, and they'll make sure you're safe. You're an important witness, and they won't let anything happen to you."

"Maybe you're right," Katie Ann said, though she didn't sound too convinced.

"I am right," Wanda Nell said, putting every ounce of conviction she could into those three words. "I'll even go with you, if you want me to."

Katie Ann shook her head. "No, I can do it by myself, if I decide that's what I should do." She looked off at the wall, seeming to drift off.

Wanda Nell didn't want to upset her, but she had to ask her another question. "Do you know which one of them killed Fayetta?"

"Who? You mean Billy Joe and Deke, and those guys?" Katie Ann shook her head. "I don't know. They didn't act like any of 'em had killed her. They just didn't want anybody to know about their little club and what all goes on there. They were all scared shitless when they found out she was dead."

"Don't you think that's why somebody killed Fayetta?" Wanda Nell asked. "I mean, wasn't she pushing them too hard for money, threatening to blow the whistle on them if they didn't keep paying her?"

Shrugging, Katie Ann said, "Maybe. But some of them guys, the kind of money they have, what they were paying Fayetta wasn't much. And they paid me and the other girls even less, the bastards." She drank the rest of her water. "All Fayetta wanted was enough money for her and her kids to get the hell out of Tullahoma, once and for all. That's all she was talking about lately. She was going to Nashville to live up there. Said the daddy of one of her kids lived there, and he wasn't married no more. She thought she might get him to marry her and take care of her and those kids."

"She never said anything about it where I could hear

it," Wanda Nell said, puzzled. "And I don't think she told Melvin any of that, either."

"She wouldn't've," Katie Ann said. She looked uncomfortable for a moment. "She didn't like you very much, Wanda Nell, and she wouldn't've said anything around you. She wouldn't tell Melvin either. She just kept stringing him along, the poor bastard."

"Well, it don't matter now how she felt about me, or how I felt about her," Wanda Nell said. "What matters is finding out who really killed her, so Melvin doesn't have to go back to jail."

"Why are you so convinced he didn't do it?" Katie Ann asked.

"I just am," Wanda Nell said simply. "He's a good man, and I don't think even Fayetta could've provoked him enough to make him kill her like that."

Katie Ann just shook her head and stared at the wall.

Wanda Nell waited a moment, then asked gently, "What are you gonna do now?"

Sighing, Katie Ann stood up. "I guess I might as well go to the sheriff's department. They'll find me anyway, since I'm driving the bastard's truck." She put a hand to her face and smiled. "But it'll be a long time before he hits another woman, you can be damn sure."

"You want me to come with you?" Wanda Nell asked, though at this point, it was the last thing she wanted to do.

"No, I'll be okay," Katie Ann said. "Thank you,

323

Wanda Nell. You've been a lot nicer to me than anybody else would have, and I appreciate that. And I'm sorry. For everything."

Wanda Nell walked with her to the door and watched as she got into Tommy Eccles's pickup and drove away. She debated for a moment whether she should call the sheriff's department, but finally she decided not to. One way or another, Katie Ann would get there.

Making sure her robe was tightly fastened, Wanda Nell stepped outside and went looking for Juliet and Lavon. She needed to be with them, to be sure they were okay, to let the horror of Katie Ann's visit fade away.

An hour later, Wanda Nell had showered and dressed and was ready to drive to Agnes Vance's house. She wanted to give the older woman the envelope of money from Melvin and check on her and the children. She wished there was something more she could do for Fayetta's kids, but there really wasn't much. It was all up to Agnes Vance now.

Juliet and Lavon were back inside, Lavon playing on the floor in Juliet's room while she did something on the computer. Wanda Nell kissed them both before she left and made sure the door was securely locked behind her.

Her cell phone rang as she backed her car out. Miranda had caught a ride with one of her co-workers that morning, so Wanda Nell hadn't had to worry about arrangements for getting them both to and from work.

She stopped the car and pulled the phone out of her purse. She glanced at the number that came up on the caller ID. It was somebody from Tuck's office.

"Morning," Wanda Nell said.

"Hey, it's me," T.J. said.

"How are you?"

"I'm okay, Mama, how are you?"

"Fine, sweetie," Wanda Nell said. From the sound of his voice, he wasn't okay. What was wrong? "I've got lots to tell you, and Tuck, too. I'll come by Tuck's office in a little while and tell you all about it. Y'all gonna be there in an hour or so?"

"Yeah, we'll be there," T.J. said. "I don't think Tuck has to go over to the courthouse today."

"You sure you're okay?"

"Yeah, I'm fine, Mama," T.J. said, but his voice still sounded funny to Wanda Nell. "But I got some things to talk to you about, too, when you get to the office. Okay?"

"Sure, honey," Wanda Nell said. "We'll talk. Bye now."

She ended the call and dropped the phone into her purse. Her heart sank. She knew what T.J. wanted to talk about. She could tell it from the sound of his voice. He'd finally made up his mind to talk to her. But what was she going to say to him? How would she be able to explain how she felt?

How *did* she feel? She still wasn't completely sure.

There was so much to think about.

Somehow, though, she'd find the words. T.J. was her son, and she loved him no matter what.

Maybe that was all she needed to say.

Feeling better, she backed her car out, then headed for Tullahoma and Agnes Vance's house.

Twenty-Nine

Another car was parked in front of Agnes Vance's house when Wanda Nell arrived. Having someone else present while she talked to Fayetta's mother might be a good thing. Mrs. Vance made her uneasy, and she was never quite sure why. Wanda Nell sat in the car for a moment, collecting her thoughts. Then she got out of her car and walked up to the front door and rang the bell.

She heard footsteps approach, and then the door swung open. A young woman of about thirty appeared in the doorway. Wanda Nell regarded her through the fine mesh of the screen door. Long brown hair streamed down her back, and she wore a plain cotton dress. Her face, bare of makeup, was plain but pleasant.

"Good morning," the young woman said. "Are you here to see Miz Vance?"

"Yes," Wanda Nell said, then introduced herself. "I have something I need to give her. And I'd like to talk to her, if I can."

"Surely," the young woman said. She pushed the screen door open and Wanda Nell stepped inside.

"I'm Elise Snavely." She held out a hand to Wanda Nell. "My husband is Brother DeWitt Snavely, the pastor of the Holy Revelation Christian Church."

"Nice to meet you," Wanda Nell said. She stood awkwardly in the hallway, waiting for Mrs. Snavely to move ahead.

Instead, Mrs. Snavely said, "My husband is here to speak with the children and to counsel Miz Vance. If you don't mind waiting a few minutes, I'm sure Miz Vance can talk to you soon."

"That's fine," Wanda Nell said. She followed Mrs. Snavely, who advanced into the living room.

Wanda Nell paused in the doorway. The scene before her was familiar. Fayetta's four children sat on the sofa, lined up by age, and a man of about forty sat in a chair nearby. He was speaking earnestly to them.

Wanda Nell thought Brother Snavely looked familiar. Maybe she had seen his picture in the paper. He was very handsome, with a strong face and thick blond hair. He wore a dark suit that fit his trim body very well.

Mrs. Vance stood behind his chair, listening and watching. She glanced briefly at Wanda Nell, then turned her attention back to what the preacher was saying.

"The Lord is looking after your mama now, and you don't need to worry about her anymore. The Lord will be watching after you, too, and you just trust in Him.

And your grandmother, of course. They'll look after you."

He had a lovely voice, strong and comforting, and Wanda Nell could see the children responding to it. All except the eldest were crying quietly, and they kept their eyes on the preacher.

"Remember, children," the preacher continued, "you are also a part of our family at the church. If there is ever anything you need, Mrs. Snavely and I, and everyone in our church, will do everything we can to help you."

"Thank you," the older girl said. Wanda Nell thought her name was Amy.

"Now, why don't you all go outside and get some fresh air and sunshine," the preacher said kindly. "Enjoy this glorious summer day the Lord has provided, while I speak with your grandmother."

The children didn't wait for their grandmother to say anything. They disappeared out of the living room and out the front door very quickly. Wanda Nell had to step aside to keep from getting stepped on as they went by. They all looked pale and tired, and some time outside in the sun would do them all good.

"Thank you for speaking with the children and taking such an interest in them, Brother Snavely," Mrs. Vance said, coming from behind the chair to stand in front of the preacher, "but I don't like the children going outside too much. They run around and get themselves all excited, and then they're real difficult to settle down."

"I don't mean to interfere," Brother Snavely said, "but I do really need to talk to you without the children present, sister Agnes." For the first time he seemed to take note of Wanda Nell's presence. He stood. "But you have company, I see."

"How do you do, Brother Snavely," Wanda Nell said, stepping forward to introduce herself. "I'm Wanda Nell Culpepper. I worked with the children's mama, and I have something I need to give Miz Vance. I'm sorry to interrupt."

"Not at all, Mrs. Culpepper," the preacher responded, accepting Wanda Nell's hand. "My wife and I are in no hurry. We're just here to aid sister Agnes in her time of need."

Wanda Nell glanced up into his face. All she saw there was concern. She was glad someone was taking an interest in the children. Someone who didn't seem as cold as Agnes Vance.

Wanda Nell dug the envelope of money out of her pocket. She held it out to Agnes Vance.

"What is this?" Mrs. Vance took the envelope and opened it.

"That's the rest of Fayetta's pay from the Kountry Kitchen," Wanda Nell explained.

"Thank you for bringing this," Mrs. Vance said. "The children and I will need it. But are you sure this is just her pay from the restaurant? I didn't think she made that much there."

Wanda Nell didn't want to lie with the preacher and his wife standing right there in front of her, but she didn't want to tell Mrs. Vance the complete truth either. "Well, she made a lot of good tips, and I guess Melvin—that's Melvin Arbuckle, the owner of the Kountry Kitchen—maybe added a little extra in there." She turned to the preacher. "Melvin's real fond of those kids."

"That's okay, I guess," Mrs. Vance said, still holding the envelope in her hand and staring at it. "I just don't want to touch any of the money she made whoring. I don't want it in my house."

Wanda Nell could feel herself blushing. There was no reason she should, but Mrs. Vance embarrassed her. Talking about something like that in front of the preacher and his wife—it was terrible. She was glad the children were outside where they couldn't hear any of this.

"Sister Agnes," the preacher said gently, "your daughter is at rest with the Lord now. Don't dwell on her sins any longer. Think of those children and their future."

Mrs. Vance stared at the preacher. "She has been washed in the blood of the Lamb."

"In a manner of speaking," Brother Snavely said. This time, Wanda Nell was interested to note, he appeared to be the one who was embarrassed. "Once they've arrested the person who did this, you will have more peace of mind, I'm sure."

"They may be doing that pretty soon," Wanda Nell said, then she wished she'd kept her mouth shut.

"Have you heard something? Is there some news?"

Elise Snavely spoke timidly, but her eyes were round with curiosity.

The last thing Wanda Nell wanted to do was start telling the preacher and his wife about the sex club and the whole sordid mess. And since she didn't know which one of the members had killed Fayetta—if one of them in fact had—she should have just kept her mouth shut.

"I can't really say much," Wanda Nell said slowly. "I mean, somebody told me something, and I can't really talk about it. But I know the sheriff's department is getting closer to figuring out who did it. I expect we'll all be hearing about it real soon."

"That's good," Brother Snavely said. "This has been such a tragedy." He touched Mrs. Vance lightly on the arm. "I know sister Agnes has been terribly distressed by the whole thing."

"Yes, it's been awful," Wanda Nell said. She decided it was time for her to go. Brother Snavely seemed more than capable of ministering to Mrs. Vance, and they didn't need her any longer.

"I guess I better be going, Miz Vance," Wanda Nell said. "And if there's anything else I can do, I hope you'll let me know. And if you'll let me know when the funeral's gonna be, I'd appreciate it."

"We surely will," Brother Snavely said after Agnes Vance failed to speak.

Wanda Nell started to say good-bye, but Mrs. Vance interrupted her.

"There is one thing," Mrs. Vance said. "There's

something else I need out of that house. I don't want to go back in there, and since you've been there, maybe you won't mind. Could you get it for me?"

"I don't mind," Wanda Nell said, though she really didn't want to go back in that house ever again either. "What is it you need?"

"Her computer," Mrs. Vance said. "It's pretty new, I reckon, and maybe we can sell it. Or maybe the children can use it for their schoolwork. I hear they're using computers a lot in school these days."

"Yes, they are," Brother Snavely said. "We even have one at the church now, and my wife is real expert at using it. I'm sure she'd be happy to instruct the children."

Elise Snavely glowed, looking almost pretty in the warmth of her husband's smile and words of praise.

"I'll see about it," Wanda Nell said, though she was a bit puzzled. She couldn't remember seeing a computer in Fayetta's house, but something about it rang a faint bell. "I'll talk to Deputy Johnson and see about going over there to get it for you."

"Thank you," Agnes Vance said. She finally tucked the envelope of money into the pocket of her house dress.

Wanda Nell turned to leave. Elise Snavely escorted her toward the front door. She was saying something to Wanda Nell, but Wanda Nell didn't hear a word of it. She stopped dead in the hall, right in front of the door.

Now she remembered what was bothering her about

Fayetta's computer. Her heart sank. There was only one way Mrs. Vance could know about that computer. Slowly, she turned around and walked back into the living room.

Mrs. Vance was listening to something Brother Snavely was saying to her. He broke off when he saw that Wanda Nell had come back.

"Is something wrong?" the preacher asked. He stared at Wanda Nell's face.

"Miz Vance," Wanda Nell said, "tell me something. I heard Fayetta was planning to leave Tullahoma and take the kids to Nashville. Is that true?"

"Well, yes," Mrs. Vance said, looking upset. "I didn't want her to do that, but once she got an idea in her head, she wouldn't change her mind."

"You hated the thought of her taking the children away, didn't you?" Wanda Nell said gently. "You were worried about what kind of life they'd be exposed to if you weren't around to look after them. Weren't you?"

"Of course she was concerned," Brother Snavely said, puzzled. "But I counseled her about that, and about what to say to her daughter, and sister Agnes told me she had convinced her daughter to stay here." His glance moved back and forth between Wanda Nell and Mrs. Vance. "Isn't that right, sister Agnes?"

Mrs. Vance ignored him. She stared at Wanda Nell. "I was fighting for their souls, and I knew if she took those children away from me, they'd be lost forever."

Wanda Nell stared at her with pity. She wished there

were some other answer to this, but now she knew there wasn't. Katie Ann had been right all along.

"Miz Vance," Wanda Nell said, her voice still gentle, "how did you know Fayetta had a computer?"

"I saw it, several times," Mrs. Vance said. Her eyes shot a sideways glance at the preacher.

"But you couldn't have," Wanda Nell said.

"What do you mean?" Brother Snavely asked. "Surely you don't think sister Agnes is lying?"

"I'm afraid she is," Wanda Nell said firmly. "Ask her yourself."

Shocked, the preacher turned to Mrs. Vance. "Sister Agnes, what is this? Is this woman right? Are you lying?"

Mrs. Vance didn't say anything. Her breathing was becoming labored. Elise Snavely took a step toward her, then stopped.

"Melvin Arbuckle bought that computer for Fayetta's kids," Wanda Nell said, looking right at Mrs. Vance. "He brought it over real late that night, the night that Fayetta was killed. After Miz Vance had already picked up the kids and brought them here. Melvin was setting the computer up in Fayetta's bedroom, because she insisted that's where she wanted it. Then they got into an argument about something. Melvin left, and the computer was there in Fayetta's bedroom. The only way you could've seen it was if you were in her bedroom that night after Melvin left."

Mrs. Vance didn't protest. She took a faltering step backward and sank onto the sofa.

"Sister Agnes, is this true?" Brother Snavely was working to overcome his shock, but Wanda Nell could tell he was having a hard time taking it all in.

Mrs. Vance began to nod. "She was going to leave here and take those children with her. I couldn't sleep, I was so worried about it. I went back over there in the middle of the night. I tried to talk her out of it, but she wouldn't listen. She said hateful things to me." She stared up at the preacher. Tears began trickling down her face. "The names she called me. I've never heard anything like it. She even picked up a knife and threatened me with it. I ran into her bedroom to get away from her."

"What happened then?" Wanda Nell asked.

"I think Satan got into her that night, and I had to stop her. I couldn't let her take those children. I couldn't let her," Mrs. Vance said. She repeated it several times. "I got the knife away from her somehow, and then I don't know what happened. I don't really remember after that."

She collapsed on the sofa, and Elise Snavely sat down beside her. She drew the older woman's head to her shoulder and hugged her, rocking her gently back and forth.

Brother Snavely turned to Wanda Nell, his face white. "I think we'd better call the sheriff's department. Would you do that, Mrs. Culpepper?" He advanced to the sofa and sat down on the other side of Mrs. Vance, his head bent and his lips moving in silent prayer.

Wanda Nell stood rooted to the spot for a moment, unable to move. Then, slowly she turned and went to find a phone.

Thirty

Sunday dawned cool and clear, and Wanda Nell decided that, after the horrible events of the preceding week, she wanted to have her family and friends around her. The image of Agnes Vance, sobbing as she was driven away by the sheriff's department, still haunted her. Maybe the bright sun of a beautiful June day would help, so Wanda Nell was planning a picnic out at the lake.

At nine she began making calls, and almost everyone agreed to come. She roused Miranda from bed—Juliet had been up for two hours looking after Lavon—and put her to work slicing potatoes for potato salad. Miranda grumbled a bit, but Wanda Nell ignored her. She was determined that it was going to be a good day.

While she prepared two chickens for frying, Wanda Nell thought about her son. She had never made it to Tuck's office the other day. After Agnes Vance's confession, she and the Snavelys had been kept busy for several hours, first dealing with Elmer Lee Johnson and the sheriff's department, then with figuring out what to do with Fayetta's children. Elise Snavely had quickly volunteered to take the children home with her, and her husband just as quickly agreed. They didn't have any children, and Elise, from what Wanda Nell could see, desperately wanted to be a mother to someone.

By the time Wanda Nell was finished with all that business, she'd had to head to work at the Kountry Kitchen. Since then, there hadn't been an opportune moment for her and T.J. to have the little talk he wanted. Wanda Nell didn't mind postponing it, though she could tell T.J. was feeling more and more frustrated. Today, though, they'd have some time to talk. She wouldn't put it off any longer.

By eleven-thirty everything was ready and loaded in the car. Her old Caddy weighted down, Mayrene pulled out right behind Wanda Nell and followed her toward the lake and across the dam. The picnic grounds lay on the other side of the dam, near the spillway, and Wanda Nell was hoping T.J. and Tuck had already staked out a spot for them.

There were plenty of other people out around the lake enjoying the beautiful weather, and Wanda Nell was happy to see T.J. and Tuck sitting at one of the large picnic tables shaded by the trees. She pulled her car to a stop behind T.J.'s truck, and Mayrene parked alongside her.

T.J. and Tuck came over to help unload. Miranda, with Lavon on her hip, wandered off, but there were enough hands to get the work done without her. Jack Pemberton arrived shortly, and Melvin Arbuckle not long after. The only person missing was old Mrs.

Culpepper. Wanda Nell had invited her, but her former mother-in-law politely declined the invitation.

"Thank you, Wanda Nell," Lucretia Culpepper said. "But I'm lunching with the Grahams. They've invited me, along with the preacher and his wife, and I can't back out now. You'll just have to have your little picnic without me."

Feeling relieved, knowing that everyone would be far more relaxed without the old witch around to make snide comments about everything, Wanda Nell had hung up the phone. No one could say she hadn't at least tried.

Standing in the shade of one of the old trees, Wanda Nell surveyed the scene in front of her. Melvin had Lavon in his lap, bouncing the laughing baby up and down. Juliet and Miranda were arguing amicably over something, while Mayrene was telling Tuck and T.J. where to put the lawn chairs she had brought. Jack, bending over a cooler, was searching for something to drink. Beer in hand, he came over to Wanda Nell, smiling. The sun glinted off his dark glasses.

"How about something to drink?" He offered her the beer.

"I'm fine," Wanda Nell said, smiling back at him.

He popped the top on the beer and sipped. "Thanks for inviting me."

Wanda Nell slipped an arm around his waist. "I'm glad you're here, Jack. Thank the Lord, it's a beautiful day. I don't think I could've stood being cooped up at home today."

"You've had a rough week," Jack said, his arm across her shoulders. He glanced down at her.

"Yeah, it was pretty bad," Wanda Nell said. "That poor woman."

"That poor woman murdered her own daughter," Jack said, his voice dry.

"I know," Wanda Nell said. "I still can't help but feel sorry for her."

"It's a terrible story."

"Let's not think about it today," Wanda Nell said firmly. "I just want to enjoy the day and having my friends and family with me."

"I'm glad to be here," Jack said. "I like your family and your friends, though I'm not sure what Melvin thinks about me."

Wanda Nell shifted uneasily. "Don't pay any attention to that."

"He's jealous," Jack said softly. "I know he cares about you. Just like I do."

"I care about Melvin, too," Wanda Nell said, choosing her words carefully. "He's been a real good friend to me. But he's a friend." She turned so she could look into Jack's face. She reached up and pulled off his sunglasses. He blinked. "I don't feel about him the way I feel about you. I care a lot about you, Jack. More than I have for any other man in a long time. But I just need you to be patient with me."

"I know," Jack said. He pulled her closer and kissed the top of her head. "I'm a very patient man, especially when there's someone worth waiting for."

Wanda Nell smiled. Taking Jack's hand in her own, she pulled him toward the picnic table. "I don't know about y'all, but I'm hungry. Let's eat." She motioned for everyone to assemble around the picnic table.

Soon everyone was seated with a plateful of food. Mayrene and Melvin occupied two of the chairs Mayrene had brought while the others crowded around the picnic table. Lavon, in his mother's lap, took a handful of potato salad off Miranda's plate and stuck it in his mouth.

Wanda Nell gazed at Tuck and T.J., sitting together beside Miranda. Her heart turned over. She wondered that she hadn't seen it before. How could she have been so blind? They were discreet, but anyone with sense could see, if only they looked. She had looked, but she hadn't seen.

Jack's hand brushed her thigh. He whispered in her ear. "It'll be okay. Don't worry."

Startled, Wanda Nell looked into his eyes. He knew, too. And it didn't bother him. She relaxed a little. "Thanks," she whispered back.

"I want to propose a toast," Melvin said, claiming everyone's attention. He stood, beer in hand. "To Wanda Nell. It's good to have a friend who'll stick by you. And to Tuck here, the best lawyer I'm glad I don't really need after all."

Tuck laughed. "To Wanda Nell, who somehow makes my work a heck of a lot easier by doing it for me." He winked and gave her a big grin, lifting his own beer in salute.

They all had a good laugh at that, and Wanda Nell blushed the whole time. When the laughter died down, she said, "I'm just glad we're all together and that we can enjoy this beautiful day." She lifted her can of Coke. "And here's to all of you. Now stop talking and eat."

Eat they did, but it didn't stop them talking. Wanda Nell had hoped no one would bring up the murder, but she wasn't surprised that the subject came up.

"Hey, Tuck," Mayrene said. "So what's gonna happen to that club now? Even if they ain't murderers, they're still pretty sorry excuses for humanity."

Tuck shrugged. "It's up to the sheriff's department. They've got statements from two people about what was going on there, but considering who all is involved, I'm not going to be surprised if it all just fades away." He picked at a piece of fried chicken on his plate. "I heard that Billy Joe Eccles and Deke Campbell want to give the land and the building to the county for some kind of camp for underprivileged kids. And I reckon that's what will happen, one way or another."

"What about Tommy Eccles?" Melvin asked. "Is Katie Ann going to jail for that?"

"It's a mess," Tuck said. "He's pressed charges against her, and she's saying he assaulted her. So I'm not sure how it's going to end up. The doctors aren't sure he'll ever be able to walk again, and Katie Ann's sitting in jail right now. Which is probably the safest place for her."

"They oughta give her a medal," Mayrene said. "That Tommy Eccles ain't nothing but scum, and everybody knows he killed his mama and daddy, no matter what his brother says."

"I can't say I disagree with you," Tuck responded. "But I told Katie Ann I'd take her case, and she hired me. We'll see what happens."

"Considering that she can't afford a lawyer, she's pretty dang lucky you're willing to defend her," T.J. said. He nudged Tuck with his shoulder. Tuck smiled back at him.

"I'm glad you're gonna do it, Tuck," Wanda Nell said. "I feel real sorry for her, after all she's been through. She's gonna need your help." She got up from the picnic table, ready for a change of subject. "Now, how about some dessert?"

Mayrene had baked a couple apple pies that morning, and she had brought some vanilla ice cream, iced down in a cooler. Soon everyone had a generous helping of both pie and ice cream, and the talk drifted on to other subjects.

Soon the afternoon heat—not to mention the full stomachs—was making everyone drowsy, and Wanda Nell decided it was a good time for a walk out under the trees. She beckoned to T.J. to follow her. Pushing himself up, groaning, from his place at the picnic table, he came to join his mother.

"Let's take a little walk," Wanda Nell said, taking his hand in hers. "Let everybody else relax a while, and then we'll come back and clean up."

T.J. looked down into her face. "Okay."

Wanda Nell waited until they were far enough away from everyone else. The air was noticeably cooler under the canopy of trees, and the noise of the other groups enjoying the afternoon faded. Here they could have quiet while they walked and talked.

"I'm sorry we couldn't talk sooner," Wanda Nell said. "I know you've been wanting to talk to me, and I reckon now's as good a time as any. You feel like it?"

"Yeah," T.J. said. He stopped walking and turned to face his mother. "There's something I really need to tell you, Mama. Something about me." He paused for a moment and swallowed hard. "It's hard for me to say. I don't want you to be mad at me."

"Honey," Wanda Nell said, stroking his cheek. "I'm not gonna be mad at you, I promise. Besides, I'm pretty sure I know what it is you want to tell me."

"Maybe so," T.J. said, "but I've still got to say it, Mama. I have to say the words aloud to you."

Wanda Nell nodded encouragement. Suddenly she found she couldn't say anything. Her throat was too tight.

T.J. turned away, gazing out into the trees. "All those years, Mama, I tried so hard to be just what you and Daddy expected me to be. I tried so hard just to be one of the guys, like Daddy was. Doing all the things that Daddy did, drinking and carousing and getting in fights, to prove how tough I was. What a man I was. Except I got caught and ended up in trouble." He sighed, and Wanda Nell wanted to comfort him. But

343

the words wouldn't come.

"And all the time I knew it wasn't me. That wasn't who I was, Mama. I had these feelings, but they were the kind of feelings I wasn't supposed to have. I hated myself for being different, and I tried to make myself the way I thought I should be. But that didn't get me anything except time in jail."

Wanda Nell could hear the tears in his voice. She wanted to reach out to him, to touch him, but she couldn't move.

"Then I ended up out in Houston," T.J. continued, still not looking at her. "I got in some trouble there, too, but there was somebody who helped me. There were several people who helped me, and I started to figure out that there were other people like me. People who accepted themselves and got on with their lives. And for the first time in my life, I started to feel good about myself."

T.J. turned back to his mother and took her hands in his. "That's when I decided to come home. I wanted to see my family and to talk to y'all. But then Daddy got killed, and so I put off talking for a while. And then Grandmama kinda took over, and I've been putting off talking even more."

"You don't have to put it off anymore, honey," Wanda Nell said, finally finding her voice again. "Just tell me."

T.J. breathed deeply, then exhaled slowly. He held her gaze with his own. "I'm gay, Mama. I hope you can accept that. I can't change who I am."

344

Wanda Nell didn't say anything for a long moment, and she could feel the tension in T.J.'s hands, see the fear in his eyes.

"Why did you wait so long to tell me, honey?" she asked.

"I was afraid I'd lose you," T.J. said. The tears began streaming from his eyes. "I was afraid to tell you, because if your mama doesn't love you, then what are you left with?"

"Oh, honey," Wanda Nell said through her own tears. "I love you, and I always will. Nothing will ever change that. You're my son." She pulled him into her arms, and she felt his body shaking against hers.

They stood like that for a while, both crying, with Wanda Nell stroking his back. Slowly the tears dried, and T.J. stood back.

"Thank you, Mama," he said, his voice rough from crying. "I know it's gonna take some getting used to." He pulled a handkerchief from his pocket and handed it to his mother.

"Yeah, it will," Wanda Nell said honestly. She wiped the tears away with the handkerchief and gave it back to T.J. "The way I grew up, everybody said it was wrong, and most people around here are still gonna say the same thing."

"I know that, Mama," T.J. said. "But I'm not going to pretend anymore."

"I'm not asking you to," Wanda Nell responded. "But I can't help but worry about what other people might do."

"I'm not gonna be stupid about it," T.J. said, smiling. "And neither is Tuck." He hesitated a moment. "Are you okay about Tuck and me? It was the last thing I expected, when he walked into the jail that day and told me you'd hired him to represent me."

"He's a good man," Wanda Nell said, "and a damn lucky one, if you really care about him that much."

T.J. grinned. "I do, Mama. And he feels the same about me."

"He damn well better," Wanda Nell said, with mock severity, "or he'll have to answer to me."

"I reckon I'm pretty lucky to have you for a mama," T.J. said.

"I've been doing a lot of thinking the last few days," Wanda Nell went on. "All that business with Fayetta and her mama. They about drove each other crazy because Fayetta couldn't be what her mama wanted her to be. And I think Fayetta did drive her mama crazy. She just couldn't handle what Fayetta was doing, and she got obsessed with looking after those children. I think she lost her mind." She sighed. "I don't want that to ever happen to me or one of my children."

"It won't, Mama," T.J. protested. "None of us are like that."

"Don't ever be afraid to come and talk to me about anything, honey," Wanda Nell said. "Promise me that."

"Okay, I promise," T.J. said.

"And you're gonna have to be patient with me,"

Wanda Nell said. "If I say something wrong, or mis-understand something, you tell me. Okay? Help me understand."

"I will, Mama." T.J. hugged her again.

"Is this still a private party, or can I join it?"

Wanda Nell and T.J. turned at the sound of Tuck's voice. He stood a few feet away, and Wanda Nell could see the anxiety in his face.

She held out her hand to him and smiled. "Welcome to the family."

Arm in arm, with Wanda Nell in the middle, the three of them walked back into the sun to join the others.

Wanda Nell said, "If I say something wrong, or mis-
understand something, you tell me. Okay? Help me
understand."

"I will, Mama." TJ hugged her again.

"Is this still a private party, or can I join it?"

Wanda Nell and TJ turned at the sound of Tuck's
voice. He stood a few feet away, and Wanda Nell
could see the anxiety in his face.

She held out her hand to him and smiled. "Welcome
to the family."

Arm in arm, with Wanda Nell in the middle, the
three of them walked back into the sun to join the
others.

Wanda Nell's
Favorite Recipes

Fruit Cobbler

1½ lbs. fresh or frozen (thawed) fruit cut in 1"
   chunks (can use berries, peaches, rhubarb, or
   any juicy fruit)
1 cup sugar
1 cup and 1 T. flour
1 t. baking powder and ½ t. baking soda
4 T. (½ stick) unsalted butter, cut into small pieces
⅔ cup buttermilk

Preheat oven to 425 degrees. Butter well 1-½ to 2 qt.
baking dish. Put fruit in dish and sprinkle with ⅔ cup
of sugar and 1 T. flour. (If you like your cobbler tart,
don't use the full amount of sugar. The sweetness also
depends on the fruit you use. For tarter results, use ½
cup of sugar with peaches and berries, ¾ cup with
rhubarb). Toss fruit in dish, spread evenly, and bake
10 minutes.

Combine 3 T. sugar, 1 cup flour, baking powder,
baking soda, and butter to coarse crumbs (you can use
a food processor, but it can be done with a pastry
cutter or by rubbing butter into dry ingredients. You

may also add nutmeg, ginger, or cinnamon to flavor the topping). Beat in buttermilk until soft dough forms.

Remove fruit from oven and drop dough on top in 6 mounds. Sprinkle with 1 T. sugar and any spice you like. Bake until fruit is bubbly and top is golden brown (20 to 30 minutes).

Wanda Nell's
Fried Chicken

1 chicken, cut up
¼ t. black pepper
½ cup milk
1 cup Crisco oil (can substitute canola oil)
1 cup flour
1 t. salt
1 egg, beaten

Combine the flour, salt, and pepper in a heavy plastic bag or a paper bag. Combine egg and milk in a deep bowl and mix well. Drop chicken (a few pieces at a time) into the flour mixture. (If you don't want to bother with the bag, put the flour, salt, and pepper mixture into another bowl and roll chicken pieces in it until thoroughly coated.) Remove and dip in milk mixture. Return to flour mixture, making sure the chicken is coated well. Put oil (about an inch deep) in a heavy skillet. Heat to a temperature of about 350 degrees. Place chicken in skillet and fry 20 to 25 minutes or until golden brown, turning chicken to brown on both sides. Remove from pan and drain on paper towels.

Center Point Publishing
600 Brooks Road • PO Box 1
Thorndike ME 04986-0001 USA

(207) 568-3717

US & Canada:
1 800 929-9108